MY CUP
RUNNETH OVER

Steve Shearwater

EM.press Publishing
Boston, Massachusetts

ISBN: 1539989976
ISBN-13: 978-1539989974

DEDICATION

To the memory of my parents

And to all the kind people at my own "coffee spots" on my various
Cumbria beats, over many years.

CONTENTS

AN IMPORTANT NOTE

For the sake of preserving some of Cumbria's fading culture and also to add some local flavour, this book contains a small quantity of dialect words and phrases as well as some period police jargon. As these may be difficult for many readers to understand, especially for people from outside Britain, there are glossaries for the two categories in the Index/Menu at my website: www.steveshearwater.co.uk I hope this proves helpful.

Chapter One

The Captain Is Dead

I never was a morning person. And I do mean entire mornings.

On that particular day my mouth felt as though I'd been chewing handfuls of dry porridge oats, straight from the box. I'd had a few beers too many with my friends the night before and an evil pain stabbed away relentlessly, right in the middle of my skull. It responded violently to the ringing of the telephone.

Be good to me, Providence, I thought. *It's five past eight on Sunday morning, for pity's sake. Tell them to go away.*

But I had to pick it up. 'Hello. This is the police station,' I mournfully acknowledged, 'This is Constable Shearwater, speaking.'

'Can you come to Scarbank?' wailed a rather frantic voice. 'The Captain's dead!'

'I beg your *pardon*?' I said. 'Who is the Captain?'

'An old chap that lives here on his own,' came back a shrill reply. 'His milk and papers have been piling up at his front door for four days so we think maybe something's wrong.'

'Four days? And only *now* you think that something might be wrong?' I asked. But my sarcasm was lost on the caller.

I didn't race to get there. I was well aware what a closed room smelled like after someone had lain there dead for a few days. Indeed, my hangover was urging me to drive in the opposite direction – to leave the country, even.

Villagers and hamlet-dwellers throughout Britain seem able to instantly form committees for almost any purpose one might care to name, and that's how it was this morning in Scarbank. I couldn't see a secretary in the gathering – well at least nobody appeared to be taking notes, yet – but the size of the group was such that I wondered whether they had been bringing spectators by coach from miles around.

I parked the police van in the cul-de-sac of council bungalows and got out.

'Who wants to tell me what's happened?' I asked.

Five of them did; simultaneously; jabberingly; loudly; *too* loudly. My brain was still insistent: *Leave the country!*

'Alright, alright; quietly. One at a time,' I pleaded but it didn't work. Maybe dropping the Queen's English in favour of our Lakeland dialect might be more effective: 'Wilst'a aw bloody whisht,' I shouted.

Only a chaffinch cheeping in a nearby hawthorn bush defied my command for silence.

'Now,' I said, turning to one of the women, 'you tell me what's going on.'

'Well, I live kind of opposite, thoo knows. And t' Captain sometimes doesn't surface for an odd day if he's not so well. But this time it's been fower days so mebby he's fettled.'

'Why "Captain"?' I asked. 'What type of captain was he? What's his real name?'

'Oh, he's known as the Captain because he was in the navy for so long that the first big ship he was ever on as a boy was wooden. He wasn't really a captain, though. That's just his nickname. Fred Blacklock, he's called.'

I went through the motions of ringing the doorbell of Mr Blacklock's bungalow – his little house was the last on the left in the cul-de-sac. Then I used my knuckles to knock – the little brass doorknocker was only ornamental and would have been no use at all – but there was no response. It was as quiet as a grave, quite literally it would seem, so I drew my truncheon and used the butt of it to hammer one last time on the door.

Still no reply. The only thing that responded to the noise was my head.

'So how old will he be?' I asked, as the self-appointed "Dead-Fred's Committee" merrily followed me around the end of the house to the back door, en-masse.

'Mebby ninety,' the spokeswoman offered.

'Nay lass, nivver. He'll be ninety six if he's a day,' came a mild rebuke from the chairman of the "How-Old's-Fred Subcommittee."

It was a forlorn hope to try to open the back door; of course it was locked. And, more ominously from the point of view of what I knew would have to come next, every single window was shut. So were all the curtains. I wanted to pat my pockets, just in case there might be a gas mask hidden away in there. But then my dad had apparently thrown away the ones our family had possessed at the end of the Second World War, about thirty years ago – I'd have to have words with him about that, because one would have been really useful right now!

'Can you all stand back, please? I'm going to smash the little flap window so I can reach in and open the main window,' I announced as I gingerly climbed onto a dustbin to gain height.

'Are you allowed to do that? Shouldn't we wait for the Council to come with a key?' asked the "Law and Order" chairman.

'Who'll pay for the damage?' the entire "Finance Subcommittee" asked me, as one voice.

'Will thoo lot shut up,' demanded a spokesman from the "Logic and Reality" group. 'It's no good calling the Council. It's Sunday and they won't come out 'til Monday, and the Captain might be dead by then.'

That served to silence everybody.

'*More* dead, more like,' muttered one of the "Philosophy" team. It was an interesting concept, but I knew what he meant.

It is very difficult to know how hard to hit glass in order to break it. The area and thickness clearly affect this, as do the type of glass, the thing you use to hit it, and how solidly the pane is held in place. There is no happy medium. The gathered throng must have thought me remarkably lacking in muscle-power when the first three blows of my truncheon all bounced off.

'Go on lad, *hit* the bugger,' came some salient advice.

Then the inevitable happened. My fourth blow shattered the glass as though a bomb had gone off. Most of the fragments went inwards but enough large shards hurtled outwards to have the gathered clans ducking and diving for cover.

'There! *That* did the job,' my adviser muttered from the re-grouping crowd.

I opened the flap-window then reached through and opened the big window. I turned to one of the men nearest me.

'I don't want anyone coming close to the window and no-one is to look through the curtains,' I said. 'So can you get everyone to go back around onto the road, please?'

He nodded. As they started to move away, I climbed onto the windowsill, and started to ease the curtain back so I could step through into the bedroom. Oh no, just my luck! On the other side of the curtains was a large old dressing table, with its ornately-shaped mirror nearly the size of the window I had just opened. It was blocking my entrance beautifully. And the room stank of stale, foetid air, just as I'd expected.

It took much judicious and painful wriggling for me to get around that mirror and into the room. At one stage, I was stuck there with one leg either side of the mirror, and the edge of it embedded in my groin, literally pressing for my attention. The soles of my boots had picked up some fragments of glass from the windowsill and were now grinding them into the woodwork of the actual dressing table. It looked like cheap, 1940's utility furniture but someone had kept it polished and in nice condition, until now. I supposed it wouldn't have to matter but it did seem a shame.

A motionless human form in the bed was entirely covered by sheets and blankets, with the sole exception of the right hand, which was hanging out over the side of the bed, palm uppermost, fingers part curled. In the dim, grey light the ancient skin looked like old parchment. A complete set of false teeth sat in a glass of water on the bedside cabinet. The body was laid out, seemingly as stiff as a plank, and in a straight line except for that one protruding hand. It would be pointless feeling for a pulse.

'Oh well, Fred, at least you got to die in your own bed,' I quietly said as I lifted the covers back off the old man's face.

But in a heartbeat, the body sat bolt-upright and shrieked at me 'What d' *you* want?'

I think I did a passable imitation of Tom, the feline half of *Tom & Jerry* cartoons. I jumped so hard it was a wonder I didn't have to prise my fingernails and toenails out of the ceiling.

'You're *alive!*' I gasped. I could feel my heart pounding against my ribcage.

Old Fred had reached over to his bedside cabinet and found his hearing aid.

'What?' he shouted, as he fumbled to put it in and turn it on. 'What was that you said?'

'I said I'm glad you're alright. Your neighbours were worried because they haven't seen you for four days, since Wednesday.'

'Oh, I see,' said the Captain. 'No, it was nowt to worry about. I just had a bit of 'flu so I put myself to bed to sleep it off.'

'I don't know about sleep it off; you damned near finished *me* off,' I said. But I was grinning at him.

'Well,' he laughed, 'you shouldn't come snooping around so quietly. You should have rung the doorbell before you came in. How *did* you come in, anyway?'

When I delivered the good news to the mourners-in-waiting, at the front door, the majority of them neatly sidestepped into the "We-Didn't-Think-He-Was-Really-Dead Subcommittee" and tried to push their way into the house to see to old Fred's every need. I let two of the women in and then, in the timeless words of policemen throughout the universe, I said to the rest: 'There's nothing else to see. You may as well all go home.'

I waited with the Captain and his two helpers for three-quarters of an hour until his doctor arrived to check him over. Fred was aggravated that the women wouldn't let him get up to make everyone a cup of tea.

'You're too independent for your own good,' one of the women declared. 'You'll be independent till the day you die.'

'If that means not being nagged by a bossy woman, that's fine by me,' he replied.

'Well judging by *that* heart, you won't be dying for a long time, Fred,' proffered the doctor as he put his stethoscope away. 'You have the heart of a bull.'

'Aye, and the thick skull of one, too,' said the other woman.

'Oh, quit yer bloody grumbling,' muttered the Captain. 'Moan, moan, bloody moan.'

The women turned away so the old man couldn't see them smiling. The doctor had clearly been right. There certainly wasn't much wrong with the old lad now that he'd got over his 'flu.

Chapter Two

A New Station

The police station and magistrates' court at Hawthwaite were in one Victorian building – built of a local, slate blocks with sandstone door and window surrounds. My first day working here had been a mere four days before the good old 'Captain' had nearly given me a premature heart attack. I had been transferred from the Cumbria Constabulary Headquarters at Penrith back to the mountains of the Lake District, one of the most beautiful places on earth.

At the age of sixteen, I'd left my home county of Cumbria and got an introduction to city policing in Kingston-Upon-Hull as a cadet for three years, although some of that time was spent in the nearby College of Commerce, gaining police-oriented qualifications. Now, after three years back in Cumbria, as a constable, I had been stationed in the town where I had gone to the grammar school, just five miles from my childhood home at Linthwaite.

Four constables, two sergeants and one inspector made up the Hawthwaite team; the PC I had replaced was having to leave the force on medical grounds after he'd suffered spinal damage as a result of a kicking he got from a gang of drunken yobs who had come up for the weekend from Manchester. That was the thing, at small stations like this one the constables often worked alone and that was a major part of the pleasure from working in a small town – the independence, and the responsibility that came from it.

'Ah, Police Constable 8-6-8 Shearwater! It's Steve, isn't it?' Sergeant Wyatt had asked, as I walked into the front office that first time.

I'd seen him previously, once or twice, at Headquarters and knew his reputation for being firm but fair. He was a solidly-built man in his early forties, a whisker under six feet tall, maybe fourteen stone and he had blondish ginger hair parted on the left.

'Morning, Sarge'. Yes, I'm Steve.'

'You're from around here originally, aren't you?' he asked.

'Yes, Linthwaite born and bred. I'm living back there again now, but I've been away from the area for a few years,' I replied.

'Right, well in that case I'll apologise for throwing you in the deep end but you haven't time to settle down for a "Welcome to Hawthwaite" chat yet, I'm afraid. I've got a job for you. There's a serious-injury message to deliver to a woman in Low Keld. Her husband is a truck driver and he's been in a big, multi-vehicle crash, down the M6, in Staffordshire. I'd go and tell her myself but we've got a mountain rescue just started up so I need to hang on here to co-ordinate that over the radio. Could you deliver that message for me?'

'Gladly. That's not a problem, Sarge'.'

'Right ho. All the details are on this telephone message.' He handed me a carbon copy. 'The van keys are hanging in that key rack by the fireplace. Got a map?'

'Yes. But I know Low Keld quite well. I should be back in about an hour,' I said.

'That depends on whether she makes you a cuppa, or vice versa if she's in shock.'

'What's my call-sign for the van, Sarge'?' I asked.

'Zulu-Three-One.'

'Okay. I'm on my way,' I said, and headed out of the back door.

Once in the van, I radioed the force control room to "book on" before I set off.

'Zulu-Three-One to BB.'

'Zulu-Three-One, go ahead; over.'

'Zulu-Three-One, on the air at Hawthwaite and mobile to Low Keld with an injury message. Is there anything else happening in the area? Over.'

'Nothing apart from the mountain rescue, Three-One; over.'

'Roger; Three-One out.'

With the radio message done, I drove out of the police station yard and turned left along Fairfield Street towards Main Street, then swung right, and headed towards the western edge of the town. It was a strange feeling to be back here as a police officer rather than a schoolboy, as I had been, six years previously. As I passed the grammar school, I could see some of the teenage boys in their dark green blazers and grey trousers, and the girls with pleated skirts in the same shade of grey. Seeing them made me smile but I wasn't sure why. A few words of the school hymn, which was entirely in Latin, echoed through my mind – "*Ad montes oculos levavimus*" – the posh version of "I lift up mine eyes unto the hills."

Once at Low Keld, it took me only two or three minutes to find the address I was looking for. It was the right-hand end-house on a terrace of four, in the middle of two other identical terraces.

I was forced to ask the worried looking blonde who answered the door 'Hello. Are you Mrs Susan Watson?'

It just doesn't do to give upsetting messages to the wrong individual.

'Yes,' she replied. 'What's happened?'

'It's alright, love; nobody's dead, but I have got a message for you,' I said. 'Can I come in?'

She led me into a modest but clean and tidy living room.

It is cruel for police officers to express platitudes and thereby make people wait for details of bad news so I'd been taught from the outset to deliver such messages carefully worded but very promptly, even if the result sounded blunt, so I came straight out with it and said: 'Your husband, Adrian, has been hurt in a road accident on the M6, down in Staffordshire. From what I have been told, his life isn't in danger but it sounds like he's in a bit of a mess. I'm sorry. I've written the name and phone number of the hospital for you, here.'

I passed her the note with the details but she just stared at me for a few seconds, looking emotionless.

'Damn. That's a pity,' she eventually said, very quietly.

'Well the main thing is it seems that he'll survive it...'

'No, I meant it's a pity that the bastard *did* survive,' she said.

My mouth was probably hanging wide open. I was speechless.

She ignored my shock and continued: 'For almost five years, Adrian has decided that it's more fun to hit me than to love me; ever since our son was born, it seems. Then, just last week, he smacked little Andrew so hard over the head that the poor little fella was knocked senseless. So I told Adrian to leave the house and never come back. I haven't seen him since. And I meant it. He's never coming back. I'll divorce him.'

'Have you only got the one child?'

'Yes,' she said. 'Andrew was born on my nineteenth birthday; the best present you could ever dream of. Then, about ten days after that, Adrian gave me another present – a smack in the mouth. He said I was neglecting him and paying too much attention to the baby. After a few weeks of that, I knew I'd never give him another child. But he never really hurt Andrew, not until last week, and that was the final straw – the little mite isn't even five yet. Would you like a cup of tea?'

'If you want to talk about it, and just as long as I'm not being a nuisance.'

'No,' she said. 'Don't be silly. Of course you're not; it's nice to have someone to talk to. And anyway, I'm curious. Don't I know you? Didn't you used to go to the grammar school a few years ago?'

'Yes. Were you there as well then?'

'No, I never got there,' she said. 'I went to Satterthwaite School. I remember your face, from seeing you around town but I left school when I was sixteen.'

The recollection, by now, was mutual. And I knew it was a good job she had no idea what a certain, over-ambitious young teenager had actually been thinking about her and her girlfriends, back then. Talk about vivid, over-optimistic daydreams! I hid a grin from her when I remembered the extent of my fantasies. Had they ever come true, I'd probably have died in the action.

We chatted for almost thirty minutes over the promised cup of tea, as the story of her husband's apparent brutality unfolded. She was coming up to her twenty-fourth birthday, making her nearly two years older than me, and it was impossible not to notice once again how attractive she was: pretty, slim, and very bubbly, despite the news. Her hair – the colour of hay – was tied back in a neat ponytail that hung half way down her back.

'Your hair is longer now than it used to be, isn't it?' I asked.

She beamed at me. It seemed that I might have scored some brownie points by remembering.

'Yes, it is,' she said. 'Did you like it shorter? I used to have it in a bob.'

'No, I didn't mean it like that,' I said. 'It's pretty. Actually, I prefer women with long hair. It looks much more se..' I stopped myself. 'Attractive,' I added.

'You were going to say sexy,' she said, grinning.

And for the umpteenth time in the course of my career, I found myself angrily wondering why on earth some men felt the need to hit women.

'Well,' I said, 'I'm really sorry you've had to go through all this. And I hope you don't mind if I say I still enjoyed our chat despite the circumstances. But I have to get back now; it's my first day at Hawthwaite so I'd better not be late getting back there.'

'Really? Where were you before now?'

'I was in the police in Hull for three years as a cadet. I went away for a bit of city experience,' I said. 'But I always knew I'd come back. I love The Lakes; I spend a lot of time fellwalking and rock climbing. Then I transferred back to Cumbria and I've done another three years at Penrith. At first, I was at the nick, in town. Then I worked at the force headquarters, which, as you might know, is just outside the town. And now Hawthwaite. It's like coming home – literally.'

'Well, thanks for bringing the news,' said Susan. 'I'm really glad you're back in the area. Really glad. And if ever you want to pop in for another cup of tea when you are passing, you'll be very welcome.'

'Okay,' I said. 'I'll definitely take you up on that if you're sure that's alright. Take care of yourself, Susan. And when Adrian eventually gets out of hospital, just let us know if he comes around causing you any problems. It will be sorted out if he does.'

'It *is* alright, and I will let you know if there are problems. You can bank on it,' she said.

We smiled at each other but hers seemed a bit more than just a smile; she looked at my eyes, then at my mouth, then back into my eyes again. My mouth went dry in an instant. I fumbled over a few words about seeing her again sometime then I left.

Low Keld was near the western end of a long, relatively shallow lake called Low Water, and Hawthwaite was a couple of miles away from the eastern end of it. I briefly stopped in a lay-by overlooking the lake, on my way back to the town, and wrote-up my notebook about the message I had just delivered. Then I drove back to the nick.

'Get it done?' asked Sergeant Wyatt, glancing at his watch. 'Seventy five minutes, eh? Either she made you a cup o' tea or you got lost.'

'Yes, it's done. And yes, I confess, I got a brew,' I said. 'Do you want to endorse the original message, Sarge', or do you want me to do it?'

'You can do it. How did she take the news?'

'With apparent delight, actually,' I said. 'It would appear that he's a wife beater.'

'Did she *really*! Well, in that case, it couldn't have happened to a nicer guy,' said the sergeant, sarcastically.

His voice had dropped low, for some reason, but I didn't say anything.

'How's the mountain rescue going?' I asked.

'No problems with it. Some chap has fallen about sixty feet off a route called Jackdaw Corner,' he replied, his voice lively once more.

'Jackdaw Corner on Farm Crag? The dozy git,' I said. 'You can just about *walk* up that route; it's only graded "very difficult" and "V-Dif" is a misnomer if ever there was one. Is he alive?'

'Still alive so far. Do *you* climb then, Steve?'

'Yes,' I said. 'I've been in the Penrith Mountain Rescue Team for the last three years although I wasn't any use to them while I was off work injured.'

'Are you going to switch over to our Hawthwaite team then?'

'Probably. I hope so,' I said. 'I haven't had time to think about it, really. I was only told I was being moved here nine days ago. The bloody *caretaker* at Headquarters knew about my transfer before I did!'

'So nothing's changed at Carleton Hall then,' he said, laughing. 'They send all the big bosses on expensive, man-management courses at that posh Bramshill Police College yet they *still* can't cope with the basics of administration, eh? Right, let's get back to serious business; come and I'll show you where we brew the tea.'

He guided me through the dog-legged corridor until there were only two doorways left ahead of us.

'The door straight ahead is the charge-room and the cells,' he said. 'But this one on the left is our nerve centre – the refreshments room! If you bring sandwiches for your refs there's a fridge in here but Ernie Robinson's butcher's shop right opposite do grand meat-and-tatie and steak-and-kidney pies, and there're a couple of good places round the corner in Main Street where you can buy stuff; but I expect you know that.'

'Yes,' I said. 'And I know Ernie Robinson's well enough. A good mate of mine from Linthwaite has worked there since we were both just fifteen. Good pies, and bloody good Cumberland sausage, too!'

Sergeant Wyatt made two mugs of strong tea then gestured to a seat.

'Park your arse,' he said. 'We'll have a chat about what's what. Do you know any of the lads that work here?'

'I don't know any of them well but I probably know everyone by sight,' I said. 'That's one of the few benefits of working at Headquarters; seeing people as they pass through, on courses and at meetings.'

'Oh yes, I was meaning to ask you about that. How did you end up getting marooned in Headquarters so early in your service? Wasn't it something to do with that injury you just mentioned?'

'Aye,' I said. 'I was stationed in Penrith town when I first started back in the county, and I did two years there, but I was the observer in a panda car one night when there was a chase and a lunatic in a stolen car rammed us. I got both my legs badly broken but once the worst was over I asked if I could get back to work on light duties, so they seconded me to Headquarters to the training department for a year. I got regular physiotherapy and check-ups and the next I knew I was coming here.

'Oh, that was you that was hurt in that crash, was it? I remember it happening but I didn't know your name at the time so I didn't make the association. They must think we're a cushy number, here in Hawthwaite,' he said. 'Are you glad you're back on the beat then?'

'Too true I am. The only thing I've got to make sure of now is that I pass my promotion exams in November. I'd look a bit of an idiot if I failed them after spending a year in the training department.'

He chuckled. 'Right, let me tell you about the people here, from the top. Our inspector is Brian Sumner, as you no doubt know. He really is a first-rate chap; looks after his lads; won't allow any back-stabbing or bitchiness. Just make sure you always tell him the full facts and he'll see you right. My fellow sergeant is Carol Clarke. She's nobody's fool is Carol and she's some sort of kamikaze-dan in karate so nobody messes with her and gets away with it. She's a good lass. The other three bobbies are Dick Price, Hamish Sutherland, and Taffy Williams – English, Scottish and Welsh; we are nothing if not international: English, Scottish and Welsh, those three. You don't have any Irish blood do you? Then we could have a full set!'

'Sorry, Sarge', I can't oblige unless you want some Canadian blood,' I said. 'I'm three-quarters thoroughbred Lakelander. But my dad's father was a Canadian forester – migrated here about seventy years ago, just before Word War 1, but he was originally of northern English ancestry – so that's where my surname came from. But the main part of our family's been in the Forndale, Overdale and Snabside valleys for at least 450 years, according to the church records, so we can definitely be classed as proper locals which probably also makes me at least 75 per cent Norse Viking. Will that do?'

Chapter Three

The Copper-Bottomed Pan

After one and a half weeks at Hawthwaite it was my turn to work a week of night shifts, 10pm-6am. On the fourth night, the Thursday, I met Sergeant Clarke for the first time. She had just got back from holiday and immediately had to stand in for Sergeant Wyatt who had gone off sick just before some 5pm-1am "half nights" he was rostered for.

'Hiya,' she said. 'You must be Steve. I'm Carol – except when one of the bosses is listening!'

'Hi,' I rather inadequately replied, but I gave her a big, beaming smile as she shook my hand. She was quite small for a policewoman – not much over five feet five tall. She had a pretty, girlish face, and her long, dark brown hair was up in a bun, on the back of her head. So *this* was the arse-kicking, karate queen. She was certainly very nice-looking for being a professional thug!

'So how's it going? Are you enjoying being back on your home patch?'

'Mmm?' I said, dragging my mind away from her figure. 'Oh, yes. Yes, I am, thanks. It's a bit weird at times though. I stopped a car the other day to tell the chap off for driving like a moron and it turned out to be my old Latin teacher from the grammar school. But then he always was an unpleasant old devil so I must admit I quite enjoyed it.'

She laughed. 'Oh, by the way, you're going to have a "special" with you for part of tomorrow night. Do you have any strong feelings about that?'

'Special constables?' I said. 'You mean "hobby bobbies," unpaid voluntary workers that take away all our chances of earning overtime money?' I grinned. 'No, not really, as long as they know what they are doing.'

'Well this one is okay,' she said. 'It's Kevin Bottomley, do you know him?'

I shook my head.

'Well his heart's in the right place, Steve,' she said. 'He's not too bad. And he'll only be with you until one o'clock.'

'Ah, the truth will out, eh Sarge'?' I said, still grinning. 'You mean you are pulling rank and putting him on patrol with me even though he's working the same shift as you!'

We both laughed.

'Listen,' she said. 'Being a sergeant has to have *some* perks, alright?'

When I came in at 9.45pm the following evening for duty, Kevin Bottomley was already there. Specials were more or less free to choose their own hours but were encouraged to help out on Thursday, Friday and Saturday nights when the drunks were likely to be out in force and all the towns were at their busiest. To my dismay, I saw that Kevin was a few years older than me. I knew from experience that older specials often either knowingly or subconsciously tried to take control in all sorts of situations even though they were only there to be lay-assistants to regular officers, whom they inevitably accompanied. I needn't have worried about Kevin though, he proved to be a nice chap and very sensible.

Carol quickly read the day's messages aloud to us in the muster room and we jotted down the necessary details in the back of our notebooks:

'*Stolen car from Kendal today, a blue Morris Marina 1.3 coupé, registered number FRM 477K. Stolen from Leatherside last night, a red Mini Cooper-S, registered KAO 105C.*'

'I know that Mini," I chipped in. 'It's owned by Stan Hewer. It's his pride and joy. We'd better catch the culprit before he does or it'll be a murder we're investigating!'

'*Observations for an Anthony Culdreth, known as Tony. Aged 30, height six feet three, heavy build, crew-cut black hair, he has absconded from Dovenby mental hospital near Maryport. To be approached with caution. He is described as a violent shit... shitso...* damn it, I can never say that word. What is it, Steve?' she asked, holding the ring binder towards me.

'Schizophrenic,' I laughed. 'But your description of a violent shit probably fits the bill perfectly, Sergeant.'

'Oh shush,' she replied. '*If seen, he is to be taken into custody as he has been "sectioned" and must be returned to a secure unit.*'

'That'll be your job – you're the professional,' Kevin said to me.

'Ha! On your bike, Kevin,' I said. 'He's six feet three – that's an inch bigger than me. That's what you Specials are here for, to get your heads kicked in so that we valuable, regular members of the constabulary don't get damaged. Anyway, from what I've heard, old Kung Foo Carol, here, would bounce him around the walls before she locked him up.'

'She would? Ooh!' said Kevin. 'Well please can *I* be a shitso-whatsits too, then?'

'Actually,' I said, 'from what I've heard, Sergeant Clarke does a rather wonderful version of the famous Bombay-chuff-lock!'

'Oooooh,' said Kevin. 'Me, please. Me, me, me, me, me!'

Sergeant Clarke fought back a smile and just said 'You two buggers behave yourselves. Otherwise you'll both end up like that famous Russian eunuch: *Ivor Bollockoff.*'

At five past the hour I donned my night helmet – supposedly less conspicuous than a day helmets because they have a black badge rather than a silver one – Kevin put on his chequer-banded cap, and we went out on foot patrol.

'So what do you do for a living then, Kevin?' I asked.

'I work at the Sellafield nuclear plant, down West Cumberland,' he said.

'So we won't need torches tonight then?'

'Yeah, yeah, yeah; I've heard it a hundred times – I glow in the dark,' he said.

We chatted about football as we walked slowly up Main Street – Kevin was a Workington Town supporter – but just before we reached the Monks Café a voice interrupted us from the unlit archway that led to the Scafell Inn:

'Steven? Steven Shearwater? Well I'll be blowed; it is an'all!'

An old chap with a border collie on a bit of string emerged from the shadows.

'What's up lad? Dun't thoo recognise me? I'se Max Knight. I used to be in a Saint John's Ambulance Brigade wid thy dad. How is he? By gum it's grand to see thoo aw dressed up like that. Thoo was still at school t' last time I saw thoo but I did hear thoo'd join't police.'

'Yes, Max, of course I recognise you,' I said. 'To be honest, though, I didn't know you'd moved from Railway Terrace at Linthwaite. Are you living here in town, now? And yes, Dad's grand thanks. How've *you* been keeping?'

'Oh, not so bad; "tewin' away" as they say. But I do miss going to t' Brigade wid your father though, now that we've both packed it in. You know, him and me often didn't get to those meetings. We always used to go in t' nearest pub first, to talk about it, and by t' time we'd finished talking, t' meetings were generally over! He used to have us all in stitches with his tall tales and his daft stories did your dad,' Max said, and he laughed to himself.

'Well I'll certainly tell him you were asking after him,' I said.

'Aye; aye do. You must. Anyways, I'd better be off. Yer dad'll tell you where I live if ever thoo wants a cuppa, sometime. You'd be welcome. Come on, Tess. We'll see you, Steven... And you, mate,' he added, for Kevin's benefit. And with that, he walked away down the street with Tess trotting alongside.

Moments later my radio broke the brief silence: 'Control to 8-6-8; over.'

It was Carol's voice.

'Receiving, Sarge', outside Monks Café on Main Street. Go ahead,' I replied.

'Report of a domestic disturbance at number five Lake Foot Lane. You two attend on foot; I'm going around there in the van. They are two regulars, Steve – Harry and Sally Smith. We can generally talk them out of fighting but sometimes it does get violent so be a bit careful. I'll see you there,' she said.

'Roger; out,' I acknowledged.

As we set off walking quickly in that direction, I asked Kevin: 'Do you know them?'

'I've never been to an incident there but I've heard plenty about them. I know the husband by sight, though.'

We arrived in less than five minutes and found Sergeant Clarke already there, standing beside the police van, clearly entertained by the loud fracas that could be heard from inside the house.

'How many *more* men are you going to screw around with while you're meant to be my wife?' bellowed the man.

'What are you complaining for?' the woman screamed back. 'At least I get paid for it. At least it means that I bring a damned sight more money home than *you*, you bone-idle lump. And what little you make you pour back down your neck at the bar in the Labour Club!'

The crashing and yells hit a new pitch while we were going up the path to the front door.

'Let me go first,' said Carol. 'They know me. But mind yourselves, they can be unpredictable.'

The door wasn't locked. We walked straight in after knocking just once. The sight as we entered the kitchen was something to behold. At the far side of a small pine table, in the middle of the floor, was Mrs Smith. She was wearing an unfastened synthetic fur coat over a grubby, rather short old nightdress, curlers in her hair, cigarette drooping from the corner of her mouth, and she was brandishing a battered but large copper-bottomed saucepan in her right hand.

At our side of the table, stark naked and wielding nothing but a small wooden spoon by way of feeble self-defence was the overweight Mr Smith, facing his fearsome wife and clearly more than a little bit apprehensive. Three chairs lay on their sides on the floor, one of them minus a leg, which was lying broken alongside it.

The bold Sally never took a blind bit of notice that there were now three police officers in her house but instead just flung the pan as hard as she could at her husband, even though we were standing behind him. He dodged left, Carol dodged right and I had time to duck, but poor Kevin, who was still in the kitchen doorway unable to see exactly what was going on, took it square in the middle of his forehead and went down as though he'd been shot. For what seemed like ages we all just stood there in total silence, staring at the motionless form lying in the hallway.

Then Sergeant Clarke said 'Right, Sally, you've done it this time. I'm arresting you for assaulting a police officer.'

As Carol cautioned and handcuffed Mrs Smith, I checked that Kevin was still breathing. Thank God he was. I rolled him over into the recovery position and then ran to the van and used the VHF radio to tell the force control room what had happened and I requested an ambulance.

Back in the house, I found Carol kneeling by Kevin's side with her fingers on his neck, monitoring his carotid pulse. The Smiths, meanwhile, were standing together by the table in the middle of the kitchen floor; him with his arms around her, and they were both crying.

'Don't arrest her,' Harry Smith blubbered, through copious tears and snot. 'It was just a lovers' quarrel. We didn't mean anyone to get hurt. Sally didn't mean it.'

'You police came in illegally; you never even knocked,' said Sally Smith.

'We did knock but we were also were entitled to enter with a view to stopping anyone getting seriously hurt, Mrs Smith,' said Carol. 'Steve, look after Kevin.' Then she stood and turned to the Smiths. 'You are coming with me to the van,' she said to the woman.

Both of the Smiths started to protest but Carol quickly interrupted them: 'One more word, just *one* more, and I'll kick both of your arses right around the town.'

Her undoubted reputation was such in Hawthwaite that they both had the good sense to shut up and within moments Mrs Smith was being led, handcuffed and sobbing, to be locked in the back of the police van. Then Carol came back to the house and said: 'Steve, you stay with Kevin until the ambulance comes then get back to the nick as promptly as you can. I'll need to stay there now that there's a prisoner but after you get back I'll need you to go and tell Kevin's wife what has happened. We can't tell her something like this over the phone. The ambulance will probably take him to Carlisle if he's still unconscious – our hospital here is far too small to deal with this kind of thing. I'll see if we can arrange for one of the traffic patrol lads to take her to him but failing that I might have to ask you to do it. I don't want her driving herself there if she's all upset.'

'Yes, by all means, Sarge'. I'll see to it,' I said.

The ambulance arrived only two or three minutes after Carol had driven away with the prisoner.

'Which hospital?' I asked, a few minutes later, as they came back out of the house with Kevin on a stretcher.

'Carlisle Infirmary,' said the older ambulanceman. 'We have to allow for the possibility that his skull may be fractured.'

By the time I had walked briskly back to the police station, Sergeant Clarke had called out Inspector Sumner from his home and was waiting for him to arrive.

'It doesn't look like the Traffic Department can spare anyone to take Kevin's wife to him, Steve. They sound as though they're having a very busy evening themselves, so I'm going to stick my neck out and ask you to go and tell her what's happened and then go off-sector and drive her straight there,' said the sergeant.

'Yes, Sarge', of course I'll do it. Can I just clarify that you'll want me to stay at the Infirmary with her until you or someone else lets me know what to do?' I asked.

'Yes, do that,' she said. 'Class it as an order from me then if anyone at division or headquarters gets their knickers in a twist about us being without our vehicle, I'll deal with it, not you. I've left his address on the telephone message pad on the table in the muster room. Kevin's wife's name is Sheila, and I know they've got two school-age children so you're going to have problems getting the kids taken care of, but I'm sure Kevin has told me before that Sheila's got two sisters in town so hopefully one of them can look after the kids. We will just have to hope we don't need the van for the rest of the night.'

Just as I was about to go out of the back door into the car park, I heard a key being turned and Inspector Sumner walked in.

'Hello, Steven. Where are you off to?' he asked.

'I'm just going to tell Kevin's wife what has happened,' I said, 'and...'

'Drive her to the hospital, I hope,' he replied.

'Yes sir, but in the heat of the moment we weren't sure if it would cause problems re the van,' I said.

'Yes, of course it's alright lad; don't worry about it,' said the inspector. 'Were you with Kevin 'til they put him in the ambulance?'

'Yes, sir.'

'So what did the ambulance lads tell you?'

'That they had to allow for the possibility of it being a fractured skull, sir,' I replied.

'Oh, dear God. Well don't let me delay you any longer. Give Sheila our love, from my wife and me, and tell her that we will be in touch tomorrow and anything she needs, she only has to ask,' he said.

I was relieved to see a downstairs light still on at the Bottomley's house when I got there, less than five minutes later. Even in just the street lighting it was easy to see that their semi-detached house was well looked after. All of the front was a rose garden with the bushes along all four sides of the lawn as well as in a central, circular bed.

Sheila Bottomley's welcoming smile started to fade the moment she saw the expression on my face when she let me into the house, and once again I started to tell a wife that her husband had been hurt.

'So how bad is he?' she asked.

Within moments, even though the hall light was behind her, I could see that she had turned an ashen shade of white.

'I'm not really sure, love, but it would be wrong of me not to tell you that one of the ambulancemen thought there's a possibility Kevin might have a fractured skull,' I said.

Sheila started to cry, silently.

'I'm going to drive you to the hospital,' I said, 'but first we'll need to arrange for your children to be looked after. You have sisters here in town, don't you?'

She nodded but was choked up and unable to speak. She picked up an address book off the telephone table right beside where she had slumped on an armchair, and she struggled to find a page. All she could do was point at a name and address. I rang the number.

'Hello?' answered a man who was clearly surprised at getting a call at 11pm.

'Mr Landers, please don't be alarmed,' I said, knowing that I was almost lying but that I had to get the news over to them without causing too much panic. 'This is PC Shearwater of the Hawthwaite police. I believe your wife is Sheila Bottomley's sister. Sheila is fine and I'm with her now, but is that right?'

'Yes, my wife Claire is Sheila's sister,' he said. 'What's this about?'

'Well Kevin was on duty with us tonight and he's been hurt,' I said. 'He's been taken to Carlisle Infirmary and I'm going to drive Sheila through there in the police van but of course we'll need someone to look after her children for the night, which is why I've phoned.'

'How bad is he?'

'It's possible, and I stress only possible, that he may have a fractured skull,' I said. 'But that's not certain yet.'

He swore and then said: 'I'll be there in five minutes. I'll bring the kids here for the night.' And he immediately hung up.

As soon as I got Sheila Bottomley in the police van and we set off for Carlisle, she seemed to calm down a little.

'You said before that it was a domestic fight and you were there, too,' she said, but can you tell me what actually happened?'

'To cut a long story short, Sheila, a couple were fighting and one of them threw a big, heavy pan at the other and unfortunately Kevin didn't see it coming and it hit him more or less between the eyes; the base of his forehead,' I said.

'A *pan*?' she said. 'For heaven's sake. I've threatened to chase him with one a few times but I never thought he'd go and get it done somewhere else!'

She was forcing herself to try and smile through a few remaining snuffly tears and I admired her for it.

Then she said: 'Do you think he'll be alright? Is it bad?'

'Well to be honest, Sheila, to me it just looked like a whack on the head,' I said. 'It was the ambulanceman that said it might be fractured so I can't really say. But I've known people recover swiftly from injuries that looked much worse.'

We filled the rest of the journey with alternating bouts of meaningless chit-chat and spells of complete silence. Getting to the hospital, half an hour later, was clearly a relief for both of us.

I parked the van near the entrance to the Casualty Department at the big, old-fashioned infirmary. As soon as we entered, one of the nurses came straight to us.

'I presume you are here about the injured policeman,' she said.

'Yes, he's my husband,' said Sheila. 'How is he?'

'Well he's still being examined at present,' said the nurse. 'I'll tell the doctor you are here so if you have a seat he'll come and talk to you as soon as he's finished checking your husband over. In the meanwhile, I just need to take a few quick details from you.'

She sat with us and jotted down all the facts she needed. Then she thanked Sheila, stood up again to leave, and then said: 'There's a drinks machine just around this corner if you want something. We'll come back to you with an update as soon as we can. Alright?'

Sheila nodded a silent acknowledgement and the nurse set off to walk around the corner she had just mentioned, so I told Sheila I would get us both a drink and walked after the nurse.

'Excuse me,' I whispered as I hurried to catch her up. 'Just to clarify something, do you know if he was conscious when they took him in to examine him?'

'No, he definitely wasn't,' she said.

I thanked her and went back to the machine for two coffees.

The ambulance had reached the hospital some time before us and it wasn't long before the doctor came to see Sheila. He introduced himself as Tony Albright and sat down beside her.

'We are just doing x-rays at present, Mrs Bottomley, and they will tell us much more. I think he probably has got a fracture but, even if he has, it's possible that it is not too significant. After the x-rays, he'll be admitted to the intensive care unit as a precaution and he may have to spend a few days here until we know exactly what the situation is,' he said.

'Is he going to be alright?' asked Sheila.

'Head injuries are always difficult, Mrs Bottomley,' said the doctor. 'I don't think it could prove fatal if that is what you are asking, but at this stage one never knows. Obviously we'll keep you up to date at every opportunity.'

'Can I see him?'

'Well unless he has to go straight to theatre we'll get him settled in I.C.U. and get him monitored, then we'll let you pop in for a minute,' said the doctor. 'But that might be a while yet. Okay? We are doing our best for him.'

I sat with Sheila for quite a few minutes after the doctor went back to see to Kevin, then I said: 'I'll have to phone the police station, Sheila. Do you want me to phone your sister as well and bring them up to date?'

'Would you? I don't feel up to that,' she said.

'Of course I will. You just wait here.'

I phoned the nick first. It was Sergeant Clarke that answered.

'Hi Carol, it's Steve. Kevin is being x-rayed at the moment. I checked with the staff and he was definitely still unconscious when they started to examine him. The doctor says that at this stage it does look like a fractured skull and that he'll be admitted to I.C.U. next unless he has to go straight to theatre.'

There was a quiet but audible gasp at the other end of the phone.

'My God,' she said. 'Is he really *that* bad? It was a pan for heaven's sake.'

'Well, all the doctor will commit himself to is that it is not likely to be fatal, but he won't be adamant about it,' I said. 'Listen, Sheila wants us to phone her sister – the one that's looking after the children – and put her in the picture. Shall I do that from here?'

'Yes, Steve, by all means,' she said. 'Just keep us up to date, okay? I think it's better that you use the phone rather than the force radio to keep in touch with us for now. We don't want the press to get hold of it yet; they'll blow it sky high. We'll give you your phone money back from petty cash.'

We hung up.

Sheila's sister, Claire, answered the phone when I rang them and she was understandably desperate for information. I gave her all the details I knew and she told me that she was going to go to collect some clean clothing and a soap bag from Sheila's house then drive to the hospital to be with her. She was with us within an hour but there was still no more news from the doctors. With Claire present, there was clearly no need for me to remain so I said my farewells and set off back to Hawthwaite.

It turned out Carol had been right about how the press would treat it. The rather conservative Cumberland & Westmorland Herald gave a serious and factual report but a journalist at the West Cumberland papers apparently had a more tabloid mentality and headlined the story:

"Copper-bottom Tops Cop!"

Chapter Four

Meeting Farmers

It was two days after the pan-throwing incident when we were told for certain that Kevin was no longer in any danger. His skull had a fracture but apparently there had been no internal bleeding. It was taken for granted at the nick that we would throw a party for him as soon as he was well enough.

After seven night shifts, followed by the Monday and Tuesday off, I was back in on the Wednesday for the first of six 2pm–10pm lates. Neither of the sergeants was there when I arrived, the required fifteen minutes before my shift started but Linda Hargreaves, the civilian typist, gave me a beaming smile and said 'Hi, Steve. Inspector Sumner is in his office upstairs and he's asked me to send you up for a quick chat with him.'

My leather-soled boots clump-clumped along the twisty, linoleum-floored narrow corridor and up the creaky old stairs. Hawthwaite Police Station wasn't a place one could easily move around in quietly.

'Come in, young Steven. There's no need to stand on ceremony, lad,' the boss shouted, before I was even within ten feet of his door.

'Good afternoon, sir. I believe you wanted to see me,' I said, as I entered.

'Aye. Sit yourself down. I just want to make sure you're settling in alright,' said the inspector as he peered at me over the top of his gold-rimmed glasses, as I sat on what looked like a very old dining room chair opposite his large, old oak desk which was positioned so that he could see at an angle out of his window down on to the street outside.

'Yes, fine thanks, sir. I think it's going well.'

'Good. I take it you've heard by now that Kevin is in no danger? He must have a thick skull; the damage was nowhere near as bad as they'd bargained for,' he said.

'Yes, sir. Great news.'

'Okay, son. Now that you are starting to settle in here, one point I want to make to you today is that this door is always open if you have any problems,' said the inspector. 'If you ever have anything that you can't sort out yourself or via the sergeants, you come to me, alright? The same applies if there's something urgent when I'm off duty; if there's something you're really not happy about and you can't resolve it to your satisfaction elsewhere then you phone me at home, alright?'

'I will, sir,' I said.

'Okay. Now from all accounts, Steve, you've got an excellent reputation for doing the job well but there are three things that I tell everyone that comes here and you'll be no exception. Firstly, when you are speaking to older members of the public I want you to remember that, even now in the nineteen seventies, older individuals may well be people who fought in the Second World War or even the Great War for our freedom, so I want you to show them due respect. That applies to everyone you speak to but I will never tolerate wise-Alec young policemen giving ordinary, decent members of the public any lip.'

'That's fine by me, sir.'

'The second point is to do with the paperwork you'll submit. This is simple. Most people labour under the sad misconception that solicitors and barristers and magistrates and judges are all intelligent people but often nothing could be further from the truth. I know you've got three years' proper service since your cadet years, Steve, but I want you always to remember that those people have to be told *everything* in all of your reports or statements. You even have to spell it out that if water is unrestrained it will flow downhill. I want you never to presume that anyone will read between the lines of anything you write. If something happened or is relevant – and is admissible in evidence, of course – then you include it and you do so in a sensible, chronological order. Happy with that?'

'That's fine, too, sir,' I said.

'Good. The last of my three points is that if you do your job properly, you *will* get official complaints made against you every now and then. You must already know that. Some people that you have to deal with think that attack is the best form of defence so they will say all sorts of lies about you. I couldn't care less if you get lots of complaints, Steven; that will just prove that you are doing your job. But I would be concerned if it turned out that some of them were substantiated and that your actions had been unjustifiable. You understand?'

'Yes, sir.'

'Right, now that that's sorted out I've got a job for you this afternoon that a few lads love but most of the lads hate. Did you do any work with farmers when you were at Penrith?'

'No, I can't say that I did, sir,' I said.

'Do you know anything about stock movement books for farm animals?'

'I've heard of them and I used to work the summer holidays on local farms when I was still at school; but I wouldn't know a stock movement book if I fell over it, sir, to be honest.'

'Right,' he said, with a faint smile. 'You can enjoy a whole new experience today, then. Basically, they are just little booklets, issued by the Ministry of Agriculture, which we have to check, supposedly on a regular basis. Every time a farmer moves stock onto or off his land he's meant to write it in the book. Now seeing that you were born around here you should be aware of how dreadful farmers are at keeping written records. The first time one of them actually *does* write anything down, I'll faint with surprise,' said the inspector.

'All my mates that are in farming hate the paperwork,' I said, laughing.

'Yes, precisely,' said the inspector. 'Anyway, I've got a couple of farms for you to do today that are overdue. The main thing is to be genial but still to impress on them the importance of getting it done. I'll guarantee you that they will ask you to leave them a couple of blank pages then sign it, so they can supposedly fill it in later. But if you look back I'll wager that there'll still be a couple of blank pages before the signature of whoever of us went last time, too. If either of those things happen today what I want you to do is tell them you can't leave anymore blank space but you'll go back again in one or two weeks' time and that you'll expect it to be completely up to date so you can legitimately sign it then. Mind you,' he continued, 'the farmers around here are generally grand folk so be diplomatic. Don't go upsetting them too much. Tell them that the inspector at Hawthwaite has had a bollocking from headquarters because the Ministry men have found some stock books with signed, blank pages and that the manure has hit the propeller. Tell them it's more than your life's worth to let it happen again this time. Happy with that?'

'Yes, that sounds fine, sir. How am I meant to know that the records are accurate, though?'

'You aren't. That's for the Ministry men to check. Our job is just to make sure that entries are being made. The two I want you to do today are Isaac Nicholson at Wren Crag Farm, Ravenscale, and Bill Hodgson at High Outgang Farm, in Snabside. The first one – Ike Nick, as he's known – can be a bit of a temperamental old bugger so tread softly with him, but the other one – Bill Hodgson – is one of nature's gentlemen. *His* stock book might even be up to date. It's generally the only one that ever is.'

It was the last day of October. The bracken on the fellsides was a rich russet brown, and the leaves on the trees were a vivid mixture of oranges and yellows. The first few days of November were always briefly the very best time to see the full glory of the autumn colours, unless a gale had already ripped the branches bare.

The sun was shining as I drove the police van along the eastern side of Nethermere. For two miles, the lake was nearby on my right. Sometimes I had trees on both sides of the road but often just on my left; they were all broadleaves, no conifers. The views over the water towards Nether Pike were spectacular, not for any grandness of scale – the highest fells only reach a little over three thousand feet high and the longest lake was only twelve miles long – but for sheer prettiness. I never needed to be reminded why I loved the Lake District so much or why it is the most-visited national park in the world. And anyway, if it had been good enough for William Wordsworth and his poetry it was good enough for me.

I stopped for a while on Netherpot car park, right by the lakeside. Thefts from parked cars were fairly commonplace throughout the Lakes – often carried out by teams of thieves from Manchester, Liverpool or Newcastle – so I had a good excuse to stop and have what was really just a pleasant walk around. Despite the autumnal sunshine, the air was as chilly and crisp as if it were still early morning. I took great lungfuls of it and enjoyed the sharp taste of its freshness. The pebbles on the narrow strip of beach ground noisily under my boots as I walked down to the water's edge. A drake pochard, trying not to be seen, paddled quietly away along the edge of a reed bed on my left. After a couple of minutes drinking in the view, it was time for me to go back to the van and continue up the valley.

After I had left the head of the lake behind, the broad, sweeping valley suddenly narrowed down and the road passed between high crags on either side of the road, less than four hundred yards apart – this bit was a rock climber's Mecca. The river wove its way back and forth through the narrows and between a couple of small grazing meadows that had long-since been cleared from the woods that were particularly thick along this section of the valley floor. There were oaks, beech, sycamore, birch, hazel and willows now, but in millennia gone by – before man changed the landscape – it would have been an impenetrable alder and willow swamp. Any footpaths in earliest times would have had to follow the high ground.

Another four miles brought me to the very head of the valley, the hamlet of Ravenscale. I drove between the six or seven houses that formed the main settlement and then turned right into the yard of Wren Crag Farm. As I got out of the van I felt a tug on the bottom of my right trouser leg and glanced down to see that a border collie had sneaked up behind and nipped at my ankle. Fortunately it had only grabbed the serge material of my uniform. I back-heeled my boot at the dog but it was far too fast for that and easily dodged aside.

'Give over, Gyp,' commanded a deep surly voice. '*I* don't mind you biting policemen but you'll likely just get sent to prison if you do.' The man was standing in the doorway of a cowshed and turned his attention to me. 'What do *you* want, then?' he said. 'Shotgun certificate? Stock books? Or just to be a general pain in the arse!'

'Are you Mr Nicholson?' I asked.

'Well is there any other bugger here? Who else do you think I might be; *Maggie bloody Thatcher*?' he said.

'Well you were right with one of the things on your list,' I said. 'It's the stock movement book that I've come to see.'

Isaac Nicholson was a stout, ruddy-faced man, maybe only 5'7" tall, and it was easy to see that despite his fifty-or-so years he was as powerful as a bull. His trousers were brown but whether that was by design or from years of accumulated grime was debatable. They were held up at the waist with a bit of coarse, creamy-coloured string of the type known as binder twine to the locals. He wore a shirt that once upon a time had possibly been white, but it had apparently been worn and washed scores of times too many. It was unbuttoned nearly to the waist and the sleeves were rolled up, rather neatly, well above the elbow, and he wore a flat cap. His bare arms and chest made it very clear that he didn't feel the chill in the air.

'Well you could always make yourself useful and shovel some cow shit out of this byre while I go and look for the damned book, but I don't suppose you'll do that so you'd better come in t' house," he said.

His hobnailed boots crunched across the cobblestones of the farmyard. It was no surprise to me that even after we were inside the back door of house he never even glanced in my direction, let alone spoke to me.

'Grace?' he bellowed. 'Grace! Where the divvel are you?'
Any sign of grace had seemingly long since disappeared from the weary face of the woman that appeared.

'What are you shouting for, Ike? I'm not deaf,' she said.
'PC Plod, here, wants to see the stock movement book. Get it for him,' he said.
'Mind your manners,' replied Grace. 'The word is "please." Come in Constable; take no heed of him.'

Mr Nicholson stomped off, going back to shovel more manure no doubt. And at that moment in time I couldn't have wished his task upon a nicer man. The back door of the house led straight into the kitchen and there was a lovely aroma, one I hadn't smelled for years, not since I used to stay for occasional nights at a friend's parents' farm at Linthwaite. Sure enough, when I looked around, there at the side of the vast fireplace was a whole side of pork, hanging up, salted and cured.

'By heck; Mrs Nicholson, that side of bacon smells grand,' I said.

A modest smile was her only acknowledgement but that smile transformed her face. She'd obviously been very pretty as a younger woman.

'Will you have a cup of tea while you are looking at t' book?' she asked me.

'Yes. That would be nice, thanks,' I said.

She switched on the electric kettle then dug the stock movement book out of an old wooden bureau that obviously amounted to Ike Nicholson's entire office.

'I'm not sure he'll have done it, Constable,' she said. 'I keep asking him to, every time he goes to the market, but I'll be amazed if he ivver has; the blighter.'

Sure enough, it only took me a few seconds to see that not only had no entries been made in the last thirteen months but, just as the inspector had predicted, there was also a blank page prior to one of my colleagues' signatures, made the year before.

The kettle had obviously been boiled once already because by the time I had glanced through the stock book Mrs Nicholson had filled the teapot and turned to ask me: 'Sugar?'

'Two, please,' I said.

'So? Is it a mess?' she asked.

'Well, I'll have to have a word with him. The inspector has been getting an earful from the Ministry of Agriculture people. They've been finding books like this, where one of us has left blank spaces and signed it, and they're putting a stop to it. I'll have to come back next week to make sure that it has been brought right up to date. This time, I'm not allowed to sign it until it's been done properly,' I said.

'Oh, well; It'll serve him right if he gets into bother. Heaven knows, I've told him often enough. Here's your tea,' she said.

We sat and chatted for a few minutes; long enough to make me feel rather sorry for the long-suffering Grace Nicholson. And then I had to be off. I stopped at the byre door.

'Can I have a word, before I go?' I shouted to the figure clattering around in the half-light.

'Will it mek any bloody difference if I said no?' said Ike Nick.

I held my tongue and waited over a minute until he deigned to put down his shovel and come to the doorway. I explained the situation again, just as the inspector had outlined it.

'Do you think I've got nowt better to do than sit filling in that bloody book before you tek it on yourself to come swanning back here next week?' he growled.

'Mr Nicholson, this works both ways. You were given more than a fair chance thirteen months ago to get that book in order so the question is whether *you* think it is reasonable that we treat you leniently and then you throw scorn in our face,' I said, trying to sound stern.

'Well do what you bloody-well like. If it's done by next week, it's done, and if it isn't it's just hard luck.'

'No, Mr Nicholson, it's not quite that easy. If it *is* done by next week, that's wonderful. If it isn't then I'm sure the magistrates will resolve the matter in court once and for all. The choice will be yours,' I said.

If looks could have killed, Isaac Nicholson's expression would have committed me to the fires of hell. He turned and stomped off, the hobnails of his boots almost striking sparks from the stones.

The valley of Snabside runs parallel to Overdale but I had to back-track down the valley for several miles then head down the west shore of Nethermere in order reach the road that links the two valleys. There were much shorter routes over the mountains but only suitable for fellwalkers and sheep. As I drove northwards down Overdale, I had the sun more or less at my back. The clarity of the air was amazing; the view of the distant mountains north of Hawthwaite was delightful. I was aching to stop again and just enjoy the views, especially over Nethermere, which by now was down below me on my right, rippling gently. But time was against me. I had no desire to blot my copybook by taking too long.

At last I swung westwards, away from the lake. The road climbed then dropped again through some coniferous forestry plantations, then suddenly burst out of the trees and I was met with the view of one of the prettier dales of the Lake District. Like my home valley at Linthwaite though, Snabside had no lake and so it was less visited by tourists – something that many of the locals would be grateful for, despite the lack of additional income that more visitors could have created.

High Outgang Farm was up near the southern end of the dale. The road was both narrow and very twisty, so the two-mile journey took several minutes. I knew enough about Lakeland's Norse heritage to know the meanings of many of the place names in all the valleys. Even the traditional layout of the fields at High Outgang was apparently typical of those found beside the fjords of Scandinavia. The ancient design wasn't hard to see for only part of the farmland was on the flat valley floor; the rest stretched away, up the hillsides and eventually led onto the open, bracken-clad fells.

A tarmac-covered lane led the quarter mile from the public road up to the farmyard, which was hidden behind the eighteenth-century, whitewashed farmhouse with its attached, stone-built barn and cowsheds. On the other side of the yard, furthest from the public road, a corrugated zinc Dutch barn was bulging to the rafters with baled hay. There was no immediate sign of life but a two-year-old, gold-coloured Austin Allegro was standing near the door of the farmhouse.

Just as I walked into the porch, the door opened and a stunningly pretty young lady emerged. She was looking down. She didn't see me until she had stepped out, and then she jumped as though she'd been electrocuted.

'Oh, my giddy aunt! Where did *you* come from? You nearly gave me a heart attack,' she said.

I lost my struggle to keep a little smile from my face and, just as I was going to apologise, she added: 'Well I'm glad you think it's funny, frightening folks like that.'

'No, I'm sorry. I certainly don't think it's funny,' I said, fighting back the desire to laugh. But then I lost the battle and my sides started to shake.

'Liar!' she yelled as she started to laugh too. 'I bet it's your hobby – sneaking around trying to scare the living daylights out of everyone.'

After a few moments, we each started to get our composure back and I said, 'Actually, I've come to see your father's movement of stock book. Is he in?'

As her giggling subsided, she eventually managed to tell me that her father was at the cattle market in Penrith and her mother had gone with him to go into the town, shopping.

'Never mind, though. I know where he keeps his books. Come on,' she said and led me into the house. From the hallway – which ran straight through, front to back, in old statesman house fashion – we turned left into the kitchen where she turned around and riveted me with a wonderful smile. 'I'm Elizabeth, by the way, Elizabeth Hodgson.'

'Steve Shearwater,' I said, and I shook the hand she offered.

'Well sit yourself down, Steve. I'll get you the records.' She left the room but was back in moments with the book. Her hair was the darkest auburn, tied back in a neat ponytail that reached all the way down to about an inch below the belt of her jeans – jeans that were tight and fitted her slim but womanly body to perfection. She was tall, too; maybe 5'8", and her white blouse set off her suntan very nicely indeed. Yet again I was offered a cup of tea but this time I accepted not for the sake of having a drink but so that I could spend a few more minutes in the company of such a stunner. I held the book up quite high so that she couldn't see which page I had open, and I even spent time studying blank pages in an effort to prolong the task. To my silent disgust, the book was apparently bang up to date. My signature could have been made and me been back on the road in about fifteen seconds flat. Under the circumstances, I think the patron saint of procrastination and delaying-tactics would have been proud of the way I stretched the job out.

Just as I had more or less run out of things to say, we heard a vehicle drawing into the farm yard, and the clattering noise that is so typical of an agricultural trailer.

'That'll be Mam and Dad back now. Just sit still for a minute;

dad always likes a chat with you police lads.' She said it as though I needed persuasion to remain. If only she knew. But then perhaps she did; I could never fathom women out. She went outside to greet her parents.

'Constable Shearwater, I believe,' boomed Bill Hodgson as he strode into the kitchen a few moments later. He started to reach out his hand so I stood up and shook it. 'Liz told me she'd got you the stock book. Was it all in order?'

'Well if I'm going to be honest, Mr Hodgson,' I said. "It's only the second one I've ever seen and it looks perfect to me. I've had to come out today though because the bosses at headquarters are on the warpath about some of the lads signing books that aren't up to date.'

'You must be new to Hawthwaite then, are you?' he asked.

'Yes. I was at the town police station in Penrith for almost two years but then I was injured so I've spent the last year on light duties at the force headquarters on the edge of town: Carleton Hall. But I used to go to school in Hawthwaite.'

'You're not related to Bob Shearwater from Linthwaite, are you?' he asked.

'Yes. He's my dad,' I said.

'Well, stone me,' he said. 'He was allus a good laugh was Bob. I used to go to Satterthwaite School with him back in the thirties. You think on to tell him I was asking after him.'

'I will, gladly,' I said.

'Are you living at home with your parents, then?'

'Just for a while. I'll probably be looking for a decent flat in Hawthwaite before too long. I've grown too used to my independence now. It would drive either me or my mother mad if I stay there too much longer,' I chuckled.

Inside, though, I was aggravated. My cue to leave was clear and I wasn't going to get a chance to have another few words alone with the lovely Elizabeth. But deep inside, I knew that it was possibly no bad thing. Plucking up the courage to ask someone like her out when I'd only just met her was probably beyond me.

Chapter Five

The Dead Centre of Town

Inspector Sumner laughed when I told him of my little altercation with Isaac Nicholson.

'You'll probably get quite a few more of those visits to do at various farms in the next few weeks, Steve,' said the inspector. 'We've got scores of hill farms on our patch, as you well know, and I want them all visited in the next month or two. But listen, I have another job I'm going to ask you to consider but it's not compulsory; it's not the sort of job everyone would be comfortable with. There'll be some overtime in it though, if you don't mind doing it. You know St Mary's Church at the bottom of the town?'

I nodded.

'Well there's a road running past the east side of the churchyard,' he said. 'You know the one?'

'Yes, sir. Larkspur Hill.'

'That's the one. So you know then that there are several houses along that road that back onto the churchyard. But if you have ever noticed, one of those houses, the one nearest the church is separated from the rest by a long building that used to be a barn but is now used for storage,' he said.

'I think I know the one you mean sir, yes.'

'Right. Well in that house there's a family of proper rag-tags; the Baldwins,' said the inspector. 'There are two sons, Peter and Paul. Peter is maybe twenty-one or twenty-two and he's never caused us any bother. By all accounts he's a reasonable lad that holds down a job and works hard. But Paul, on the other hand, is a proper little rat. He's nineteen and already has loads of convictions for burglaries, thefts, receiving stolen goods, and some assaults, too. But social workers made sure the magistrates have been too lenient with him. There has been a recent spate of burglaries around the west end of town and I'll put money on it that it's him.'

'You want someone to do observations on the house, sir?'

'Yes, precisely,' he said. 'But it won't be a comfortable job. I want observations on the *back* of the house and that can only be done from the churchyard. Do you fancy it?'

'Gladly. Will it be full nights?' I asked.

'Yes. Now that the clocks have been put back, it's getting dark early,' said the inspector. 'You'll be on 6pm to 6am so it will be four hours overtime per night. With luck you might even see him go out after dark and then come back home later. But you'll need your granddad's long johns. And you'll need to be well hidden, too, because a lot of people from the Hill Foot housing estate take a shortcut through the churchyard on their way home from the Laughing Lord pub each night.'

'I'll do it, sir,' I said. 'And I've got mountaineering thermals so I'll be fine.'

And so it was that two days later, on the Friday evening, I found myself sneaking into St Mary's churchyard just after 6pm. I had driven to a nearby lane in my own car so that nobody would see a police car in the vicinity or an overdressed policeman carrying a small rucksack. Apart from alpine-quality thermals, I had a dark blue sweater on, under my tunic, then my double-breasted greatcoat over the top, with its black buttons for night time and, I had my police cape with me too, to go over the top of everything if I got really cold. I loved that cape, even if it did make me look like Batman. It was warm even on the coldest nights.

I had been to the churchyard in civilian clothes the previous day and while I'd been pretending to study the headstone inscriptions I had worked out where I needed to be. It was a prickly option. The only well-hidden place where I could sit down was under a holly bush that had largely overgrown one of the older graves. The leaves were virtually right down to the ground but there was a hollow area under the spikey canopy, with no branches, and I could sit with my back against the headstone, which – in turn – would be between me and the path, about two feet away.

After making doubly sure that there was nobody else around, I crawled into the bush, apologised to the long-deceased occupant above whose head I would be sitting, and got settled. As long as I kept still it was unlikely that anyone would see me, even people using the path so close behind me. A street light in Larkspur Hill was casting it's orange-tinted glow across the churchyard and despite it faintly illuminating my holly bush it would serve me well if anyone did try to sneak across the grounds. Close by, on my left, was a thick, heavily trimmed yew bush. Twenty yards to my right was a sycamore tree with many of its leaves now fallen. But I was in the oldest part of the churchyard so there weren't many other headstones to block my view.

In my rucksack, thanks to my mother, I had enough sandwiches to feed an army and two flasks full of scalding-hot coffee. I swapped my night helmet for a dark green mountaineering balaclava which at first I kept in its rolled-up shape so that I actually had three layers of woolen hat around the top half of my head, and my ears were kept nice and warm. The inspector had told me to keep my radio turned off unless I needed assistance and I had it in my greatcoat pocket rather than in the rucksack. It would be no good in my bag if I needed it in a hurry.

One thing above all else was certain: It was going to be a long night.

By 2am, the sparse procession of people taking a shortcut home from the pub had long since finished and to my relief none of them had spotted me there, hunched up under the bush. The risk of them having a bad fright must have been high if they had done so. And by that time I was starting to get stiff. There wasn't enough room to stretch out, all I could do was check there was nobody around then wiggle and stretch each limb, one at a time.

About ten minutes after I heard the distant town hall clock strike 3am, I glimpsed a swift yet totally silent movement to my right. It startled me but when I turned my head to look, I saw nothing. This much I didn't like; there were plenty dry, fallen leaves on the ground, that should have alerted me to anything moving other than on the footpath. I sat there pondering what on earth it was that I could have seen. It was only when I looked upwards and saw a tawny owl sitting on a low branch of the sycamore that I realised my senses had been deceived. I must have glimpsed its silent flight. The owl sat there, staring squarely down at me. Holly bush or no holly bush, it could undoubtedly see me and was watching intently. I'd always liked watching birds so the fascination was mutual.

Without any warning the owl let out a shrieking, bonding call: "ter-whit." I knew that a response would probably come from its mate, somewhere nearby, and sure enough the answering "ter-woo" came from the far side of the churchyard. Most people think just one solitary owl goes "ter-whit-ter-woo," without ever knowing that what they actually hear is a pair of tawnies communicating. Had I not caught sight of that silent shape ghosting through the churchyard before it announced its presence with that loud, startling call, I would probably have jumped out of the holly bush with shock and taken the Lord's name in vain. I chuckled quietly to myself at the thought.

Suddenly, the owl's head turned quickly to its right. It was watching something moving somewhere in front of me. I felt my heart quicken. Was the job on? Was I going to get my man?

The owl was rocking its head side to side, increasing its 3D vision. It was certainly intent on something. I moved my own head as slowly as I could, trying to peer through different holes and gaps in the holly leaves – movement itself is always the biggest give-away on outdoor covert surveillance. Nothing! But the owl was still watching.

Those few seconds seemed like an eternity. But then I saw the truth; Inspector Sumner had described Paul Baldwin to me as being a rat but I was fairly sure that even the inspector wouldn't expect the young miscreant to adopt that bodily form. A small rat was scuttering back and forth near a headstone about 20 yards ahead and slightly to my left. I wasn't sure whether a tawny owl would try to tackle a fully-grown rat but even to my eyes this was clearly a small youngster. The bird swooped down in deadly silence. There was a momentary little scream as the owl's talons speared the little rodent through and then the tawny was up and away with its supper, just as silently as it had arrived.

Four o'clock came and went, and then – seemingly about a week later – so did five o'clock. At 5.30am I slipped quietly away, climbed over the far wall of the churchyard, dropped into the overgrown lane that passed it by and went back to my car.

Back at the nick, two of my new workmates were changing over. Taffy Williams was just finishing an ordinary night shift and Dick Price was just starting earlies.

'Here he comes – Officer 'Orrible, the graveyard ghost,' laughed Dick.

Taffy showed a bit more empathy. With his wonderful Welsh lilt, he said: 'I bet you're flaming perished, boy-oh; it's been a cold night.'

We chatted for a few minutes then the Welshman and I headed off to our respective homes and well-earned beds.

I got up at 3pm. My mother had heard me moving around and by the time I got downstairs she had a steaming-hot dish of porridge waiting for me.

'That'll warm you up, Steven,' she said.

'Thanks, Mam, but it's nearly dinner time.'

'Never mind that, I'll do you something else hot before you go out. I don't know what your inspector is thinking about making you sit out on the cold ground all night at this time of year. You'll catch your death of cold!'

'Mam,' I protested, 'I'm not Private Pike off "Dad's Army!"' But he loved fussing over her boys, did my mother.

That night I got settled once again, in position by about 6.15pm. My only difficulty was getting under my holly bush without being seen by some of the people who were on their way out to the pub. I ruminated on the fact that not only was I going to see those same individuals coming back past me in five or six hours' time but that in the interim they would be having a much more enjoyable time than would I.

Sure enough, all those hours later, those same individuals were the next high spot of my voluntary solitude. There had been no sign of movement near the Baldwins' house. Shortly after 1am, I looked around to make sure it was safe to move a little then unscrewed the cup and the lid from my flask and started to pour myself a coffee. There was a gasp behind me. A young couple had come up the path – they must have had training shoes on or something equally quiet, because I hadn't heard them coming. They had seen me move. And now the boy, all full of late-teens bravado was coming right towards me to have a look. It was decision time. If he came to me and found out who I was then not only would my cover be blown but the surveillance could never be repeated.

I drew my arms up high as I stood up, spreading my cape like a giant bat from hell, and I burst out from the bush as quickly as I could, doing my best impersonation of a deranged growl... I was sure that the soles of those youngsters' shoes would ignite, judging by the speed at which they fled. Now my only worry was whom – if anyone – they would tell. I could do without angry fathers or brothers coming to sort out the lunatic in the churchyard. The only good thing had been their silent exit – too busy running to scream. Anyway, there was precious little I could do about it right now so I quickly settled back into my hiding place.

Only another ten minutes or so elapsed before I heard footsteps approaching – trotting then stopping, trotting then stopping. *Damn*, I thought, *here comes the trouble*. I slipped my balaclava off and picked up my night helmet from its place beside the rucksack. At least I might get the chance to identify myself to them before I got thumped. Somebody stopped directly behind me; I could even see their hand resting on the top of the headstone and I could hear their heavy breathing.

'It's all clear,' one of them whispered.

'Oh, no it bloody isn't!' I snarled as once again I stepped out and stood up and shocked the living daylights out of two people. 'What have you got in your bags?'

They were momentarily frozen with shock, so I grabbed the nearest man with my left hand and pressed the transmit button of my radio with my right. I almost yelled: '8-6-8 ten-nine, St. Mary's; 8-6-8 ten-nine, St. Mary's.'

"Ten-nine" was our force radio code for "officer requires urgent assistance." Taffy Williams and I had discussed exactly what he would do if and when I called it in but in the few minutes it would take him to reach me I knew I was going to have an interesting time. As I was finishing my call for back up, my radio was sent flying. The man I had hold of had swung his bag at me and knocked the radio from my hand. I could see the second man lunging towards me from a few yards away, on my right. I knew there was no way out of a battle so I let fly with my right fist at the one I had hold of and punched him solidly on the left temple. To my great relief he went down like a fallen tree. My pleasure was short lived, though. The blow that hit my own temple from the guy on my right knocked me down, dazed. He was obviously a bit too sure of his punching prowess though because as I looked up I could see him struggling to pick the other man up, apparently convinced that I was out for the count. I stayed still for just a moment to gather my wits, then stood up and asked: 'And where do you think you're going?'

At that moment, we both heard Taffy's two-tone siren as the police van turned onto Larkspur Hill. The second man dropped his colleague and turned to run. I managed to grab him around the neck but couldn't bring him down. He was trying to punch over his shoulder into my face so I just clung on tightly to let him tire himself.

After a lengthy wrestling match, I heard Taffy's very welcome Welsh accent as he shouted: 'Steve, where are you, boy-oh?'

'Over here, Taffy, near the church door,' I yelled back.

At least I was in a good place to thank god that assistance had arrived. I didn't want to lose either of my suspects. Taff' got to me and helped me push my man face-first against the trunk of the sycamore tree so I could handcuff his hands behind his back. Then we took him back to his fallen comrade.

'Sit down,' ordered Taffy, and he did. 'Let's have a look in these bags. Have you got your torch, Steve?'

Mine was still under the holly bush. Taffy picked his up from where it had been dropped in the scuffle. I unzipped the nearest of the two black sports bags... Bingo!

I turned to the man in handcuffs: 'You are under arrest on suspicion of theft. You are not obliged to say anything unless you wish to do so but what you say may be put into writing and given in evidence.' I paused. 'Do you want to explain where you got all this jewellery?'

'Get stuffed,' he said.

'What's your name?' I asked.

'Father bloody Christmas!'

Taffy shone his torch in the man's face. 'Well, well, well,' he muttered. Then he examined the still unconscious partner. 'Ten out of ten, Stevie, boy-oh. The one you clobbered is the infamous Paul Baldwin and this lippy one is none other than his allegedly innocent elder brother, Peter Baldwin. The boss will be delighted.'

At that, Taffy went back to his van to use the force VHF radio to request an ambulance; Paul Baldwin, meanwhile, made no appearance of regaining consciousness. From where he was lying, it looked as though he might have hit his head on a kerb stone on the edge of the path when he had fallen.

As soon as Taffy came back to where the three of us were at, I asked him to keep an eye on my two prisoners so that I could go and use the van's VHF radio myself. It would get me through to the force headquarters at Penrith; our personal UHF radios only worked locally. I walked through the church gates onto the road and was amused by how many curtains were twitching in the nearby houses.

'PC 8-6-8 to BB,' I called in.

'BB receiving; go ahead 8-6-8.'

'My colleague who was using call-sign Zulu-Three-One has just requested an ambulance for one of my prisoners, currently at St Mary's Churchyard, Larkspur Hill, Hawthwaite. The man was knocked unconscious during a fight with me and I therefore request that you contact Inspector Sumner, here in Hawthwaite, or any other appropriate officer in case they wish to attend the scene to review what happened; over.'

'Roger, 8-6-8. Will do. Over.'

'Received. 8-6-8 out,' I replied.

And just at that, an ambulance turned into the street. Another set of blue flashing lights to excite the neighbourhood.

I locked Peter Baldwin in the back of the police van then saw Taffy helping the ambulancemen lift Paul Baldwin, on a stretcher, into the back of their vehicle. I heard Taffy asking them which hospital they would take him to, but we all knew the answer. If someone was unconscious they had to be taken to the Infirmary at Carlisle. There wasn't an option unless the C.I.C. was too busy, in which case they would go to the West Cumberland Hospital at Hensingham.

Just as the ambulance doors were being closed a scruffy, heavily built man pushed his way through the now-gathered cluster of onlookers.

'Oh, good. I'm glad you've got the bugger,' he said to me. 'He frightened my daughter half witless in that churchyard, pretending to be a bloody ghost or something. I was just going to go and smash his bloody head in!'

Chapter Six

Return Visits

The C.I.D. had instantly pushed me aside in the Baldwin case so that they could try and make it look like their victory. O n the same morning that I had made the arrests, they searched the house on a warrant. What they found was nobody's business and they were now busy linking together the many retrieved valuables with the various burglaries that each item had originated from. Paul Baldwin had remained in hospital for two nights, for observations, but was arrested as soon as he was discharged.

By the following Tuesday, my black eye from the churchyard scuffle was rather prominent. I'd been put on 9am-5pm for the day. Soon after my new starting time, I was sitting writing up the relevant observations messages into the back of my notebook when the phone rang. Linda answered it. She chatted to the caller for a minute or two. I could tell she was surprised by whatever she was told but I wasn't paying any attention to what was being said.

When she hung up, she said: 'Steve, wasn't it you that delivered an injury message to a Mrs Susan Watson at Low Keld?'

'Yes,' I said.

'Well it looks like you're going to have to go there again,' she said.

I read the message on the pad that she held out to me, and muttered: 'Oh, God; I'll do it right away.'

I drove to Low Keld immediately. Susan was in the front garden, hanging washing out on the line. She beamed when she saw me.

'Hi, Steve. You've decided to come for a coffee have you? I'd nearly given up hope. What on *earth* has happened to your eye?' she said.

I said as little as possible until we were in the house, then I had to come straight out with it: 'Susan, Adrian is dead. I'm sorry.'

I had to catch her arm to steady her.

'But you said he was only injured... How?'

'They had to do a small operation on him – you probably knew that – but apparently a blood clot formed afterwards and they think it shifted to his lungs,' I said. 'I believe it's called a pulmonary embolism and I'm afraid it killed him instantly.'

Suddenly, she burst into sobbing tears. 'You must think me dreadful. I told you I wished he was dead and now he is. Oh, my God,' she said.

'Don't do that to yourself,' I said. 'It's okay. I don't think anything of the sort. All I'm concerned about is doing what I can to help. Have you any family nearby, or any good neighbours?'

'My mam lives up the village but she's at work at the Bield Retirement Home in Hawthwaite until five o'clock.'

'Well I presume you'll need to think about getting Andrew from school so what about the neighbours?' I said.

'Jane might be in, next door,' she said, indicating the house to the right.

'Will you be alright while I go and see?' I asked.

She just nodded.

At the next house, a woman in her thirties answered my knock.

'Hello, you must be Jane,' I said. 'You might have seen that I've been to Susan's house next door. I had to give her some bad news, I'm afraid. Obviously you'll know that Adrian was in a bad accident but following an operation, I'm afraid that he has died, very unexpectedly.'

'Oh, good grief; poor Susan. What a shock... But I don't know; on second thoughts maybe she's well rid of the bastard,' she said.

'I wonder if you'd mind coming round to Susan's to help me get her sorted out, please?'

'Aye. Of course I will,' said Jane.

She came with me immediately then, between them, they arranged that Jane would collect Andrew from school. Moments later, without warning, the front door opened and an older woman walked in.

'Mam!' said Susan. 'What on earth are you doing home so soon?'

'I was due a few hours' time off and I didn't feel... Whatever's the matter? What's going on? When I saw the police van I thought he'd come for coffee. You said you hoped he...' Her words tailed away to silence.

'Mam, Adrian's died, in hospital.'

'Oh!'

'Well, ladies, I really am sorry to be the bringer of news like this but unfortunately, Susan, I have to get back now that you've got people here to help you,' I said.

Her mother butted in: 'Now, young man, it's alright. You've only got your job to do. And frankly that wicked man dying is no great loss. Little Andrew won't understand that, though, God love him. But thank you for coming.'

'Mam, would you take Jane through into the kitchen and make us all a cup of tea, please? I just want a word with Steve,' said Susan.

She ushered the other two away, closed a door behind them, and then turned to me.

'Like I was saying, Steve,' she said to me, 'I'm so ashamed of the way I've acted. You must think me dreadful.'

I started to speak but she raised her hand to silence me, and continued: 'After you left here last time I sat wondering what on earth you must think of me saying it was a pity that Adrian hadn't died. And now he has. I'll feel guilty for saying that, as long as I live, but that's not half as bad as knowing that you actually heard me say it. I'm not a vindictive person, honest I'm not.'

She moved right up to me. Two big tears rolled from her sad, blue eyes and slowly down her cheeks. Sympathy for a weeping woman came between me and professional good sense. I wrapped my arms around her and gave her a hug.

'It's okay, Susan.' I said. 'Please don't upset yourself. Under the circumstances what you said was very understandable. It might have surprised me at the time but I certainly don't think anything bad about you because of it.'

She took her head from my shoulder and looked up into my face. With her fingertips she reached up and touched my blackened eye. With a stifled sob for breath, she said: 'And *you've* been hurt.'

'That's nothing, and it's the last thing *you* need worry yourself about. You have enough to think about. Now, you have still got the telephone number for the hospital, haven't you?'

She nodded her head mutely, as I eased her way from me.

'Good,' I said, 'but I'm sorry, Susan, I really do have to go now. You take care of yourself, alright? If there's anything I can do, just phone the police station, okay?'

'You *will* still call in sometime, won't you?' she asked.

'Yes, I will. I promise.' And with that, I left.

Twenty minutes later, I was back in the office.

'Done?' asked Linda.

'Yes, done.' I nodded slowly, a bit lost in thought about Susan Watson.

'Well there's a list gone up on the noticeboard since you went out. Kevin's back on his feet and he's having a small party on Friday night for any of us that want to go to his house. Put your name on if you want to go. Have you someone to go with?' she said.

I laughed. 'No, Linda, I'm footloose and fancy-free at present.

No woman.'

I endorsed the telephone message and the Station Occurrence Book – known to all as the S.O.B. – to show that I had delivered the message to the Watson household, then I put my name on Kevin's party list. And then I knew I had to get on with a task I would rather have ignored: a trip back to Ike Nicholson's farm to see whether he'd brought his movement of stock book up to date. My drive up the valley was quicker than the last time. I neither had the "time to stand and stare," as the old poem by W.H. Davies recommends, nor was the weather very nice. The clouds were low and grey; in local terms it was a greasy day.

When I got out of the police van at the farm, I was watching out for Gyp, the ankle-assassin, but it wasn't daft; it knew I was ready for it and it kept out of reach of my boot. The bold Ike was rather less full of himself, too. Whatever the cause, he wasn't offensive when I arrived. That outcome always threw me when I turned up somewhere expecting aggression or abuse but the people concerned were reasonably well behaved. It was as though my adrenalin level was up in anticipation and I had no way to burn it off.

'Oh, you're back are you,' he said, matter-of-factly. 'Your eye's a good un. Somebody 'parenttly doesn't like policemen! Anyway, the book's not quite done but I can finish it now if you'll wait ten minutes.'

'That's alright, Mr Nicholson.' I said. 'If we can get the job done today it'll be grand. Do you want me to go away and come back again shortly?'

'Nay, lad; thoo'd best come in t' house. I'm sure you could manage a cup o' tea while yer waiting,' he said.

He really was subdued. His hobnails crunched once again as we headed across the cobblestones and I followed him into the farmhouse.

'Grace? Where the bloody hell are you?' he shouted. 'Come and make this policeman a cup o' tea. He wants a drink while I finish that stock book off.'

Grace Nicholson came into the kitchen, once more with a deadpan expression on her face, but as soon as Ike's back was turned she grinned at me and made a "yack yack" gesture at him with her fingers and thumb. It didn't take a genius to work out that she was well pleased that he'd felt forced to back down from his aggressive stance.

Maybe this was a good time for me to strike up a bit of a rapport with Ike. It would certainly make any future dealings with him a lot easier.

'So how's your year going, Mr Nicholson? Any good?' I asked.

'Like t' parson's nose, lad. Good in parts, but the rest's nobbut been middling.'

'What about the lambs? Did you have a good spring?'

'Gaily good, but I lost eight to damned foxes. Gawen Crosier brought the foxhounds twice and we got one of the blighters the second time. Yon's the little bugger's brush, yonder.' He pointed to a fox's tail hanging on the wall. 'It was an old dog fox, a bit past his best but they still ran him twelve miles afore they could catch him.

'And are the auction prices any good, this autumn?' I asked.

'Could be worse, I suppose. Could be worse.'

'So are they your herdwicks, two fields back? Or do you stick to Swaledales?'

'Nay,' said Ike. 'My father was a herdwick shepherd and I've followed him. I'm not one for Swardles at all.'

'Did you show any at the Hawthwaite Show in August?' I asked.

At this, Ike Nicholson put his pen down and turned to look me straight in the eye.

'Was thoo browt up aroond sheep, lad?' he said. 'Thoo seems to know at least summat about them.'

'Well if I do, it's only from helping on my mates' dads' farms before I left school,' I said. 'I don't know that much, but Ah's nobbut frae Linthwaite,' I said, falling back into the dialect.

'Come wid me,' he said and he led me through to the parlour. A large part of one wall was decked with brightly coloured rosettes, although some were a bit faded.

'Lookat!' he murmured, proudly.

'All from your *herdwicks*?' I said, genuinely surprised.

'Aye, ivvery last yan o' them. Come back through to t' kitchen and finish yer tea then afore you go I'll show you some of t' best herdwick tups you've ivver seen.'

Over the next few minutes, the difference in the man was remarkable. Completely gone was the belligerence. He became affable and animated. He even went so far as to smile! It wasn't hard to see that even the tolerant Grace was taken aback as she busied herself bringing us our cups of tea.

Suddenly, he turned on his chair, thrust the stock book at me and said: 'That's it done. Sign it, or do what you must.'

I signed it.

'You'll have some Wellington boots in your van, have you?' he said.

On many days I could have answered yes, but not today. As the pair of us left the house, I caught a little glimpse of Grace smiling to herself as she tidied up the cups.

'Oh well you'll just have to mind where you're walking then,' said Ike. 'Come on.'

He led me through a mucky part of the farmyard and round the back of the byre. There, in a stone-walled pen, were four marvellous herdwick rams: thick-set curly horns, white faces and fleeces still tinted the typical dusty deep pink he'd rubbed in when he'd taken them to the various autumn shows.

'Theer! Watt's ta think o' *them*, then?' he asked, clearly confident that even other shepherds would have been hard-pushed to criticise such fine beasts.

'Ah's nee expert, Mr Nicholson,' I said. 'But they look first rate. Absolutely first rate.'

But he wasn't listening. He was far too busy beaming at his beauties. I had just discovered what Isaac Nicholson lived for. It was neither money nor comfort, because Lakeland hill farmers rarely got tolerable amounts of either. "Ike Nick" had shepherding in his blood; it was as simple as that. And, despite all the odds, it appeared that I was also part way to making friends with him.

After a couple of minutes of his contented silence, the farmer turned away from his sheep pen. A couple who'd been out on the fells were walking past, on the road, about twenty yards away. A bit surprisingly, they were both wearing shorts and the shapely young lady was also wearing a tightly fitting, turquoise top. Their trek over the high ground had obviously been enough to have kept them warm in the chill air.

'By hell,' said Ike. 'Just look at that.' He was staring at the woman. 'Why do you think it is that flies and midges bite the likes of you and me when they could be chewing on *her*?'

He stared for a while longer, then added, 'Aye, well, I can't detain you any longer. No doubt we've both got work to do.' Then, as an afterthought as we walked back towards the house, he added 'And when you're up at this end of the valley just come in if you want another cup o' tea.'

'Thank you, Mr Nicholson, I will. You can be sure of it,' I said.

On the Friday, I had another 9-5 day shift so I was able to go to Kevin and Sheila's party at eight o'clock. Only a handful of people had got there before me – everyone else had gone to the pub first. Kevin opened the door but Sheila, standing close behind him, said: 'Out of the way, Kevin; I'm just gonna snog one of your mates.' She was true to her word, too. She gave me an enormous kiss, then said: 'Thanks, Steve. Carol's told us that you did all the first aid when Kevin got clobbered, and you were very kind to me that night, too. Thank you.'

I said: 'If it'll get me another kiss like that, can I get a brick and knock your husband out again, please?'

'Oy!' piped up Kevin, grinning. 'Put my wife down. I'm not sure I like you being *that* kind to her!'

We stood in the kitchen for a few minutes, laughing and chatting. And Kevin was delighted that I had a much more visible mark from the remnants of my black eye than he had suffered at all with his damaged skull.

About ten o'clock, Linda the typist and her husband Mick came bundling through the door together with a slightly smaller, pretty, dark-haired girl who looked remarkably like her. They were all laughing and fooling around, and when they had said their hello's to the hosts Linda pointed at me and said: '*There* he is, Louise. That's Stevie-baby, Hawthwaite's most eligible bachelor. Steve, come here.

This is Louise, my sister, and I've told her *all* about you.' Linda giggled; Louise blushed.

'How much have you had to drink, Linda?' I teased.

'More than me,' chipped in Mick. 'In fact probably more than an average fish,' he added, with a hiccup and a silly grin.

'Well, *I* am not drunk, even if *they* are,' Louise protested to me, although I wasn't convinced.

'Good for you. Those two will probably end up getting arrested, anyway! Can I get you a drink, though?' I asked her.

'Gin and tonic, please,' said Louise.

'What about you two? Shall I get you a drink, too?' I asked.

'I'll come with you,' offered Mick, and the pair of us went back through into the kitchen to raid the drinks table. 'Do you fancy Louise, then?' he asked me, as we poured the drinks.

'Hell, Mick; slow down. I've only just met her. But yes, she's very attractive,' I said.

'Well, I sometimes used to wonder which one of them I'd most like to marry,' he confided. 'But don't tell Linda I said that!'

'Don't be daft. Course I wouldn't but that must be worth fifty quid for me to keep quiet! So how old is Louise?' I said.

'Twenty. Two years younger than Linda. And have you seen her *arse*!?'

'Well I certainly won't try to compare it with Linda's while you're around. I don't want another black eye,' I said. There was only a large bottle of Schweppes tonic water on the drinks table so I didn't have the option of taking Louise a small bottle to let her mix her own. 'How does she like her drink, Mick?'

'Two thirds gin, one third tonic. And don't mess about with a small amount of gin; she wouldn't thank you for it.'

'Mick, you're incorrigible. If I do that she'll think I'm trying to get her plastered.' I went to the door between the kitchen and the living room and shouted, over the sound of the music: 'Louise, how do you like your drink mixed?'

'Two thirds gin and one third tonic, please. Plenty! In a big glass if there is one.'

Mick just stood smiling, looking down and pretending not to notice while I was pouring a huge G&T in a tumbler. I was trying not to laugh, myself.

'Stop smirking, you git. Either that or just say it and be done,' I said.

He grinned at me and said, 'Told you so! And you'd better watch it, too. She's likely to try and take advantage of you if she gets you tipsy, so don't go getting brewers' droop.'

Before I could say another word, Mick had turned and taken Linda's drink, and his own, back through into the lounge.

He proved to be right about Linda drinking like a fish, and it obviously ran in the family – to the extent that I started surreptitiously mixing shandies for myself because I was in grave danger of her drinking me under the table.

I knew I could never keep up with the number of drinks the girls were having. But the surprising thing was that it didn't seem to be affecting Louise at all.

The night wore on, the music got louder, and the secretary's sister got closer and closer. The pair of us ended up sitting on the floor in the corner of the room – me right in the corner and her close beside me, on my left. Her skirt had slid a little way up her slightly bent legs, revealing very nice thighs.

'You got a girlfriend, then?' she asked.

'No. Not guilty, Your Honour. I'm totally single.'

'Fancy a snog, then?' she asked mischievously, as she rolled onto her side to bring her mouth to within two inches of mine. And who was I to argue? Her tongue dived straight for my tonsils. Damn; talk about getting my attention quickly.

'Put him down love, he's nearly married.'

The voice was that of Dick Price, who was swaying merrily at the other side of the couch and slurring his words without a care in the world. I felt Louise go tense, then she pulled away.

'What do you mean?' she asked him.

'Well I had a cup of tea with his mother-in-law-to-be today, that's all,' he said as he turned away to stagger his way upstairs to the bathroom, chuckling to himself.

'What the hell are you on about?' I shouted after him, incredulously.

'Yes. Would you care to tell *me*?' Louise demanded, looking straight at me. And for the first time I could see that she was getting to be the worse for wear from all of her drinks.

'I have no idea, Louise. But I'll get him to come and explain as soon as he gets back. He's only joking. In fact, I'll go now.'

I was waiting for him as he staggered out of the bathroom. 'Hey, you dozy pillock,' I said. 'You've upset Linda's sister. What was all that nonsense about a mother-in-law?'

He laughed. 'I was only teasing. I was at the old folks' home for a brew, earlier and Mrs Goss, Susan Watson's mother, said Susan fancies you.'

'Well come and tell Louise, you daft prat,' I said. But Louise wasn't there; nor were Mick and Linda. I went through into the kitchen.

'Sheila, have you seen Louise?' I asked.

'They all left, Steve. She looked a bit upset. What happened?'

'Nothing that me killing one of my own colleagues won't cure,' I said.

Chapter Seven

Veteran of Violence

I left my car in Hawthwaite, after Kevin and Sheila's party, and got a taxi home to Linthwaite, so I got the bus back into town the next morning, well before my 2pm starting-time. I went straight to the nick to get Linda Hargreaves' home address then went around there to apologise to Louise.

Mick answered the door, with the heel of his hand pressed hard against his temple. His thinning hair was as yet unbrushed and almost vertical. He fit perfectly the old description of looking like someone who'd been dragged through a hedge backwards.

'Too late; she's gone,' he muttered, before I could say a word. He looked at my blank expression. 'Louise,' he added for emphasis. 'She thought you were trying to con her last night. She left early this morning. She's seriously peeved with you, mate.'

'Is Linda in?' I said.

'Linda,' he bellowed, loudly enough to make himself wince. 'Casanova's here from last night.'

Linda came to the door, bedraggled, and looking as though she had fallen into the dressing gown that she was wearing.

'When you next see Dick Price, Linda, will you please garrotte him for his tom-foolery last night? He was talking a load of nonsense

63

and thought he was being funny,' I said.

'So you aren't seeing Susan Watson, then?' she said. She had obviously been asking questions of somebody to find out what Dick had been implying.

'No! For pity's sake, Linda; her husband died this week. They haven't even buried him yet. Even if I was interested, what do you think I am?'

'Oh.'

'Please tell Louise that I'm sorry that it happened but that it's all a load of nonsense,' I said.

'Yes, I'll tell her. But she lives in York and she's going back there tonight, after she's been to see our parents,' said Linda.

'Okay, thanks. I won't keep you at the door any longer. Just tell her that, please. I'll see you at work sometime next week.' And with that, I headed to the police station. .

I was on foot patrol in town that afternoon. The weather had changed; there was a bitter chill in the air and it wouldn't be many more days until the surrounding mountains got their first dusting of snow. I wore my woolen greatcoat.

Moments after I turned onto Main Street, I was approached by two middle-aged couples.

'Gee, are you a reeyal, live English Bobby?' asked the woman with curly, white hair, and a strong American drawl.

I wasn't too sure what other possibilities there could be for someone who was wearing the uniform I had on, but I smiled and said, 'Yes, madam. I am.'

'C'mawn, Tammy. Let's have our photograph taykin with this fine young man. George, git the camera out. George! Wotcha waitin' fer?'

As the women each clasped one of my arms tightly, George dutifully obliged, with about a dozen pictures from every conceivable angle.

And then it was Tammy's turn to speak: 'How d'you git to yer gun under that big coat?'

'The British police don't carry guns, madam.' I said. 'The only weapon we carry is a truncheon and even that is almost never used.'

'Ooh, officer; show us your truncheon then,' the white haired one purred.

'Ohh myyy,' said Tammy a few moments later. 'How're you meant to defend yerself with that little piece a' wood? What if the bad guy has a hayndgun?'

'It's not as bad as it seems. We've always had strict gun controls in Britain so crimes involving firearms are very rare. Which of the States are you from?' I asked, trying to change the subject.

'Texas,' replied Tammy's husband. It was the only word that either of the two men managed to inject in several minutes of photographs and conversation.

As the four of them walked away down the street a few minutes later, I could still hear Tammy's voice. 'I think he's kidding, Bobbie-Sue. He *must* have a gun!' The word actually sounded like "muyust" but I took it to be must.

Outside W.H. Smiths, I nearly collided with a woman who was hurrying out of the doors with her head down. It was Grace Nicholson from Wren Crag Farm, clutching a copy of Farmers Weekly.

'Hello Mrs Nicholson, how nice to see you. How are you both keeping?' I said.

'Fine thank you,' she said. 'But you dun't have to call me Mrs Nicholson, call me Grace. And aye, we are both awreet.'

'Well I'm Steve.'

'Well, Steve, you sorted our Ike out last week, good and proper! It made me chuckle, you getting him to sit down and do that damned book. An' then when he took a shine to you and took you to see his tups, well that was a capper, that was. Him, being friendly with a policeman! I've seen ivvrything now. Just tell your boss that anytime summat needs checking on oor farm, he'd better send *you*. Ike'll grumble like billy-oh if anyone else turns up, mark my words,' said Grace.

We stood and chatted for many minutes and at the end of it my respect and liking for her had gone up even higher.

'Well, I'd best be off,' she eventually said. 'If I don't git yam in time to make old grumble-f'yass his tea there'll be hell to pay.'

But the fact that she was very fond of the cantankerous old Isaac was plain for all to see.

A few minutes later, as I was walking past the cinema, my radio came to life.

'Control to 8-6-8; over.' It was the voice of Sergeant Clarke.

'Receiving, Sarge'. I'm outside the Mecca, over,' I replied.

'Roger, Steve. Come in and collect the van and go down to the bungalows on South Hill. There's a report that an old man has collapsed in his house and nobody can get in to help him, over,' said the sergeant.

'On my way, Sarge'. He isn't a retired captain, by any chance is he? I'm getting a run of these cases, over,' I said.

'Not to my knowledge, Steve. Oh, you mean the old chap you went to out at Scarbank? No, it's not another captain; out.' She was laughing as she replied.

This time, when I arrived at the bungalow concerned, there were only two people waiting. One was the neighbour that had called for the police, and the other was Susan Watson's mother, Mary Goss. It was only a hundred yards from the retirement home where she worked as a nurse.

'Oh hello, Steve,' she said. 'What a nice surprise. They came for one of us to help Jack but we can't get into his house. He seems okay, though. He fell and pulled the curtains down with him but he says he hasn't hurt himself. I've been shouting to him through the letter box.'

I bent down and took my turn at shouting to the old chap.

'Jack, can you hear me? This is the police. Do you think you might have broken any bones?'

'Nay, lad. I'm sorry to be sec a nuisance to you,' he called back. 'No, nowt's brocken. I've just gitten sort of twisted like, and I can't git back up.'

'Do either of you know how old he is?' I asked the two women.

'He'll be eighty or mebby a bit more,' replied the neighbour. 'Oh, and his last name is Dash. Mr Dash.'

'Jack,' I shouted through the flap once again, 'I'll have to break one of your windows around the back of the house to get in so don't worry when you hear the glass go, alright?'

'Aye, lad. Just do what you must. This is gittin tedious,' he called.

I was in the house within a few moments and opened the front door to let the neighbour and Susan's mother come in.

'Hello, you old divvel,' said the neighbour. 'You'll have to stop frightening me like this. It put the fear of God up me when I realised your curtains had been pulled off the rail. This is Mrs Goss, she's a nurse from the retirement place over the road. She's come to check you over and see if you need a doctor.'

With that, the lady from next door set about trying to fix Jack's curtains while Susan's mother and I picked the old chap up and got him sat on a big, comfortable chair.

'What happened?' Mrs Goss asked.

'Oh, I just did summat stupid, lass, that's all,' he said. 'I tried to git over there to adjust the heating thing without using my walking frame and I tumbled; it's as simple as that.'

'Have you got any pain at all? I really think we should get the doctor out to see you,' she said.

'Well my home help doesn't come to put me to bed until eight o'clock and to be varra honest I feel like going and having a lie down now. It's shaken me up a bit,' said Jack.

Mrs Goss looked up at me and asked: 'Would you mind helping me? I know it's not your job.'
'Of course I will,' I said.

We got Mr Dash through to his bedroom where I supported

him as she undressed him. Neither of us expected what we saw. A huge lump of his right thigh had long been missing; a trench across the muscle big enough to hold the thickness of a woman's forearm. And his left bicep had a smaller but similar-looking, deeply-gouged scar.

'Dear Heavens, Jack; however did you get those wounds?' Mrs Goss asked.

'First World War, lass, when I was eighteen.' He replied, bluntly.

A minute or two later, when Susan's mother went through to the living room to phone for old Jack's doctor to come and check him over, he beckoned me to stay with him.

'Want to know how I got them?' he asked, pointing at the area where his pyjamas were covering his horrendous thigh injury.

'Yes, if you want to tell me,' I said.

'Aye, well it would nivver do to say owt in front of women, because they would git all upset and squawky about it,' he said. 'The battle of Paschendale Ridge, Belgium. We'd been ordered to go ower the top and try to capture a German trench about a hundred yards away. Well, we ran and we ran. Most of my mates were slaughtered – cut in half or blown to bits, some of them. Anyway, I dived heed first into a shell hole that I thowt was empty but there was a Jerry still in there wid three of his dead mates. And as I jumped in, he shot wildly at me, point blank, and that's what blew that lump out of my leg. Then he stuck me with his bayonet but in the panic he was a bad aim and just got my arm. The next I knew, my mate Jimmy popped the muzzle of his rifle ower my right shoulder and blew that Jerry's heed wide oppen. It blew my eardrum out too, so I've been stone deaf on that side ivver since. Then a Jerry sniper got Jimmy, right in the chest, and he fell in the hole beside me. I nobbut just had time to say thank you to him afore his eyes glazed over. "Thank you," I ask you – how feeble is that? We didn't get that Jerry trench, either. I had to wait for dark then I crawled back through no-man's land to our own side. And that was the end of my war. I was bloody lucky not to have bled to death.'

I listened in silence and total respect. Jack Dash didn't know that what he told me that day would stick with me for life.

Susan's mother was happy to stay with Jack until the doctor arrived so I left to get on with my work. But before I did, I received two open invitations to call in "any time" for a drink – one from Mrs Goss for both the retirement home and her own house at Low Keld, and the other from Jack, himself. After his fall, the old chap started to leave his back door unlocked during the daytime and I started calling in regularly – as much to make *him* a hot drink as to have one myself.

The timing of his war story turned out to be a coincidence. When I got back to the nick, Carol Clarke told me that Dick Price had been off sick, following the Bottomley's party and had now phoned to say that he wouldn't be in tomorrow, either. And that was a problem; tomorrow was Armistice Day, with its Service of Remembrance – the eleventh hour of the eleventh day of the eleventh month. Sergeant Clarke asked me to change shifts to another 9am-5pm and to march with her at the back of the town parade. Inspector Sumner and Taffy Williams would be at the front.

'Helmets, not caps,' she instructed. 'Well-polished boots, and don't forget your white, dress gloves.'

So Remembrance Sunday had special meaning for me that year; old Jack's recount weighed heavily on my thoughts.

On the Monday, I was on yet another day shift. It swiftly became common knowledge that PC Dick Price went in front of the boss and got a roasting for getting himself absolutely plastered at the Bottomley's party, and making himself too ill to work his early shifts, over the weekend.

I was completely taken aback when I was called up to the boss's office immediately after Dick came out, though. I was wondering what I might have done to get *me* in the queue for a bollocking.

'Come in, lad. Have a seat,' said the boss. Then he noticed my expression. 'It's okay. You're not in bother. Just a few things I have to sort out with you, that's all. Are you still enjoying it here? Still settling in alright?'

'Yes, absolutely fine thanks, sir,' I said.

'A bit different to your cadet years in Hull, I take it?' he said.

'No comparison at all, sir. Hull was a much nicer city than I expected it to be but I wouldn't go back to city policing for anything,' I said.

The Inspector raised his eyebrow, quizzically, so I carried on: 'The thing is that in the city they were so busy with a never-ending string of urgent jobs that there wasn't a hope of having any time to just help folk with day-to-day problems like we can here. I recognised that, even as a cadet. It's a great balance in Hawthwaite. A few biggish jobs to keep the adrenaline flowing and the rest of the time we can just be helpful. And we can have a laugh with folk, too.'

'Fair enough,' said Inspector Sumner. 'I can't argue with you on that. Anyway, I have a couple of bits of news for you and the first is a little pat on the back so that's why I asked for you to come and see me. You will remember that headquarters are running a one-week crammer course in a few days' time for the thirty constables who have consistently achieved the best results in the training papers that they've been sending out all summer?' I nodded that I did and he continued: 'Well I'm pleased to tell you that you are going on the course, although they haven't given us much notice. And more importantly, I'm pleased to tell you that you weren't just in the top thirty, you were in the top five. Well done.'

'Thank you, sir. I'm chuffed,' I said.

'Keep at it, lad,' said the inspector. 'Bramshill Police College – the so-called "Brands Hatch" – beckons if you work hard enough and if that's what you would like. Right; next. I am having to re-shuffle the shift rota system in December so as soon as you get back off the course I'll want you to have Saturday and Sunday off, work three earlies, have Thursday and Friday off, then work five more earlies. It means that from then on you'll have your long weekend a week later then you would normally have done. This will be a permanent change. Will this cause you any major problems with any holiday bookings you may have made?'

'No, sir. Not at all,' I replied.

'It'll mean you'll be on nights at Christmas but at least you'll be off at New Year,' said the inspector. 'Is that Okay?'

'Yes, sir. It's fine. I had nothing planned.'

Chapter Eight

Cross Country

Tuesday was day three of the national Lombard R.A.C. Rally and they were coming right through our patch. Except for a Ford Escort RS2000 driven by local man Malcolm Wilson who was doing well, all the other leading cars were being driven by Scandinavians – Stig Blomqvist, Ari Vatanen, Hannu Mikkola and Bjorn Waldergaard – and they were followed by the rest of the remaining ninety eight competitors. The first of them was due to reach the Black Wood forestry stage about 9.30am. We were all out on patrol, right after six o'clock, to stop the early wave of spectators from abandoning their cars all over the roadsides. There were special car parks in fields all around Black Wood and several thousand followers were expected. The event was big enough for the Constabulary to have issued a Force Order to specify which personnel had to be at certain locations. Ours was the first of three special stages in the county so it was all very precisely planned. Traffic Department personnel were everywhere, most of them in patrol cars but some on Norton Interpol motorbikes.

I had drawn a lucky straw. I was given point duty, controlling the competing cars where they re-emerged from the end of the stage onto the public road. And from where I was standing, I had a perfect view of a long, downhill section of Forestry Commission gravel road in Black Wood, prior to the finish. I was going to see some spectacular dashes for the line.

The next few hours were as frantic as they were exciting. By the time all the competitors had come through, at their roughly one-minute intervals, the majority of the spectators had gone on their merry way to other stages. We all needed a cup of tea.

I set off to drive back the three miles to Hawthwaite but just where my road crossed the town by-pass, I saw a young man waiting at the roundabout, trying to hitch a lift towards Penrith... I thought I recognised his face, but who was he?

I just had time to steer right and keep going around the roundabout once more as it hit me that I'd seen his face on a Criminal Records Office bulletin. He was wanted.

As soon as he saw me coming back around the roundabout for the second time, he was off. He climbed a nearby, five-bar-gate and was jumping off the far side of it into the field as I pulled up. I grabbed the radio handset; I had no time to worry about interrupting anyone else: 'Zulu-Three-One, out of the vehicle on foot pursuit of a wanted person at the top roundabout on Hawthwaite by-pass. Request assistance.' And, with that, I took the van keys and ran to vault the gate after my suspect.

He was quick, and even after we had crossed two large fields, mostly uphill, I had gained no ground on him. He was still about fifty yards ahead of me but I wasn't too bothered; I had always been a distance runner – always done best at cross-country. At the far side of the second field, he climbed the fence into dense trees. We had gone up the steep hillside about another four hundred feet by the time I caught him. I grabbed the dangling hood of his Parka jacket. He stopped instantly and lunged around with his fist. We were both far too breathless to say a word. A big scuffle started and we ended up rolling around in decayed pine needles and loam. He managed to get a thumb into one of my eyes and then kneed me in the stomach as we rolled over. A scuffle was one thing but going for my eyes was quite another. I managed to get a handful of the hair on one side of his head and a fistful of ear on the other, and gave his head a good thump against a convenient bit of fallen wood. It dazed him long enough for me to 'cuff his wrists behind his back. I dragged him to his feet by his neck. My right eye was hurting like fury.

'What's your name?' I asked.

His muttered oath in response was accompanied by an attempt to kick me in the groin. Now I was really vexed. I used his long, curly hair to pin him, face first, to the nearest tree while I searched his pockets – none too gently – but there was nothing there to identify him.

It soon became very obvious that he was going to resist me every step of the way back to the road and in the end I had to bundle him head-first over the fence at the edge of the trees. As I climbed over after him, he picked himself up off the ground and had another go to kick me in the stomach. This was getting a bit much and I gave him a good kick up the arse for his troubles. Eventually, I grabbed hold of the handcuffs and pulled his arms upwards. It forced him into a bending position so that the 'cuffs would bite into his wrists enough to hurt.

'As soon as you tell me you've calmed down and that you'll walk back to the van without any more fighting, I'll let go,' I told him. 'What's your name?'

'Fuck off.'

So I dragged him.

With one field to go, we were joined by one of the traffic motorcyclists who had still been nearby when my request for assistance had been broadcast by control room. After we got my suspect into the back of the van, the bike officer followed us to Hawthwaite nick – another man who could sniff out a free cup of tea, no doubt!

The two of us took my man into the charge room at the nick, where Sergeant Wyatt was waiting.

'So who have we got here?' he asked.

'I don't know his name, Sarge', but I have reason to believe he's wanted,' I said.

'What's he wanted for?' asked the sergeant.

'I'm not sure. But I've seen his face in the C.R.O. bulletins,' I said.

'What's your name and address?' Sergeant Wyatt asked the prisoner.

'Mind your own fucking business.'

'Oh, but son, it is my business and rest assured that you are going nowhere until we find out. Steve, can I have a word outside with you?' I followed him out into the corridor and closed the door. 'Steve, you are going to have to do better than this. If there's any chance that you have made a mistake, then we have a false arrest on our hands. Has he committed any other offence that we can hold him for?'

'Obstruct police, assault police, I suppose, Sarge',' I said.

'Yes, okay. But under the circumstances it's still a bit tenuous. The resistance only happened because of the arrest. You'd better find that C.R.O. bulletin that he's in, and find it now!'

Lancashire was the northernmost county in England that issued Criminal Records Office bulletins really relevant to Cumbria – LanCRO's – and I went right through several months' worth with no success. It was almost as a despairing afterthought that I turned to the Scottish bulletins. But there he was; listed three months previously, wanted for armed robbery in Glasgow.

I went back through to the charge room. Andy Wyatt still hadn't placed him in the cells for fear of a possible backlash.

'Got him, Sarge'. Gregor McVitie, wanted in Glasgow for an armed robbery in July. Age 27, numerous convictions for serious assaults, burglaries, thefts and robberies,' I said.

At this, McVitie – still with the handcuffs on – launched himself up from the bench to body-charge me against the wall but Sergeant Wyatt and I grabbed him.

'Into the cells, then,' said Andy. 'And if he's going to be like this, we'll leave the 'cuffs on him.'

When we had finished the paperwork and left McVitie to stew in the cells, Andy stopped me in the corridor and said: 'Well done, Steve. I'm starting to think that if you fell in a bloody sewer you'd come out smelling of roses. But don't do that again, please. You'll give me a premature heart attack if you make a habit of arresting people without knowing what the hell you are locking them up for! Now go and phone Strathclyde Police and ask them to come and drag that bastard back up into Scotland.'

Chapter Nine

After Last Orders

My week of nights went very quietly indeed, until the Friday – or to be more accurate, the early hours of Saturday. I had just got into the police station at 1am for my sandwiches, when the phone rang.

'Hullo. My name's Lewis. I've hired a holiday cottage for the weekend opposite the Drovers' Inn at Linthwaite and I think there are still some people in there, drinking.'

'Oh, I see. Are they creating any noise or disturbance, sir?' I asked.

'No. I just thought you should deal with it. That's all.'

'Very good, sir. I'll be there in a few minutes.'

I sighed as I got back into the police van. The Drovers and the Birch Hill Arms pubs at Linthwaite were my "locals" and I really didn't savour the prospect of having to deal with my own friends. It was only a six- or seven-minute drive, and on the way I decided to treat the matter as lightly as possible without failing the gentleman who clearly thought that late, quiet drinking in a country pub was a terrible thing.

I parked the van about a hundred yards away from the pub when I got there, just so that it wouldn't be seen, then I walked quietly down the deserted street and around to the back door of the

Drovers. Amongst many other knick-knacks, I always carried a length of string in the big pocket of my tunic. I lifted one metal dustbin to one side of the pub's back door and another bin to the other, then fastened a single piece of the string across between them. It was a variation of a trick I'd been shown at the Bruche police training centre by a rookie British Transport Policeman called Barry, and it sometimes came in useful.

I crept back around to the front of the building and then – pretending to adjust my cap, so that my hand hid my face, in case my imminent arrival was seen through the windows – I walked up to the front door and knocked loudly.

'Police. Open the door,' I commanded, in my deepest voice.

Just as the landlord, Chris Kendall, opened the door, looking woebegone, there was a crashing noise from the dustbins at the back of the pub. I couldn't stop myself from laughing.

'Who did I get with the bins, Chris?' I asked.

'Oh, thank God it's you, Steve,' he said, puffing out an enormous sigh. 'I thought we'd been nailed.'

As he closed the door again, behind us, I said 'Don't worry. Someone phoned to complain that you were all still drinking so now I've dealt with it. That's all. That's the end of the matter.'

As we entered the public bar "Big Bill" Underwood came in at exactly the same moment, from a door at the opposite end of the room. He was rubbing his knee and muttering curses.

'Which bloody git booby-trapped the back door?' Then he saw me and, as everyone burst out laughing, he said 'Oh, it was you, ya bugger, was it?'

Apart from Bill, there were four other after-hours drinkers in the bar.

'Well I just wanted to give you something harmless to remember tonight by,' I said. 'It was just good luck that it was me on duty and not someone that would have nicked the lot of you, so please think about that for the future. Next time it might not be me.'

'Thanks, Steve. It's appreciated,' said Chris.

'I'm glad *you* all bloody appreciated it,' grumbled Big Bill, still rubbing a grazed knee. 'You're not the ones that went arse over elbow!' Then he turned to me and said, 'But at least *I* wasn't the one in my birthday suit when I had *my* pride injured.'

Everyone looked at "Ginger" Peel, sitting on one of the bar stools, and there was a roar of cheering and laughing.

'Oh, thanks,' said Ginger. 'You buggers would have to tell the bloody *law* about it, wouldn't you.'

'No, Ginger,' said Big Bill. 'Tell him yourself, then we can just quietly piss ourselves laughing at you again.'

'Bugger off.'

'Go on, Ginger!' Several of them were egging him on.

'Bastards,' he replied. 'But I *will* tell him, 'cos if I leave it to you lot, you'll exaggerate it beyond belief.' Then he looked at me and continued, 'I fancied getting my leg over the other night so I offered Sandra Yaffe twenty quid for a quickie in my car. I drove us up Calva Lane and got my money's worth but then she said she wanted forty quid 'cos I'd taken too long, so I told her to get stuffed. And somehow in all of this, we'd ended up in the wrong seats; she was in the driver's seat. So I got out to run round to that side of my car, and the bloody bitch drove off with it. And I hadn't got a stitch of clothing on, so I had to run home through the village and hide behind bushes every time I thought I heard someone around.'

'There's a rumour going round that "Old Mother Dinsdale" saw him flashing past, quite literally, and she's still recovering from the excitement,' chuckled Bill.

'So do I report you for breaching trade descriptions with your too-slow quickie, Ginger, or will you sue Sandra Yaffe for breach of contract?' I asked, trying to keep my face straight.

'I dunno, but you're still gonna have a field day, aren't you; catching us drinking after time and all,' said Ginger.

'Don't be daft.' I said. 'You really think I would nick you for *that*? I've already said I wouldn't. Just sup-up and get away home. I won't tell anyone if *you* don't. And I mean that. Keep your mouths shut or I'll get into trouble for being nice to you.'

While they gulped the last drops from their glasses and started to leave, Chris said: 'I'll make you a coffee before you leave, Steve.' I could tell by his expression that there was more to it than just a coffee, though.

Minutes later, he and I were sat alone in the kitchen and he handed me a steaming mug of Nescafe's finest.

'I needed to speak to you boys anyway, Steve, so I suppose it's just serendipity that you turned up. I overheard something in the snug-bar earlier. Two lads were sitting in there – I suppose they thought they were on their own, but just by accident I was able to hear what they were saying. Unless I'm gravely mistaken, there's going to be a burglary tomorrow night at the Countryman's Club in Hawthwaite. You know it's their annual Shooters' Ball tomorrow, right?' said Chris

I nodded.

'Well from what I overheard,' he said, 'these two think that there'll be a lot of cash left in the club overnight, after the ball, so it sounded like they are planning to turn the place over.'

'Hell! Thanks, Chris,' I said.

'One good turn deserves another, Steve, but nobody will find out who told you, will they? It would damage my trade if it got out that I told the police when I overheard stuff,' he said.

'That's a guarantee, Chris. Nobody – not even another copper – will ever find out where this info' came from – *ever*.'

Back at the nick, I decided this was one of those occasions when the inspector wouldn't mind being woken up in the middle of the night.

'Hello,' muttered Brian Sumner, when he picked his phone up.

'Sorry to disturb you at two in the morning, Sir. It's Steve Shearwater and I think you'll want to hear what I've found out, despite the time.'

'Oh, do tell,' he replied with a distinct lack of enthusiasm.

I explained everything I'd been told about the rumoured plans for the burglary.

'Alright, Steve,' the inspector said, at length. 'Do you trust your source? Is it good info, do you think?'

'Yes, Sir, I trust him totally but it was an overheard conversation so he was at pains to say that he couldn't be a hundred percent certain about all the details,' I said.

'Okay. Well we'll certainly give it a shot,' said Inspector Sumner. 'And seeing that it's your info', I want you to be on the inside, at the club, tomorrow night. When I come in, this morning, I'll make all the arrangements to get you inside and I'll also arrange for a dog handler to be there with you. I'll fix up for someone to cover your night shift out on the beat, too. Although, coming to think of it, I may just quietly do that myself. The less people who know about this, the better. In any event, son, just come to work for ten o'clock as normal. You'll be on the obs' team. Don't mention it to anyone else at all, alright?'

'That's fine by me, sir. I'll look forward to it,' I said.

Dick Price was on late shift the next day, as was usually the case when I was on nights, but he'd left for home at least fifteen minutes before the inspector and the dog handler turned up. By then it was twenty past ten. There were still a couple of hours left before the Countryman's Club would be closing its doors.

'Do you know Ken Vipont, the dog handler?' Inspector Sumner asked me.

'Only by sight, sir,' I replied to the boss. 'Hi, Ken.'

'How-do,' he answered, as he shook my hand. 'So have you got a decent job for us? Not just a wild goose chase?'

'As best I can tell, Ken,' I said.

Just after 1am, after all the Shooters' Ball revellers had gone home, Ken and I were let in at the back door of the Countryman's Club by Henry Abrahams, the caretaker, who lived with his wife in a flat on the top floor. The place was already in darkness, as the inspector had requested.

'I'm glad you lads are here,' Henry said. 'We've never had burglars in the fifteen years we've been here. Our lass thinks I'm too old to go fighting thieves these days so if they do come tonight, she'll be ever so glad you're downstairs. Thank you.'

'That's fine, Mr Abrahams; it's what we're paid for. Oh, and by the way, Inspector Sumner sends his regards,' I said.

Mrs Abrahams had left a pile of cushions and blankets for us, and there were two flasks which I took to be either tea or coffee, plus a huge plate of left-over vol-au-vents and sandwiches, so we were all set for a comfortable night.

The club was down a tree-lined drive, maybe sixty yards long and the back of the building faced out onto woodland, so potential intruders would either have to come through the woods or over adjacent properties by the side of the club, or perhaps they would just come down the drive. The two main bars in adjacent rooms were effectively back-to-back. The rather posh lounge bar was at the front of the building and a public bar, with snooker tables and dartboards, was in the back room. Ken wedged open the door that joined the two serving areas and we settled down, with him behind the public bar and me behind the one in the lounge. His big, black Alsatian, Spartan – apparently the size of a pony with teeth – wandered back and forward between us. I was just praying that it wasn't feeling too mean, each time it stared at me with its baleful expression. I had a bit of light coming into the lounge from distant street lights and both of us had the dim green glow of emergency exit signs to help us see in the gloom. And then we sat. And we sat. And we sat.

The muffled crash of breaking glass jolted me alert just after three-thirty. It sounded like the noise had come from a toilet that led off the lounge bar. I could see through to where Spartan was now acting more like a pointer than an Alsatian; he froze, facing the noise

– every muscle of his body seemingly locked rigid. Ken appeared at our joining door on his hands and knees, whispering to Spartan, and slowly Ken got hold of dog's collar. There were a few small noises coming from the toilet, including the sound of someone's shoe grating on broken glass. I turned on my radio and quietly pressed the transmit-button three times, then three more. It was a pre-arranged signal. Inspector Sumner would hear the clicks and know that we had intruders on premises. And he also knew not to transmit to us; radio silence was paramount now and nobody else had radios on the Hawthwaite frequency. The toilet door was opening. Whispering. I could hear whispering. So we definitely had at least two intruders inside the club. More than two was unlikely. They were approaching the bar; the shuffling noises were getting closer. One of them bumped into a chair or a table.

'Be careful, you prick,' murmured the other.

Ken and I stood at the same moment, and Spartan pulled against his collar, growling.

'It's too late to be careful,' I said. 'This is the police, and you are under arrest. We have the dog so don't try running.'

If a film director had said: "Cue dog-bark," Spartan's timing would have been perfect. Sadly, though, it had no effect on any common sense that our two miscreants had. They both fled; one back towards the toilet and one towards the front door. Ken immediately slipped Spartan, who leapt towards his "supper" at the toilet door. That left me free to chase the other chap without fear of being bitten by our canine colleague. Naturally the door of the club was locked so I'm not sure where my man thought he was going. As he grabbed the door handle, I grabbed him. He didn't struggle; he just froze, pressed firmly against the door as I handcuffed him. Back through in the bar, we could hear his mate begging Ken to get the dog off him.

'Come on, Spartan,' said Ken, calmly. 'That's not a "Scooby Snack." Leave go of his buttock!'

I radioed the inspector: '8-6-8 to Inspector Sumner; over.'

'Receiving, Steve. Go ahead.'

'Two prisoners in custody, inside the club. Not known at this stage whether there are any more outside; over.'

'There isn't anyone else,' said my man, far too quickly.

I pressed transmit again: 'Sir, from what I've just been told, I would guess that there *is* at least one accomplice out there; location unknown. But these two entered via a window on the west side of the building and without using the drive so I would guess that they may have someone waiting, possibly with a vehicle in Mill Lane, down the riverside.'

'On my way. Out!' said the inspector.

A few minutes later, after Ken and I had walked our two prisoners up the drive to the main road, the police van pulled up alongside us. Inspector Sumner got out. A little blood was dribbling from the left hand side of his mouth.

'You were right, Steve. He was down Mill Lane. It's a while since I've had a good scrap like that.'

We put our two prisoners in the back of the van where their so-called getaway driver was already sitting, handcuffed and dejected. Ken wanted to walk Spartan back to the nick and give him some exercise, so I went in the van with the boss and our three hapless burglars.

'That was a good night's work, Steve,' said the boss, after we'd put them in the cells. Would you mind staying on duty until all the paperwork's done? That way, I can let Sergeant Clarke charge them, with you present, when she comes on duty at 9am, and everything'll be done and dusted.'

'I don't mind at all, sir,' I said.

'Good lad. Remind me never to give you a bollocking for going for a cup of coffee somewhere if this is the sort of info' you can pick up,' said Inspector Sumner.

I couldn't stop myself from grinning at him.

Chapter Ten

Lost and Found

'Is that the police station? Some bugger's nicked mi taxi!'

The voice on the phone was a mixture of bewilderment and indignation.

'Where from, sir?' I said.

'Tarn Close, off Lakefoot Lane. That's weer Ah's calling from. It's a red Volvo estate, MHH 171K. I just dropped old Mrs Mitchell off at number sixteen, a few minutes back. I carried her shopping bags into her kitchen for her, then when I kem oot it hed gone. Some bugger nicked it. The bloody *cheek*! La'al gits!'

'If you wait there, I'll be up to see you in three or four minutes. Flag me down when you see the police van. One of my colleagues here is already passing the details of your car to the force control room so that an observations message can be put out for it, over the radio,' I told him.

Alan Young proved to be a happy-go-lucky sort of chap, although his expression when I pulled up beside him on Tarn Close precisely matched the tone of his voice a few minutes earlier, on the phone – a blend of indignation and bemusement.

'I bet I wasn't in t' house sixty seconds. I nivver even heard the blighters start the engine, and that's a capper 'cos the exhaust's been blowing. I shouldn't tell a policeman that, should I? But I suppose it's okay if the car's been nicked 'cos you can't prove it now,' he said, grimacing at his own joke.

He'd obviously not lost his sense of humour completely, despite losing his car.

Ahead of us, from where we were sat in the police van, there were only two more houses on the left before a beech hedgerow started, between the road and the south side of the Gandy Memorial Gardens, which were named after a well-known artist who had lived in the town. The road itself curved gently away to the right, down a slight hill. It was whilst I was taking Alan's statement that I first noticed a slightly deformed section of the hedgerow.

'Mr Young, before we finish writing this,' I said, 'would you mind if we just go and look at that hedge? There's something I think we should take a look at.'

He gave me his bemused look once more, as we got out of the van and walked down the road.

'Oh, hell. That's nutt watt Ah think it is, is it?' he said, as we looked over the hedgerow at two lines of tyre marks running away from us, down a slope of damp, neatly manicured lawn.

A gate led into the gardens about twenty yards from where we stood, so we walked through and followed the marks down the grassy incline. The tracks passed safely between two large flowerbeds and, even more remarkably, between two of the frames on the crazy golf course, until they disappeared into the base of a huge clump of rhododendrons. We pulled back branches and there, nestled cosily out of sight in the heart of the shrubbery, was the missing taxi.

'How the hell did you know it was going to be doon here?' asked Alan.

'Oh, that was easy in the end,' I said. 'While we were sitting, I saw where the hedge had been damaged. The car must have run away, right through it, and the hedge sprung back up into place after it had gone. Didn't you put the handbrake on?'

'Well, bugger me! I hope I can get it out of here without my mates finding out about this. I'll never hear the end of it otherwise,' he said.

A voice from behind us immediately dashed his forlorn hopes: 'Hey up! Who's been parking in my bushes?' It was Derek Levens, the head gardener, and a mate of mine from Linthwaite, who clearly knew Alan Young well. 'Look, Alan,' he continued. 'If you've fallen on hard times, mate, I'll give you a free pass for the normal car park. You don't have to hide your car in one of my rhododendrons so you can avoid paying.'

'Oh ha ha. Get knotted,' said Alan.

'Now, now, Alan,' said Derek. 'Don't be like that. Just tell folk your car got ambushed, or bush-whacked but Special Branch found it. Your tale will be a runaway success on the bush telegraph. It might even win a few laurels.'

'Will you *get stuffed*!' said Alan.

But Derek was clearly enjoying his puns and hadn't finished yet.

'Oh, Alan,' he said, 'you'd better be careful, or this constable might arrest you for taxi-vasion.'

'He'll arrest me for shoving my bloody taxi right up your arse if you don't leave off!'

I left the two of them embroiled in banter. Derek clearly wanted every possible ounce of fun from Alan's embarrassment. I could have reported Alan Young for "failing to correctly set the hand brake" and also the collision with the hedge that followed but later that day I contacted administrators for the park and cleared it with them that they would simply go through the taxi driver's insurance if there was any cost for repairing the hedge or the turf. It was clear that Mr Young's friends would never let him forget his negligence and that taking him to court would serve no purpose.

My next job, less than twenty minutes later, was an entirely different matter – a car had reportedly hit a pedestrian on a fast section of the town by-pass. It was a sirens-and-blue-lights job – often known as "blues and twos" – and I was the first of the emergency services to reach the scene.

A man in a dirty old raincoat was lying by the roadside with three people kneeling beside him. A blue Saab car was parked on the grass verge about fifty yards further up the road and even from that distance the damage to its windscreen was obvious. As I reached the group of people, I saw that it wasn't just the coat that was dirty, the elderly man that was wearing the coat was grey with embedded grime too.

'Do any of you know him?' I asked.

'He says his name is Bert,' answered the only woman in the group.

'Thanks,' I said. 'Bert? Bert, can you hear me?'

His eyes met mine for an instant, as I spoke, but he merely grunted in response.

'Bert, the ambulance will be here in a moment but I want you to tell me what hurts, alright?' I said.

The old man's eyes met mine for another second or two.

'Bert, does your back hurt, or your neck?' I said.

His "No" was a whisper but at least it was clear.

'Listen, Bert, I want you to try to wriggle your feet for me; just gently,' I said.

Two tatty socks, peeping through big splits in two even tattier shoes became surprisingly active for a few moments. The pupils of his eyes seemed to be equal in size and, together with his level of awareness, everything seemed to suggest that old Bert had fared far better than might be expected, given the nature of the incident. Anyway, the sound of a distant siren told me that his physical welfare would soon be in the hands of experts. Before the ambulance pulled up beside us, I had managed to coax Bert's surname and address from him; he was from Workington. But I needn't have bothered.

'It's Bert Jones again,' said the first of the two ambulance men, as they got out of their vehicle.

'You know him?' I asked.

'Yes. Come over here and I'll tell you about him,' said the second of the ambulance crew, while his colleague checked the old man over. We walked a few yards along the roadside. 'He's unique, is Bert,' he began. 'He tries to commit suicide once every two or three months. He always has a good go at it but somehow he always cocks it up and fails. I'll bet you a pound to a penny that he jumped in front of the car that hit him.'

'How many times has he tried?' I asked.

'I'm not sure if anyone is keeping count, but it's a few. He threw himself off the dock wall in Workington Harbour once, at low tide,' he said. 'But he landed on a sheet of corrugated tin, in among the rocks, and just broke both his legs. He's tried overdosing on tablets at least twice but was found each time. He tried to electrocute himself once but only managed to burn all the skin off his arm. The last time *we* saw him, he'd thrown himself into Nethermere off one of the tourist launches but his raincoat trapped a lot of air and kept him afloat till they pulled him out. He's banned from all the boats, now. Poor old bugger; no doubt he'll succeed one of these days but no-one wants him to. He's a harmless old sod. Likely neither God nor the devil wants him just yet, eh?'

'Oh, well that'll probably be due to his socks!' I said. 'I'll bet that even the devil wouldn't want *those* socks for company.'

The ambulance left the scene minutes later, complete with a remarkably uninjured Bert Jones. It turned out, later, that he had nothing but mild concussion and grazes, despite the head-shaped impression that he'd left in the splintered windscreen of the Saab.

I took the driver to one side and asked what had happened.

'You wouldn't believe it! We had just set off from Low Keld to go to Manchester Airport and fly to Tenerife on holiday, and that old man just jumped right in front of the car; I *swear* he did. I'd been able to see him walking along the roadside from way back. I was giving him a wide berth but he just jumped right in front of me. It was on purpose, it must have been. He's nuts!' he said, with obvious exasperation.

'It's alright,' I said. 'Obviously we'll have to investigate the incident fully but let me just say at this stage that I don't disbelieve you. If I take a quick statement from you – maybe fifteen minutes – will you still be able to get to Manchester and catch your flight?'

He checked his watch and said, 'Yes, and actually, while we're doing that, maybe my wife could take the Saab back home and get our other car. The driver's side of the widescreen looks undamaged enough for her to be able to drive it slowly. Fortunately I always leave a big safety margin for us to be able to get to the airport, thank heavens.'

I finished writing his statement just a few minutes before his wife arrived back with a different car, and away they went on what would hopefully, thereafter, be an incident-free holiday.

I got back to the police station just after 5pm, less than halfway through my 2pm-10pm shift, and it had already been eventful. Linda Hargreaves had gone home, as had the inspector, who had been on 9am-5pm. Sergeant Clarke, on 5pm-1am, was nowhere to be seen and had presumably arrived and already gone out on a job. I was just settling down to my sandwiches in the refs room when I heard someone knocking at the front door. It turned out to be a drably dressed woman in her late twenties, looking rather fraught.

'Can you help me, please?' she said. And I could see that she had been crying. 'My ex-husband has got my kids and he's not meant to have them, and he scares them. He was meant to have them for just a few hours yesterday – the court order says he can see them every other Sunday – but he phoned me last night and said he was keeping them overnight and that he would take them to school himself this morning. He wasn't meant to keep them but I'm scared of him and…'

'It's okay, try to calm down,' I said. 'Come on in and sit down and tell me all about it, alright? Then you can tell me exactly what happened.'

I'd just brewed a fresh pot so I gave her a cup of tea and got her settled.

'I got divorced last year,' she started. 'My husband used to beat me up and then, when he started getting too rough with our two children, I left him. I told the courts about the children but they said he could still see them every second Sunday afternoon. At first it had to be supervised but then they started letting him see the kids alone. I knew something would go wrong and it has. He came for them at one o'clock yesterday and he was meant to bring them back home by six o'clock, but at half past six he phoned me to say his car had broken down so he would keep them overnight and walk them to school this morning. Here,' she said, as she thrust a piece of paper into my hand. It was the court order about custody and visitation. It confirmed her description of his visitation rights.

'Can I ask why you didn't phone us last night?' I said.

'I dunno. I suppose it was partly because I was frightened of what he would do if I did, and partly me wanting to let him have enough rope to hang himself with. I think I thought that you would all take more notice of me if he kept them much longer than he should have, rather than just a little bit beyond his limit,' she said.

'So, Mrs Montgomery,' I said, as I checked through the details on the court order. 'Your daughter, Emma, is seven and your son Jasper is five. Is that right?'

'Yes,' she said. 'And they are both frightened of him, too. Please don't call me Mrs Montgomery, though; I'm getting my name changed back by deed poll. Just call me Cathy. I'll soon be Sinclair again; that was my maiden name.'

'So,' I said. 'Did he take them to school this morning, as he promised?'

'No. I went to collect them at three thirty but one of the teachers told me that he had phoned this morning and said that they were ill. So I went home and phoned him and he lied to me and said that they really had been ill and that he was keeping them again tonight and he would take them to school again tomorrow. You've got to help me get them back, please. I'm so worried about them. He never has taken any care of them and if they get upset he'll hurt them, I know he will.'

'It's alright,' I said. 'We'll go and get them back right now, and then we can tell Social Services what has happened.'

Colin Montgomery's house was only a few hundred yards from the police station, via one of the old yards and a side-alley, so I suggested that we walked there rather than take the police van. The last thing I wanted to do was put the children in the back of a police van to drive them away from the house – it might frighten them even more. Cathy agreed with me.

'Listen,' she said, as we got close to the house. 'Can I suggest that you stay out of sight, around the corner, while I go to the door, so that me having a policeman there doesn't wind him up to boiling point right away? If ever I called the police because he was hitting me it used to make matters ten times worse until they could calm him down or they arrested him. If I need you, I could just shout.'

'Well, I'm not too keen on that idea,' I said. 'But I'll do it if that's what you really want. I don't want you to get hurt.'

'It's not me I'm bothered about,' she said. 'I just want him to stay calm while the kids are still in his house.'

As soon as Cathy walked into the tiny back yard, though, I could hear two little voices crying 'Mammy, Mammy,' from inside the house.

She knocked at the back door and I heard it open. Immediately, I heard a smack and the sound of a metal dustbin crashing over. As I hurried around the corner the man was growling: 'Piss off, bitch.'

I was just in time to see Cathy, with a bleeding nose, picking herself up from amongst the scattered contents of the fallen bin. My appearance on the scene clearly startled Colin Montgomery and took his attention away from her. In the few seconds that it took me to stride across the yard, she stood up and punched him as hard as she could. It was a good one, too. Now there were two bloody noses. He turned, to retaliate.

'Don't you *dare*,' I said. 'You know precisely why we are here. We have come for the children. The fact that you have broken the orders of the court will be reported; you have committed a contempt of court. Touch her again and I'll lock you up.'

'I'm not having that bitch in my house,' he said, as he mopped blood from his nose with a handkerchief. '*You* can come in, but that bitch isn't.'

The children were only a few feet away, inside the house but watching all this through the window and undoubtedly hearing every word. Both were sobbing, but both only for their mammy.

'Mind your language,' I said. 'Have you forgotten that the children can hear you? Anyway, you've said I can come in, so I'm coming in for the children right now. You wait here, Cathy; I'll bring them out.'

Montgomery turned and went back inside his grubby little terraced house, and I followed him.

'Get your coats, Emma, Jasper; you're going home with Mammy now. It's alright,' I said.

Jasper pushed past us and ran outside. Emma went to pick up two little coats. She was a pretty little thing, very small for her age. Like Jasper, she obviously hadn't had a wash in the last twenty four hours or more, but that was no fault of theirs.

'I hate you. You always hurt us,' she sobbed at her so-called father as she came towards us.

He was a man my own size, about six feet two and maybe twelve stone – a big man. Without a word, he drew his hand up, high above his head, to hit her. Before he could, I punched him on the head and he fell to the floor. He was still in the process of picking himself up as I left the house. I knew I shouldn't just have left it at that but all I was concerned about was getting the two toddlers away from him without any more distress for them.

After the two children finished their rather frantic, teary-eyed hugs with Cathy, the four of us walked back to the police station, then she phoned for a taxi and took them home. It wasn't for me to tell her that the red Volvo that came for them had spent part of the day hiding in rhododendron bushes, but I smiled when I saw that Alan had failed to remove all of the twigs and leaves from the grill and the bumper.

Chapter Eleven

On the Scent

For November, it certainly wasn't a bad morning – fine and quite bright, but with high-level stratus cloud that completely hid the sun. The bracken on the fellsides had lost its golden tints now and was a more mundane shade of brown. The higher summits had a light dusting of snow.

I was with my lifelong friend, Sid Ritson, a butcher from Linthwaite. He wanted me to come foxhunting with him; with the Forndale Foxhounds in Snabside.

When they encountered a fox hunt in the Lake District, visitors from down south or overseas inevitably asked where the horses were, but the terrain is far too steep and too rough for horses; they and their riders would be probably crippled or even killed if anyone were stupid enough to try it.

That particular day, the hounds were "loosed" at the aptly named Terriers Inn but I soon lost some of my interest in them when I spotted Elizabeth Hodgson in the gathered onlookers. I tried to look nonchalant as I worked my way through the crowd towards her.

'Hiya,' I eventually said, trying to act surprised to see her.

'Ooh, hello!' she said, looking a bit puzzled. 'Oh, yes. The policeman. Steve, isn't it?'

'Yes. Guilty, as charged. That's me,' I said.

'I didn't know you were a hunting man,' said Elizabeth.

'Well I can't really say that I am. I've been to hunts with my dad, but not regularly. I'm here today 'cos my mate wanted me to come. And the fresh air won't hurt me,' I said.

'Is it your day off, then?' she asked.

'No. I'm on two-to-ten, this afternoon,' I said.

'You are?' she said. 'I'm on one-thirty to nine-thirty at the Cottage Hospital.'

'That sounds promising. What're my chances of a coffee then?' I said, grinning at her.

She smiled. 'Well everybody else from the police station comes for a brew regularly so I can't see why you shouldn't jump on the bandwagon. Ooh, look!' Her attention had turned to the mountainside. The hounds had picked up a drag and were running fast across the fell breast. One or two at the front were "giving tongue" and even if one's sympathies lay with the fox – which would be a rare sentiment in hill-farming country – it couldn't be denied that it was a glorious sight. The noise echoed around the slopes. I started scanning the mountainside a few hundred feet ahead of the pack, with my binoculars, and eventually spotted the fox. It was cantering almost casually towards Blea Crags – it was either an experienced veteran, with little fear of the hounds, or it was a foolish youngster. My money was on the former. It was soon in among the rocky outcrops at the side of the main crag and it quickly climbed higher, hopping lightly from boulder to boulder. Definitely a veteran. The hounds came to a standstill as soon as they got in amongst the rocks. Bold "Reynard" had broken his scent trail beautifully. It took several minutes before the hounds had cast about and found the spot where the fox had eventually come down off the boulders, maybe three hundred feet further up the hillside. All the watchers had lost sight of the fox, too. As it came off the rocks it had gone to the left, into a mixed patch of juniper bushes and gorse. The hounds, with the new drag to follow, went charging in after it and soon Master

Reynard was spotted walking carefully along a narrow ledge – a "benk" – on an almost sheer face of the cliff.

Within minutes, there were hounds above him and hounds below him; hounds to his left and hounds to his right; but only a couple of them could actually see him, and clearly none of them could find out how to get at him. I'd heard many times of the cheekiness of the hunted fox, but this was spectacular. He sat there as though he were a king, holding court. Even the two hounds that could see him and were baying frantically left him apparently unconcerned. It took another ten minutes before one hound found its way onto the ledge.

'Go on, Bellman, sort him out, lad,' Elizabeth half whispered, as she watched through her binoculars.

I didn't dare lower my own binoculars from the scene. It was hard to know whose side to be on. Many times I'd seen the carnage left by foxes that got amongst a farmer's lambs, but the coolness of this one was unrivalled. The fox casually stood as Bellman came in from the right, then it sauntered almost jauntily around behind a big rock and was lost to sight. The hound, being bigger than the fox, had to pick his way with extreme care along what was obviously a narrow approach ledge – one slip and he would be done for – but eventually he reached the wider part where Reynard had sat, surveying his kingdom until so rudely disturbed, and Bellman dashed around the back of the rock in pursuit of his arch enemy.

Several seconds elapsed. Maybe fifty people on the roadside and another thirty or so who were up on the fellside waited expectantly – all no doubt presuming that all hell would suddenly erupt from one side or the other of that boulder. The gasps and mutters from people when the fox came walking casually back out from behind the rock, exactly where he had gone in, were priceless.

'Cheeky little bugger,' said one man.

'Well I'll be damned,' said another, while a third chap just laughed.

'I've seen everything now,' added Elizabeth.

And to confound the onlookers even more, the fox sneaked surreptitiously off the ledge, without any hounds spotting it, then slipped away through the junipers and wasn't seen again. Maybe the collective indignation was made even worse when Bellman eventually re-emerged, appearing to be completely baffled, from behind the boulder and then struggled to find his own way back off the ledge.

I turned my attention back to Elizabeth. She wasn't wearing any makeup or perfume this morning, which was no doubt just as well. Farmers' daughters certainly didn't get dressed up for hunting. She was in workaday clothes – a pair of green wellies, green corduroy trousers, a rather battered brown sweater, an unzipped, olive-coloured waxed-cotton jacket, and a flat cap. Dressed like a farm worker and drop-dead gorgeous – a novel combination. I was staring, and I knew it. And I couldn't stop myself, either.

'… that's done the damage. Steve?' she said.

'Pardon?' I replied, embarrassed.

Once more, she laughed. But it was with a glowing, kind, gentle smile. 'I was just saying that I hope it wasn't that fox that killed some of Dad's lambs. That's all. Are you coming to the Hunt Ball tomorrow night?'

'There's a Hunt Ball?' I said. 'Where at?'

'Geordie Bell's farm, down the valley – Low Hollows,' she said. 'But most people will be here in the pub till at least ten o'clock if you're not on another late shift.'

'Well in that case, I'll be there. Thanks for telling me,' I said.

She smiled again, then turned away to answer a woman who was calling to her, from among some parked cars.

The next day, my afternoon at work started so quietly that I was able to take the van and just go for a drive and see what turned up. I did a trivial, vehicle taxation enquiry in Overdale then set off to drive towards Low Keld. I'd only gone two miles west of town when I saw a slim young woman with long blonde hair, hitchhiking. She was wearing jeans, stack-heel shoes, and an Afghan coat – a reminder of the hippy fashions from a few years ago. She had to be worth a check for drugs so I pulled up alongside her.

'Hiya, love,' I said, through the passenger-side window. 'Just sit in the van a minute while I have a word with you, please.'

She got in without saying a word, but doing her best to smile and look coy.

'Where've you come from, love?' I said.

'Manchester,' she said.

'And you are going to where?'

'My friend's house at Maryport.' She said.

'And what drugs are you carrying?' I said. It was a bluff, of course, but it was amazing how often bluff worked. Her jaw dropped and the smile faded.

'What?' she said as she nervously pulled at the edge of her coat.

'What drugs are you carrying?' I repeated.

'What makes you think I'm carrying…'

'That smelly oil that you're wearing.' I said. 'You lot will never learn that it might cover other smells but it is the giveaway. So what are you carrying?'

'Nothing,' she said, but it was obvious from her fidgeting that she was lying.

'What's your name?' I said.

'Sylvia.'

'You know I need more than that,' I said.

'Sylvia Quinn.'

I took the rest of her details and passed them to HQ, by radio, for a persons-check.

While we waited for the result, I said, 'So, let's go back to the original question. What are you carrying?'

She had unfastened her Afghan since getting into the van. She got hold of her sweater and the t-shirt underneath it and pulled them up, she had no bra on, so her breasts fell free. And very pert breasts they were too.

'I'm carrying these,' she said. 'You can take me somewhere quiet and fuck me if you'll let me go.'

'Put them away,' I said. 'I'm arresting you on suspicion of carrying controlled substances, failing which you've just tried to bribe a police officer.' And I cautioned her. She said nothing but slowly lowered her clothing.

'You have two choices,' I continued. 'Either you can stay in the front and keep your hands on your knees, completely in my sight, so that you can't try and shove stuff down the back of the seat, or I can handcuff you, search you at the side of the road, and take you to the nick in the back of the van. Which is it to be?'

'Front, I suppose,' she mumbled, then ever so quietly added 'fucking pig.'

I watched her carefully as she fastened her seat belt, then I said 'Okay. Keep your hands on the very tips of your knees. Move them from there at all and you'll be wearing handcuffs. Do you understand?'

She nodded. I radioed control room and asked them to arrange for a female officer to attend Hawthwaite police station to search a female prisoner in connection with drugs. As we got into town, I radioed direct to the nick on my U.H.F. pocket radio. Andy Wyatt answered so I told him to expect a female prisoner within the next three or four minutes. He was waiting at the back door of the police station when we arrived.

As soon as we were all in the charge room, I said 'Sergeant Wyatt, I have arrested this woman on suspicion of carrying controlled substances. For my own protection, I want to point out in her presence that she bared her breasts to me and offered me sex if I would let her go.'

'You liar,' she yelled. 'He tried to rape me.' She jumped to her feet.

'Sit down,' Andy said to her. 'A policewoman will be here shortly and will take a statement if you have a complaint to make about this officer.'

Then Andy turned to me and said 'Steve, I want you to stay in this room, in my presence. No matter what we think of it, what this woman has alleged must be investigated.' He then rang through to the front office and asked Linda to contact control room to find out if the results of the woman's person-check had come back yet. Then he asked her to request a Scenes of Crime officer to attend at Hawthwaite, preferably the SoCo sergeant, and to contact "Complaints and Discipline" at H.Q. to request that a senior officer also attend, without delay. What had looked like a straightforward arrest was turning into a major event.

About half an hour later, a policewoman from the town police station in Penrith, whom I knew only by sight, came into the charge room. She was obviously the one they'd sent for the purpose of searching a female prisoner. Before she took Miss Quinn through to the privacy of a cell, to conduct the search, she spoke to the sergeant and to the prisoner: 'Not only is there no-one of the surname of Quinn registered at the address you gave us in Manchester, but it turns out that the street was totally demolished a few months ago. Come with me, and we'll see what you're carrying.'

'Before you go through there, Karen,' said Andy to the police woman, 'this lady has alleged that Constable Shearwater attempted to rape her so I want you to check for any signs of bruising or other relevant marks or injuries. I will be sending for the police surgeon in just a moment so that her story can be confirmed or refuted. Take a statement from her as to what happened. And as for you,' he said, to the woman I had arrested, 'if what you say is correct then you can rest assured that it will be fully dealt with. If, however, you are lying, in an attempt to deflect any charges then you may equally rest assured that you will be charged with wasting police time. Do you understand?'

Sylvia Quinn just turned away without a word, as though she actually wanted to go through to the cells. I stayed there with Sergeant Wyatt until the SoCo sergeant came, then I had scrapings taken from behind my fingernails and swabs from my hands. Then I had to put a spare uniform on so that my tunic, trousers and shoes could be bagged, ready for forensic examination.

At the end of it, the SoCo sergeant called Andy Wyatt back in and said, 'I have all the samples that I need. I've photographed Steve to show that there are absolutely no scratches, abrasions, bruises or other marks present.'

The SoCo man left the room after Andy muttered something to him, then Andy turned to me and said, 'Superintendent Dunlinson from headquarters is here to interview you about this girl's allegations. There's no way around this, Steve. You know it has to be done. Just remember that he has a job to do, alright?'

I nodded.

Just at that, the policewoman came out from the cells. She said, 'I've completed my search, Sarge. I've found what looks like a lot of drugs on her – mostly LSD at a guess, but there's some cannabis too – and there doesn't appear to be a single mark on her in relation to her allegations against Steve.'

'Right, Karen,' said Andy. 'Given that this is now a serious matter, I want you to contact Drugs Squad and ask them to come and take possession of the substances that you've found. The handover should be done in the presence of the prisoner and yourself, okay? I want you to allow her to get dressed again, now, and then I want you to stay with her whilst the SoCo officer takes nail scrapings. And he can take that flea-ridden Afghan coat away, too. We'll have to arrange for some spare clothes for her before he can have her other garments though.'

With that, I was despatched to the inspector's office, upstairs, where Superintendent Dunlinson had taken up temporary residence. The door was open. I knocked and waited.

'Shearwater? In! Si'down!' he said. He paused whilst he looked at some papers in his hand. Then he looked over his glasses and said: 'Well?'

'Sir?'

'Don't fucking "sir" me. Did you grope her?'

'No,' I said, indignantly.

'Don't mess me about, boy. The forensics will show up if you touched her so if you did it'll be better for you if you admit it now,' said the superintendent.

'Superintendent Dunlinson,' said Brian Sumner as he walked in, 'I'm glad my office is suitable for you. You won't mind if I sit in whilst you interview one of my officers will you, sir?'

I glanced up at the clock – five past five – I'd forgotten that the inspector was on 5pm-1am.

The superintendent gave a cursory nod and carried on: 'What happened, Shearwater?'

I ran through the full incident in as much detail as I could possibly remember, then Dunlinson said, 'I want a statement from you. That's not a request, it's an order. A full statement by ten o'clock tonight. Clear?'

'No, Superintendent,' said Inspector Sumner. 'I'm afraid it's not clear. You know as well as we all do that nobody can be ordered to make a statement. That is duress and I cannot permit one of my men to be given an unlawful order. May I take it that you will accept a written report from Constable Shearwater for the time being? He may, of course, wish to consult a lawyer before he considers whether or not to make a statement in due course.'

'How dare you interfere when I'm questioning him,' said Superintendent Dunlinson, clearly furious.

To this, Harry Sumner said: 'If you have finished your interview with Constable Shearwater, Superintendent, may I suggest that he be allowed to go downstairs before you and I finish this conversation?'

Dunlinson looked at me. 'Right. Piss off,' he said. 'I'll be seeing you again soon.'

A couple of minutes later, even above the noise of people talking and phones ringing in the front office, it was soon clear to everyone on the ground floor that the inspector's conversation with the "soft shoe" superintendent was very heated.

It was almost three more hours before the police surgeon was able to attend. His job, in the presence of a female officer or nurse would be a close examination of the prisoner and the taking of internal swabs. Only a few minutes after he went in, the policewoman came out and said to Sergeant Wyatt: 'She has completely withdrawn her allegation against Constable Shearwater and she has signed a statement to that effect, witnessed by the doctor.'

I could have wept.

'The boss says if you haven't already had your sandwiches, Steve, have them now, then go up to see him in about half an hour.' It was Andy Wyatt speaking but, for the second time that day, I wasn't really listening to what someone was saying to me. He put his hand on my shoulder, repeated it, and added: 'It's alright, lad.'

I went to the refs room for half an hour but I struggled to eat anything. Being subjected to untrue allegations was all part of the game but none-the-less this one had shaken me.

I sat in the same chair in the inspector's office for the second time in four hours.

'Right, Steve. Let's get this afternoon's nonsense right out of the way. It was a load of bollocks; everyone knew that from the outset. Everyone except Superintendent Dick-Prick, or whatever his name is, but at least you will not be seeing him again, even though he erroneously predicted that you would.'

'Yes, the superintendent did seem a bit overzealous, sir,' I said.

'Overzealous? He's a twat, excuse my language; a bloody Bramshill career boy – nothing more,' said the inspector.

'Thank you for…'

'Steven,' Harry interjected, 'this afternoon might be done with, but I'm afraid that it's not the only serious allegation that has been made about you.'

'What?' I said, stunned. 'What else is there, sir?'

Inspector Sumner paused, looking me straight in the eye: 'Does the name Montgomery mean anything to you?'

Chapter Twelve

The Hunt Ball

I went back downstairs to the front office in a daze after the right, royal bollocking that Brian Sumner gave me. His closing words were in my ears and would stay in my mind for years: 'If you have to strike someone, Steven, you have to arrest them. What you did was stupid. It's just lucky that I was able to get it sorted out or you'd have been fighting to keep your job.'

Carol Clarke was in the front office, and she'd clearly overheard the bits where the boss had raised his voice at me.

'Not your day, is it,' she said. 'You look as though you don't know whether your arse has been punched, bored or blasted.'

Ever the one for subtlety was Carol.

'No, Sarge,' I said. 'You're right; I've known better days than this.'

She started to laugh.

'Forgive me if I don't see the funny side,' I said.

'If only you knew… If only…' She couldn't finish her words for the hilarity that had overcome her.

'Why? What do you mean?' I said.

But she just raised her hand in an attempt to silence my question, as her whole body shook with her now silent giggling. Then she snorted and had to wipe her nose.

After a few minutes, she managed to tell her tale: 'I came in the back door, yesterday, just as your friend, Mr Montgomery, was leaving after making his complaint. And he had Brian Sumner's boot stuck firmly up his arse. Brian was going mad. "Don't you *dare* attempt to brutalise a child then come and complain about one of my best officers for giving you a lot less than you deserve, you little shit-bag. Now bugger off before I beat the bloody daylights out of you," he said.'

She started to laugh again, then turned towards the office door and froze.

'Oops,' she whispered.

I turned too and there, stood in the doorway behind us, was Inspector Sumner.

He kept an entirely straight face as he said: 'Sergeant Clarke, you have just destroyed my entire credibility with this young man. You ought to be ashamed of yourself. And the next time you see me assaulting a person without arresting him, perhaps you had better remind me that I am being a trifle rash.'

A few minutes later, over a cup of tea, I said to Carol: 'I was going to go to a hunt ball in Snabside tonight, after work, but I'm not sure I feel up to it after today.'

'Steve, you can be such a gormless prat sometimes,' she said. 'Get yourself to the bloody dance. Will that farmer's daughter be there?'

'Who? What do you mean?' I said.

She smiled. 'Give it a rest, you pillock. You know fine-bloody-well who I mean: Miss Hodgson.'

'What?' I said.

'I've heard how you go all dreamy-eyed whenever the Hodgsons are mentioned,' she said. 'The folk around here do notice things like that, you know. It's our job! So don't try and kid *me*, kiddo; you'll never succeed.'

I went to the Terriers Inn first. They were having a hunt singsong when I arrived. John Jackson, an old chap from Forndale, was singing "John Crosier's Tally Ho," about a hunt master from the 19th Century. I stayed a while and enjoyed the "crack," over a single pint of bitter, then drove down the valley to Low Hollows, to the hunt ball, in one of their buildings.

It was being held on the wooden upper floor of a huge, old, stone-built bank-barn that had been cleared of its baled hay. Strands of grass seeds in the gaps between the floorboards and the lingering smell of the fresh hay added an extra touch of atmosphere and charm to events such as this. A single row of chairs had been put around the walls, facing what was now temporarily a dance floor. A small, makeshift stage had been built at the end furthest from the door, for the four-man, local band. About eighty people were there when I arrived, with just over half of them standing around watching the rest dance. I looked all around; Elizabeth was nowhere to be seen. Three of my mates from Linthwaite – Sid and two other single men – were standing over by the far wall, so I went to join them.

It was another twenty minutes before Elizabeth arrived, and she was holding onto the arm of the whipper-in.

'Are those two courting?' I asked Sid.

'I doubt it. That's her brother, Danny. It'll be a damned queer job if *they're* courting!' he said.

A few moments later, the huntsman followed them in and my mate continued: 'Now *that's* her boyfriend – or so folk say, because they've never seemed really serious; they just go a lot of places together.'

The huntsman and the whip – known by an old title as the "hunt servants" – were still in their hunting attire, as was expected of them at hunt socials, and that made them the only two of the younger men in the room to be wearing ties. Only the older men still got dressed up for events like these; many of the under-forties were in little better than their working clothes.

The two hunt servants, together with Elizabeth and a few friends, stood chatting in one corner for much of the time but the huntsman was obviously expected to do his bit and socialise so while he was dancing with one of the older ladies, I asked Elizabeth for a dance.

'I'd love to,' she answered. And then she sucked all the energy from me with one of her wonderful smiles. We stayed on the floor for three dances and for most of the time I knew I was waffling and burbling on about trivia – farming, nursing, yesterday's hunt – it was only towards the end of the third dance that I plucked up the guts to ask her out.

'Thank you, Steve. I'm flattered, but I'm going out with someone at present, I'm sorry,' she said.

'Oh, I apologise,' I said. 'I'd been told that you were just friends, not serious.'

A few minutes later, with my embarrassment in over-drive and my ego rather dented, I slipped out of the barn and drove home. It hadn't been one of my better days.

Chapter Thirteen

Once Bitten

Being bitten by an Alsatian dog was one of the three highlights of my week at headquarters. Those of us lucky enough to get a place on the promotion exam crammer course had from the Monday to the Thursday in which to make a last, concerted effort to cram selected information, ready for the sergeants' promotion exam on the Friday – the same day the exam took place around the whole country.

On the Tuesday lunchtime, in order to escape the building and get a breath of fresh air, I had a walk down the sports field, past the new social club. As I rounded the corner of the club buildings, I found three of the dog-section men there, training two of their dogs. There was Mick Thornton, with whom I had done my initial training when we both joined the force, Ken Vipont, and their sergeant, David Relph, another Linthwaite man, who was about eight years my senior.

'Ah, just the man,' shouted David. 'Come here, Steve, there's a good chap!'

I walked over towards them, grinning. I knew I was going to be set up for something.

'Stevennnn,' he said, with a deliberately ingratiating smile on his face. 'Do us a favour, my old son.'

'I reserve judgment,' I said. 'Tell me what it is first.'

'Well,' he said. 'You know how all the dog handlers look after each other's dogs when someone is on holiday or off sick? Well the problem is that the dogs obviously get to know all the handlers. Now, to put it simply, they need somebody new to bite, so that the training is more realistic. And when *you* came around the corner they both started licking their lips. So how about it? Are you game?'

Ken and Mick were standing beside him, by now, exchanging smiles with each other and subtly defying me to refuse.

'Yes. Okay. I'll do it,' I said.

I'd got the last laugh. It was easy to see that not one of them knew whether to believe me. Then it dawned on me that now I'd committed myself to doing it, maybe it would be Spartan or Mutts that would really get the last laugh.

David gave me his ancient Barbour jacket to replace my tunic whilst I was doing the running, then at least only my trousers would get messed up if I fell. He briefed me that the first run would just be a "stand-off" – that when he shouted for me to stand still, I really had to.

'You won't need the leather sleeve for a stand-off,' he said. 'The theory is that as long as you stand still, the dogs won't bite. Sometimes they can't resist a bit of a nip, though, so as soon as you stand still, cup your hands over your family valuables then the worst that can happen is that you'll get your fingers chewed rather than lose your manhood.'

'Oh, wonderful!' I said. 'Anything else I need to know?'

'Just that if one of the dogs actually *does* bite you, don't retaliate. Just stand still and scream silently till one of us gets there to drag it off. Just keep turning to face the dog as it circles around you, that's all,' he said.

That wasn't very reassuring, and I wouldn't have much choice if one of the damned things had me by part of my anatomy.

I did two stand-offs, first for Spartan, who circled me only about eighteen inches from my body but never came closer. His barks were seriously daunting though. It would take a lunatic to ignore him. When Mutts came after me, I froze as soon as I heard Mick shout 'Stand still!'

I turned to face the hairy express train that was bearing down on me and for a moment thought the dog was coming in for an all-out attack. At the very last moment, Mutts turned very slightly and bashed against my side so hard that he nearly knocked me over as he passed. I spun around to face him as he rounded to come back at me, his eyes fixed on mine. This was a seriously hard dog. It was as though he deliberately manoeuvred to get me between him and Mick, so that Mick couldn't see what was happening, then Mutts came in quickly. He grabbed my right forefinger and middle finger, across the knuckles, and gave them a wicked nip, then he grabbed at the soft bit on the inside of my right thigh and gave it the same treatment. If I had been indoors, at least I would have a roof to go through. If these were just nips, I would dread a real bite!

'Leave!' bellowed Mick, as he ran up. 'You okay?' he asked me, casually, seemingly quite unconcerned that Mutts had gained my attention so painfully.

'I'll live,' I said. But my facial expression probably spoke volumes.

The next I knew, Dave was strapping a leather sleeve onto my right arm. It was entirely closed off at the hand end and had a handle inside for me to grip. There was also a strap from the top end that went around my chest to help secure the whole sleeve in position. It was made out of leather, maybe three quarters of an inch thick.

'Don't be surprised if you feel the bite, Steve,' said Dave. 'If they get a good grip it can still sting through this.'

'Oh, now you tell me!' I said, trying to grin.

I must have run thirty or more yards before I heard Ken shouting the regulation phrase: 'This is the police. Stand still or I'll send the dog.'

I knew that Ken would have slipped the dog as soon as he had finished speaking. They had told me not to look back but when I heard what sounded like a cavalry charge gaining on me quickly, I made the mistake of glancing around. For all the world, Spartan looked like a low-flying crocodile. All I could see was a huge teeth-ridden maw. And it was me he was going to eat. Fortunately for me, though, the huge Alsatian had already been airborne when I looked back. It was only a split second before he caught me and sank his teeth deeply into the sleeve. I hadn't enough time to panic and do something instinctive like trying to snatch my arm out of the way – good enough reason for telling beginners never to look back. Spartan had an incredible grip. I could feel my forearm being progressively crushed as he sank his teeth further and further into the leather sleeve.

'Give him a fight, Steve. Swing him around a bit. Make him work,' shouted Ken.

Swing him around? Ken might as well have asked me to swing a truck. Spartan had his feet planted in the turf and he wasn't for swinging. He told me so, too, with his growls. And I believed him.

Before I did a second run for Mutts, Mick said: 'My dog is a totally different cup of tea, Steve. Spartan is what we call a vice; a hard gripper. Mutts is what they call a piano player. He'll bite repeatedly, up and down the sleeve. Just make sure you keep the sleeve held out towards him, whatever happens, otherwise he'll use your flesh as a substitute. In person.'

Mutts took me down. He took me down humiliatingly, comprehensively, and bone-jarringly. Despite me being a good runner, he gained on me so quickly that he simply knocked me right off my feet. But what upset me most was that his momentum, when he had grabbed the sleeve, brought him round far enough in front for me to land right on top of him. And now I was lying across him; my stomach was holding him down by his head, to be precise. An ominously deep growl from my carnivorous colleague seemed to shake my whole body as it rumbled right through me. And I could feel that he had lost his grip on the sleeve, too. Those teeth of his were going to do me some serious damage unless I was lucky.

'Steve, roll off him but for Christ's sake give him the sleeve,' yelled Mick.

Too *right* I gave him the sleeve. As I rolled to my left and Mutts wriggled out from under my right-hand side, I nearly rammed it down his throat. And to my eternal relief, he took it. Mutts was having a whale of a time, though; I could tell he was enjoying himself because he started his "piano playing," up and down my arm. The fact that he didn't stray beyond the end of the leather of the sleeve was my second stroke of luck. Afterwards, however, what struck me the most was just how much I had enjoyed working with these dogs. Crazy but true; it was brilliant.

On the Thursday evening, we were all going to go down to the police club for an end-of-course drink, and there was talk of going to Carlisle later, to a nightclub, but nobody wanted to get plastered or stay out too late with the promotion exams happening the next morning. When we got to the social club, it soon became obvious that there was a presentation ceremony happening in the adjacent gymnasium – eighteen of our older colleagues getting long service and good conduct medals.

About 10pm, I was leaning on my left elbow, propping up the bar, chatting to Terry Mayo, the only constable on our course who wasn't still in his twenties. In fact Terry was only just still in his thirties so he was the "old man" of the group. Without warning or an "excuse me," somebody pushed firmly in between us. I was just about to speak my mind about his bad manners when the pusher half turned and I saw it was the chief constable. And he was well-oiled, too, which wasn't a rare event. Seemingly a lot of the middle-ranking officers had been hovering around him all evening, topping up his gin-and-tonics at regular intervals. That was the norm for these events, and the Chief never refused a gin, even if he did have a habit of being very dismissive towards whichever obsequious junior officer had bought it for him. I had worked at HQ long enough to know the pattern but it seemed that they either never learned or they hoped that despite the sarcasm they suffered, the boss would eventually reward their fawning with a promotion.

He saw me looking at him.

'Evening, young man. Are you on a course?' he said to me.

I stood up straight and took my elbow off the bar.

'Yes, sir. I am on a one-week crammer-course, leading up to tomorrow's promotion exam,' I said.

'Ah, yes.' he said. 'The top thirty studiers in the county. So it's a reward for grovelling, eh? Are you staying in our new accommodation block, then?'

I ignored his probing sarcasm about grovelling and said: 'Yes, sir. Apart from two local officers, we are all staying here.'

'Good, isn't it!' he said, emphatically.

'Yes, sir. Very comfortable.'

'So, what's your name?' he said.

'Shearwater, sir.'

'Ever been in trouble with *me*?'

'No, sir; never.'

'I seem to know your face; that's all. Where are you from?' he said.

'Well I worked here for a year on light duties, sir, which is probably why you might know me by sight, but I'm now working at Hawthwaite. My family are from Linthwaite, though,' I said.

'Hawthwaite, eh? Linthwaite; hmmm.' He sighed, as though deep in thought, and took hold of the bar to stop himself swaying so much. Then he completely foxed me with: 'Tell me; have you ever met the Chairman of the Police Committee?'

I had to pause for a second to be sure that I had heard him correctly.

'No, sir. I haven't,' I replied, trying not to sound bewildered.

Without further ado, the Chief turned towards the large crowd of hangers-on that were standing a few feet away. Rather imperiously he raised his left hand high above his head and snapped his fingers.

'Colonel Bromhead, a moment of your time,' he loudly commanded.

The Colonel came over immediately.

'Colonel Bromhead, I'd like you to meet Constable Hawthwaite from Linthwaite.' And with that, the great white chief turned and lurched away towards some more glasses of G&T that were being held ready for him.

The Colonel and I were no doubt equally baffled by our introduction.

'Good evening, sir,' was all I could manage.

'Good evening, Constable Hawthwaite. How are you?' said the colonel.

The head of the Police Committee was less given to excess than was the big boss but even he had clearly had a few, so I didn't even try to argue the point over my surname.

'I'm fine, sir, thank you,' I said.

'Jolly good,' said the colonel.

We made small talk for a few minutes, about the weather, the course I was on, the police service in general, and how we would each solve current matters of world peace ('Shoot all the troublemakers; that's what I say, what?' was the colonel's solution.) Then he turned to me, looking seriously, over the top of his splendid, white, handlebar moustache, and said, 'So what is it that I can do for you?'

'Sir?' I said.

'Why did you need to see me? What did the old goat introduce us for?' said the colonel.

'I'm sorry, sir. I have no idea why we were introduced. It just sort of happened; rather out of the blue,' I said.

He laughed. 'Well, at least it got me away from those other patronizing blighters, what? And you made a lot more sense than most of them, Constable Hawthwaite, I'll warrant. Anyway, you get back to your mates.'

'Thank you, sir. It was nice meeting you,' I said.

Terry was having a difficult job not spluttering in his beer. He'd been watching my discomfort throughout, and had heard most of the conversation.

'Oh, God,' he said. 'Your face, when he asked if you'd ever met the Chairman of the Police Committee; it was priceless.'

A few minutes later, somebody put the word around our group that we were all going to Carlisle. It was only when we were all leaving the club that I saw Terry holding back, obviously not intending to come with us.

'What's up?' I said to him.

'You youngsters don't want an old bugger like me with you in a nightclub. I'll just have an early night,' he said.

'You think we are just gonna leave you on your own?' I said.

'Well it looks like the rest have,' he said. And he laughed.

I turned around and he was right. All the rest had gone.

'Well I'm not going to stay out late because tomorrow's so important, and I'm bloody-well not going to leave you on your own on the last night of the course, so you can just shift yer arse and come to Carlisle,' I said.

He didn't argue, but he insisted on driving, so I got chauffeured to the city in an immaculate, old Triumph 2000 that was his pride and joy. Our only problem was that we weren't sure which club everyone had gone to, so the pair of us took a chance on the Twisted Wheel disco. We were wrong; none of our group were there.

'Oh, well,' said Terry. 'If there's just the two of us, we need a strategy. Keep your eye out for any two birds that look the right ages to be a mother and daughter coming in together. I'll distract the mother and you can tackle the daughter!'.

Chapter Fourteen

Having a Ball

I went back to Hawthwaite on the Monday following my course and the promotion exam, in time for my last four "earlies," and spent most of the time doing a lot more stock movement books. On the first of the four shifts, I had to do three farms near Low Keld so I took the opportunity to call in on Susan.

The smile on her face was a picture as she opened the front door to me.

'Well, stranger, I thought you'd forgotten all about me,' she said.

'No, Susan, I'm barely likely to do that. But I admit that after what happened I did want to give you some breathing space. How's young Andrew doing?'

'Oh, he's fine, thanks. I had to take him to the funeral, of course, so that was very hard for him but you know there was a woman there that nobody seemed to know and it turned out that it was Adrian's bit of stuff, his bit on the side,' she said.

'Oh, for pity's sake,' I said. 'I'm sorry you had to go through that as well.'

'That was Adrian for you,' said Susan. 'Typical of him.'

She showed me into the living room and went to make two

coffees. I was sat in an armchair and Susan sat on the nearest end of a three-seater settee, on my right.

'I'm glad you've come,' she quietly said as she passed me my cup.

I had a question to ask her but, as so often happened for me at moments like this, I was struggling to say the words. We ended up chatting about everything and nothing for maybe twenty minutes. And then I managed it.

'Susan, after what's happened I hope you don't think me awful for asking you this but it's the Hawthwaite Police Ball on Friday evening, at Castle Hall, and I was wondering whether you might like to come with me.'

'Of course I would like to, silly!' she said. 'Will it be long dresses and bow ties or not that formal?'

'Only if you have a bow-tie that will match your long dress,' I teased. 'Yes, it is meant to be full evening dress but a lot of the ladies wear shorter dresses at police dances so don't worry about it.'

'Wonderful. I can't remember when was the last time I went to something nice like that. Certainly not since I got married. And I know mam will have Andrew for the night so there'll be no problem there… Ooh, I'm all excited,' she said.

A few minutes later, as I stood up to leave, Susan stood up with me so that we were face to face and very close. She looked into my eyes and quietly said: 'I don't want to wait till Friday night to kiss you.'

My arms slipped around her waist a fraction of a second before hers wrapped around my neck and we kissed for what seemed like an age. I let my hands stray up to the back of her shoulders then eventually right down onto her jeans, over her buttocks. At that point I knew I had to go, before things got out of hand. And I *was* on duty, after all. It seemed like a rather fast start to our potential relationship, but I wasn't complaining.

I had two more early shifts to complete before my days-off started on the Thursday. All was quiet on the Tuesday, but on the Wednesday morning my 9am refreshments break was suddenly interrupted by Linda Hargreaves who burst into the refs room at five past and asked me to go to deal with a member of the public at the enquiry desk.

'Either he's taking the piss out of us or he's to be pitied, but I'm sorry, Steve, I just can't deal with him,' said Linda.

'Why? Whatever's the matter?' I said.

'I can't tell you.' She was leaning back against the wall, struggling to speak and nearly helpless with silent spasms of mirth. 'Oh God, I hope he doesn't hear me laughing.'

I had no choice but to leave her to her private hilarity and go through the front office to the enquiry desk.

'Good morning, sir,' I said. 'What's the problem?'

The man waiting there was probably only in his mid-30s but had thinning black hair, grown deliberately too long on the left and brushed sideways, right over the top of his head to try to camouflage a bald patch. His spectacles had thick lenses and thick, black rims, and his top teeth projected forwards at a dramatic angle.

'The pwoblem is your secwetawy. She was laughing at my speech impediment. It makes me feel wetched when people do that,' said the man.

'Oh, she was?' I said. 'Well I'm sorry about that, sir. How can I help you?'

'I want to weeport a lost wallet,' he said.

'When did you last have it, for certain, sir?' I asked.

'Wight before we went out for a stwole in the park, last evening,' he said.

'And when did you notice that it was missing?' I said.

'When I went to bed in my hotel woom, last night,' he said.

'You said "we" when you mentioned the stroll. Who else was there?' I asked.

'My fiancée. But we have seppawat wooms at the hotel, you wealise,' he said, rather sternly.

'Yes, sir, of course,' I said. 'And how much was in the wallet?'

'Thwee thousand two hundwed pounds,' he said, with no change of expression.

'Three thousand two hundred pounds? What on earth were you carrying that sort of cash in your wallet for?' I asked.

'Well, not that it's wellevant, but we are on our way to Gwetna Gween to get mawwied. We wanted something womantic and as soon as the cewemony is over we are meant to be flying away on honeymoon,' he said.

'Do you have *any* idea exactly where you may have lost the wallet, sir?'

'Well cleawy not but, in confidence, Constable, I suppose I ought to tell you that after it got dark, we lay down on the wivverbank, in some twees in the park, about thwee hundwed yards below the footbwidge, for a cuddle. You wealise what I'm saying?' he said.

That answer made my mind race but I refrained from saying "you mean you had a shag by the river?" Instead, I merely said, 'I think so, sir, yes. And have you been back there to have a look?'

I was really struggling not to allow myself to even smile otherwise I knew I would burst out laughing and I was desperate not to be that rude to him.

'Yes,' he said. 'But just quickly this mawning, and on my own. My fiancée is waather embawassed about it all, you see.'

I took a description of the wallet and its contents in the lost property book and made a note of the hotel and room number.

'All I need now is your full name, please sir,' I said.

'Wankin... *Pwofessaw* Wodger Wankin, if you want my full title,' he said, deadpan.

And at that point neither he nor I could have failed to hear not only Linda Hargreaves but also Sergeant Clarke – who had obviously come in the back door while I was at the desk – explode into helpless laughter just around the corner from where we were standing.

'Very good, Professor Rankin,' I said. 'Please ignore my

colleagues; they are talking about a party they went to, last night. Anyway, given the amount of money in the wallet I think you are in the lap of the gods as to whether anyone hands it in. We'll just have to keep our fingers cwossed…Oh, bugger, I didn't mean to say that, I'm sorry.'

And at that point – with Carol and Linda now hysterical not far behind me – my own composure failed and I had to fight back my own laughter. It was immensely embarrassing but there was simply nothing I could do about it.

The professor's disgusted expression said it all as he left the police station.

After he had gone, Carol and Linda stumbled from their hiding place, both crying with laughter and holding onto each other.

After two or three minutes, Sergeant Clarke managed only one question: 'Why did the Pwofessaw have to have seppawat wooms if he had alweddy given her a wodgering in the twees by the wivver?'

'Maybe just wanking,' said Linda.

And the pair of them exploded into howls and giggles once more.

When a degree of sensibility had returned, Carol called Dick Price on the radio and asked him to call in at the nick for details of a job. Dick was on 9am-5pm, town foot patrol, and she asked him to go and search the trees on the riverbank in the park for the missing wallet. I was going back out to do more stock movement books; it hadn't taken the boss long to realise that I got on quite well with farmers.

Unsurprisingly, Dick Price said the wallet was nowhere to be found, and nobody handed it in.

On the Friday evening, I went to collect Susan from her home a little after seven o'clock, as we had planned. Her long blonde hair was fastened up in a loose, attractive bun on the back of her head. She was wearing an ankle-length, side-split, glittery silver dress with silver shoes to match.

'Blimey, Susan, you look lovely,' I said. 'I hope you don't think me too old-fashioned but I've brought you this.' I gave her the corsage that I had kept hidden behind my back.

'Oh, wow, Steve, it's so pretty. I haven't put my lipstick on yet so let me say thank you first, then I'll do my lips in a minute,' she said. Then she reached up and kissed me.

'Now,' she said, 'you'll have to help me pin the flowers on.'

She took the pin from the corsage and passed it to me. 'About here, do you think?' She held the narrowing strap of her low-cut dress, just above her left breast.

'Be careful what you do with the pin,' she added, teasingly.

Fastening those flowers to her dress proved impossible without the back of my left fingers brushing a few times against her skin. By the time the pair of us left that house, a few minutes later, I felt as though I had hormones coming out of my ears.

There were quite a few guests and town dignitaries at the ball, so there were nine tables of eight in the private dining room at the Castle Hall Hotel, arranged around three sides of the dance floor. On the table to one side of ours, were Inspector Sumner and his wife, Joan, together with Lord and Lady Nethermere – Lord Nethermere being the chairman of the local magistrates, and Master of the Forndale Foxhounds.

On our table with Susan and I were Carol Clarke and her husband, Dave; Taffy Williams and his girlfriend, Amanda; and Kevin and Sheila Bottomley.

Taffy and I ordered two bottles of wine but we each had only one glass full during the evening and let the girls drink the rest. He and I were paying the price of abstention for being drivers that night.

The conversation and the laughter bubbled all around us throughout the meal, but on two or three occasions people had to call my name a little loudly to get my attention away from Susan. She looked wonderful and my troublesome hormones were still being very enthusiastic.

'Ladies and Gentlemen,' a sonorous voice boomed out as soon as the tables had been cleared. It was Lord Nethermere, standing with a glass in hand.

'Ladies and Gentlemen,' he repeated, 'as you know, your good inspector asks me each year to say a few words to you all at the annual dinner.' He turned to look down at Inspector Sumner. 'There, Brian; is that enough words for this year?... No?...Bugger. Thought not!' And he returned his attention to everyone.

'That's another point. Are they dinners, dances or balls?' said Lord Nethermere. 'Balls, Brian, d'you think?'

By this stage the combination of the wine and the speaker had people chuckling.

'Right. Where was I?' he said. 'Oh, yes; balls. Anyway, irrespective of all your balls, I am actually here to try and be sensible for once and to express the gratitude and congratulations of all we Justices of the Peace – and that, of course, potentially includes the big blonde piece that has the red light down by the bus station – our congratulations to you all, from the inspector, here, down. And that's for the successes and professionalism that you have displayed over the last year. Before I sit down, I have to tell you that there was a newsflash on the BBC just as we were about to leave the house, this evening. It was a case of good news and bad news, I'm afraid,' said Lord Nethermere. 'The good news is that an entire bus load of defence solicitors and barristers, on an outing, crashed over a cliff near Hardknott Pass, earlier today. The bad news is that at least one of the blighters survived. Anyway, now I shall hand over to your inspector. He's a keen golfer, as you will all know, but I am reliably informed by the captain of the golf club that the only time Brian here ever hits *his* balls straight is when he accidentally stands on the wrong end of a garden rake.'

Lord Nethermere's jokes went down well and Inspector Sumner had to stand and wait for over half a minute before the laughter and clapping died down enough for him to have his turn to speak.

'Thank you, Lord Nethermere,' said Inspector Sumner. 'I think I can safely say that your philosophical words will leave us all contemplating the sad fact that our wives only get to our balls once a year – less often than the handle of my rake, it would seem. I too, however, would like to add my thanks and congratulations to you all for a job well done. There only remains one other formality before the dancing starts, and that is the Loyal Toast. Now as you know, we have a tradition of springing this task – without any warning – on the newest member of our team, so this year I am going to call upon Steve "the gravedigger" Shearwater to perform the task. As many of you will know, last week Steve secured convictions in court against both of the Baldwin brothers, for a string of burglaries and thefts. Over fifteen thousand pounds worth of property has now been recovered, and no matter what the C.I.D. might pretend about who deserves the credit, it's all down to Steve's ghoulish, graveyard surveillance. Steve, will you please propose the Loyal Toast.'

Susan squeezed my thigh, a moment before I stood up. Then everyone rose to their feet. I was amazed at how nervous I suddenly was and it made me pause just long enough to give Taffy the chance to chip in with: 'What's up? Don't you know the monarch's title, Steve?'

As the laughter died away, I took a deep breath and said: 'Ladies and Gentlemen; The Queen.'

While the tables were all being cleared, after the meal, Dick Price came over to our group. He was already the worse for drink again and he was starting to be too loud.

'Steve, my old *son*. Is this *another* of your girlfriends?' he said.

'Dick, give it a rest please,' I snapped at him.

He looked at Susan. 'Oops, sorry, didn't you know he was a bit of a lad, then? Oh, don't I *know* you?' he said.

I'd had enough. I stood up and said, 'Dick, go away. You made a fool of yourself at Kevin's party and you're not going to spoil our night tonight.'

I sat back down with Susan as Dick muttered something

impolite then wobbled away to torment somebody else.

'What did he mean, Steve?' she asked me.

'About the supposed girlfriends?' I told her the whole story, including the fact that it was her that he had been referring to at Kevin's party. She seemed to brush his stupidity aside and the rest of the night went brilliantly.

After the dance ended, I drove us back to her house at Low Keld and we laughed and chatted all the way there.

'Come on in,' she said as I stopped the car, outside. As soon as we got inside and I closed the door, she turned to kiss me. Then she reached out and switched off the light, leaving the room lit only by the dim glow from the coal fire, which had burned down low.

'Stay with me tonight,' she whispered. And as she did so, she slid both the straps of her dress down and off her shoulders.

Chapter Fifteen

Crashes and Crushes

Starting work at 10pm on Christmas Eve wasn't much fun, and it soon deteriorated. Only a minute after I arrived at the nick someone knocked at the front door. Hamish Sutherland was the constable on 2pm-10pm but he was obviously still tied with a job as he hadn't come back in to finish duty yet. Carole Clarke was out somewhere, too; she was on 5pm-1am supervisory duty. I opened the outer door. A young couple were standing there; both in their very early-20s, and it was obvious that the girl had been crying.

'Come on in,' I said. 'What's the matter?'

'Our new car,' she sobbed.

Her young husband gave her a hug and said, 'It'll be alright. It's only a car. We are alright, that's all that matters.' I got them sat down and then he continued: 'We went to meet some friends in the Terriers Inn at Snabside and the car park was full so we left our car half up on the grass verge on the main road with its sidelights on. I wasn't drinking, by the way; I don't drink and drive. Well, anyway, after we'd been there a while we all heard a car reversing fast up the road – reversing from the Hawthwaite direction towards Snabside. I think he must have missed the junction or something and was backing-up to have another go. Then there was a hell of a crash and through the windows we saw it. It was a blue Mini van and it looked like it had hit our car. Then it drove forwards again and turned left around the corner of the pub towards Low Water. Two or three of us went outside and I found that our car had been rammed really hard. That was obviously what the bang had been. It was all smashed in on the driver's side.'

The girl burst into tears once more.

'It's okay, love,' I said. 'As your husband said, at least no-one was hurt, and that really is the main thing.'

'It's not that,' she sobbed. 'We only got married two months ago and rather than going on honeymoon we decided to get a new car instead because we knew that if we used our money for something else and didn't get it now, it would be years before we would ever be in a position to get a good car. But we got the sums wrong when we bought it and we couldn't afford fully comprehensive insurance cover so we got third-party-only. And now the car is wrecked. There's no *way* we can afford to put it back on the road.' Her crying got worse.

I looked at the lad. 'Is it really that bad?' I asked him.

'Aye,' he said. 'One of my mates that was at the Terriers is a mechanic and he reckons it might even be an insurance write-off. The chassis is twisted, around the driver's door area.'

'Did anyone see the number of the Mini van?' I said.

'No. The only thing that anyone saw was that it had a roof rack and there was a ladder fastened on the rack. It must have been his rear driver's side that hit our car though,' he said.

'Do you know what time it actually happened?' I said.

'Bang on half past nine. Oh, sorry, that was a bad choice of words,' he said.

I took a short statement from him. It turned out that they were called Andrew and Jill Ivinson and lived on Gale Hill in Hawthwaite. Their own car was a brand new yellow Ford Escort Popular.

I phoned the headquarters control room and asked for all vehicles in the area to be given an observations message regarding the blue van but it was nearly certain that it would it already have been hidden away out of sight.

After that I told Andrew and Jill: 'Obviously, there's not much I can do now until after Christmas is over but I'll do everything I can to try and find it for you. If I do find it and that's an awful long shot – then we'll just have to hope that the driver has got some insurance himself that you can claim off.'

I got the name of the garage that would be recovering their wrecked Escort, and the name and address of the witness who had actually seen the roof rack and ladder. I needed to check every possible detail if I was to stand any chance of catching the clown who'd done it. I hated people who did dirty tricks like that. The Ivinsons' Christmas had been spoiled and, for all I knew that much worse things happen in the world, it put a bad taste in my mouth that Christmas Eve. If I could get him, I would.

As soon as the Ivinsons left the nick, I called Hamish Sutherland on the local, UHF radio: 'Control to 1-7-9; over.'

'1-7-9 receiving; go ahead.

'Have you got no home to go to on Christmas Eve, 1-7-9?'

'Yes, I have, Steve. But unfortunately I've also got an R.T.A. to sort out, too. I should be back in about ten minutes; over.'

'Hard luck, Hamish,' I said. 'Is Sergeant Clarke there, too? Over.'

'Affirmative, Steve; it was a nasty crash – a two-car collision. Three people removed to West Cumberland Hospital by ambulance, but we've got the scene cleared and "Traffic" are here and they've taken over so we'll be back with you shortly; over.'

'Roger, 1-7-9. Control Out.'

By the time they did get back to the police station, I had gone out on foot patrol in the town centre, to keep the revellers in check. When I went back in at 1am for my refreshments, Sergeant Clarke was just tidying up ready to finish duty and go home.

'How bad are the injuries from that road accident, Sarge?' I said.

'One of them's nasty; a possible "foxtrot",' she replied.

"Foxtrot" was just the word for "F" in the phonetic alphabet but, in accident and injury situations, it was official police jargon for "fatal". And no doubt some poor family were now beside themselves with distress. Some Christmas it had turned out to be for them. Road crashes: *La plus ça change, plus c'est la même chose* – festive season or not.

Carol wished me Happy Christmas then left. And the rest of my night, thankfully, was uneventful.

Christmas afternoon was spent with my parents, at home in Linthwaite. It was difficult eating a full Christmas lunch for what was – for me – my breakfast, but I wanted to keep things as normal as possible for Mam and Dad. My brothers Robert and Chris were both there for the dinner, with their wives, Sandra and Felicity, and all was good humour and affection.

In keeping with my parents' usual routine, we finished the meal just in time to get settled for the Queen's Speech from Buckingham Palace, on television at 3pm.

A couple of hours later, on the Border Television news they announced that an eighteen year old girl, who had been involved in a road accident near Hawthwaite the night before, had died in the West Cumberland Hospital. It was hard for me to share in the family's festivities after hearing that but at the same time I made sure that I didn't let them see that it had affected me. I was really grateful that they didn't ask me any questions about it, either.

When I walked into the nick, on Christmas night, Hamish Sutherland was sitting finishing off his statement about the crash.

'A quiet day apart from that, Hamish?' I asked.

'Yes, not too bad, Steve. And now that this one's a fatal, the Traffic Department has officially taken over the investigation,' he said.

The rest of that week was uneventful until 5.30am on the Saturday morning, when I got a radio call from the headquarters control room to go to the Netherpot Car Park, beside Nethermere because there was a report of two people trapped in a car. It seemed rather an odd message because it apparently wasn't a road accident but that was all they could tell me. There had been a 999 call but the caller had refused to leave his name and address even though he had said it was urgent.

It only took me ten minutes to drive up the lakeside to Netherpot and to my great surprise the only car that I could see there was a dark blue Bentley. But that was nothing like the surprise I got when I went to the car and found that there was a huge man lying face down on the reclined, front passenger seat, stark naked. When, moments later, I saw a woman's face peering out from just over his right shoulder it was a couple of seconds before I was able to ask a loud but rather silly: 'Are you alright?'

'I am – almost – but it's a bit hard to breathe,' she shouted. And then she added, quite matter-of-factly: 'I'm fairly sure *he's* dead though.'

I tried to open the car door but the central locking was on; all four doors were secure. I went back to the passenger side and said: 'Is there any way you can reach the door lock?'

She simply shook her head at me.

'I'm going to have to smash a window to get in; I have no choice. Keep your eyes closed; the glass will make a tremendous bang when it goes,' I said.

It took me several very hard whacks with my truncheon to smash the driver's door window. As soon as I popped the lock and got in, I checked the man's bulbous neck for a carotid pulse but could find nothing. And his arms were fairly stiff, too – partial rigor mortis.

'I have to go back to my van and call for assistance,' I told her. 'I'll be back in just a moment.'

'Please hurry,' she said. 'It's getting really hard for me to breathe.'

Once at my radio, I called in: 'Zulu-Three-One to BB; over.'

'Zulu-Three-One, go ahead.'

'Zulu-Three-One, I'm at Netherpot Car Park as instructed,' I said. 'I require an ambulance, a doctor, and you'd better send an undertaker, too. I have one casualty here – almost certainly a "foxtrot," in which case the ambulance crew will refuse to convey him. The second person is seemingly unharmed but is currently unable to leave the vehicle. Will you also ask the six o'clock starter at Hawthwaite to travel immediately to the scene to assist me, please; over.'

'Roger, Three-One, will do, but the Control Room Inspector is asking for more details of the incident; over.'

'Zulu-Three-One to BB, I request that I wait until I'm back at Hawthwaite to give you details by landline. I would prefer not to pass details over insecure radio channels as it is rather delicate; over.'

'Roger, Three-One, noted; BB out'

Back at the Bentley, I cleared broken glass from the driver's seat then knelt on the expensive leather.

'What's your name, love?' I asked the woman.

'Cassandra Hemmingway,' she gasped.

I jumped so hard at hearing the name that I banged my head on the car roof.

'The *solicitor*?' I said.

I was even more dumbstruck now. Cassandra Hemmingway, of Hemmingway, Parsonby and Clunes, was one of the north of England's top criminal defence lawyers.

'Yes, I'm afraid so. And before you ask, no this man is not my husband; it's somebody else's,' she said.

'Well we'll worry about that later. I'm going to try to roll him off you so I can get you freed before anyone else arrives, Miss Hemmingway, alright?' I said.

'Yes, but it's Mrs, not Miss,' she replied.

I reached over the man and got his right arm and shoulder. I dragged, and heaved, and pulled. My God, was he heavy! All I could think was that after this I could maybe get a job at an American rodeo, wrestling steers; it would probably be easier. Eventually, though, my perseverance paid off and I gradually rolled him over towards me so that the bulk of his weight landed on the driver's seat, which was already reclined.

'There you go, Mrs Hemmingway,' I said. 'Get yourself dressed before the other chaps arrive.'

At that point her modesty was secure for the simple reason that I could not see her undoubted nakedness because of the size of the man and – keeping well back, for that very reason – I busied myself trying to find his carotid pulse once more.

'Oh, shit. I'm sorry, I can't move,' she cried. And for the first time there was distress in her voice. 'You are going to have to help me please, Constable. I simply cannot move. I have been pinned down under his weight too long.'

'Do you want me to come around to your side of the car?' I said.

'You'll have to, I'm so sorry,' she said.

I wouldn't have been a normal man if I had failed to steal glances at Mrs Hemmingway. She was perhaps about 28-29 years old and she was beautiful too. I had seen her before in court. Everyone fancied her but here, in the light of my torch and the interior light of the Bentley, she was just an acutely embarrassed and vulnerable woman.

Her voice was subdued and it cracked as she repeated: 'I'm so, so sorry. You're going to have to help me.'

'It's alright, Mrs Hemmingway. I'll help you get dressed before anyone else arrives if that's what you want me to do and I'll tell you this, too: Nobody else will ever find out about it, alright? That's a promise, so don't worry yourself about that,' I said.

She even had the prettiest underwear I think I'd ever seen – peach coloured, lacy, and very skimpy – and it looked expensive. I managed to get her dressed as far as her slacks and her blouse, and got her shoes back on her just before the ambulance arrived. As they pulled on to the gravel of the car park I was just slipping her cardigan around her shoulders and I'd managed to get her up into a sitting position, with her feet on the ground outside the car and her circulation was coming back. I helped her to my van and sat her inside it, with the heater running.

'You'll realise, of course, that I'll have to ask you a few questions about the incident, later?' I said to her.

'Yes, believe me I know,' she said.

'For now, can I just ask you the name and address of your friend, and his age and occupation, if you know them,' I said.

'Yes; of course. He's Peregrine Chatsworth-Dean; that's Chatsworth-Dean with a hyphen – Perry to his friends. He's 52. He has a holiday cottage in Snabside; his wife is there right now. Their proper home is in Cheshire. Oh – occupation, yes – he's a barrister,' she said. Her voice was composed but the occasional tear ran down one or other of her cheeks.

'Okay. You just stay there and get warmed through. I'll be back shortly,' I said.

By the time I got back to the Bentley, a local G.P., Doctor McDermott, had arrived and pronounced Mr Chatsworth-Dean's life extinct. And sure enough, the ambulancemen refused to convey the body to the mortuary. It simply wasn't their job because ambulances needed to be kept available for live casualties. Just then, Joe Stuart – a Hawthwaite undertaker – arrived in his hearse and my 6am relief, Taffy Williams, pulled up in his own car.

Dr McDermott left us. He'd had three call-outs during the night and was desperate to try to get a little more sleep before he was due to run his Saturday surgery at 8.30am. But we managed to get the ambulance crew to hang on a few minutes to help us try to get Mr Chatsworth-Dean's body into the fibreglass coffin that undertakers use to collect the victims of sudden deaths. The shell, as it was known, proved far too small for such a huge man. We estimated that he weighed about eighteen stone. But the ambulancemen still refused to use their vehicle to carry him.

'It's more than our job is worth to do that,' one of them protested.

'Well,' said Joe, 'there is one alternative that I've had to do before. We'll have to dress him, put him in the front seat of the hearse with a seat belt on, and take him to the mortuary *that* way, as though he was just a passenger. There won't be many folk about at this time of morning to see him.'

And that was how it was; we simply had no choice. It was decided that I should leave the scene immediately and take Mrs Hemmingway with me so that she didn't have to watch her friend suffer such an undignified departure.

'It's okay, boy-oh,' said Taffy in that wonderful Welsh accent of his. 'Get you away. I'll come back to the nick in my own car then we'll have to come back later for the Bentley. There's no other way around that.'

As we drove back to Hawthwaite Police Station, I said to my passenger: 'Right, may I call you Cassandra?'

'Of course. After all, we *were* on rather personal terms back there,' she said, trying to force a smile through some more of her silent tears.

'Okay, Cassandra,' I said. 'I can't make you any promises but my own instinct is that there is no good to be served whatsoever by telling Mrs Chatsworth-Dean the full circumstances. It would presumably just distress her all the more. Do you think she had any idea about you and Perry?'

'No, I doubt it,' she said. 'But what do you mean?'

'I mean that I am going to ask my inspector whether we can reserve the full details solely for the coroner and simply report the matter – as far as the public are concerned – as Mr Chatsworth-Dean just being found dead in his car at a well-known Lakeland beauty spot,' I said.

'You can't *do* that, can you?' she said, surprised.

'Well, no matter how I feel about it, you are right in that I couldn't do it just for your own sake, or for the sake of your career. But I have known it to happen before where a coroner was prepared to accept such associated evidence *"in camera"* to reduce unnecessary distress for the next of kin,' he said.

'If you are able to do that, for whatever reason, I shall be more indebted to you than you could ever comprehend,' she said.

'Well, with respect, I'd certainly not be doing it for you or your indebtedness. You do realise that in order for me to attempt this I would have to ask you some extremely personal questions which will have to be included in my own report? And it would have to include every detail of what happened in the car,' I said.

'Yes, but unless I'm much mistaken, you would have to ask me those questions in any event,' she said.

'True, but I think I'm just trying to prepare us both for what is bound to be an uncomfortable interview. Alright, well as soon as we get back to the nick, I'll call my inspector out. He's a really decent chap and totally discreet. If what I'm suggesting is feasible, he'll smooth its passage,' I said.

'Thank you.'

'Where are you staying?' I asked her.

'My husband and I have our own holiday home in Hawthwaite – up on Lake Bank, to be precise – and I stay there alone, sometimes, when I have cases up in this neck of the woods. My husband and I have nothing left between us. We effectively lead separate lives. Perry and I sometimes ended up there, at night, but tonight we went up the valley for a drink at the Kirk Riddings Hotel. And then on the way back we stopped on that car park to see the mountains and the lake in the moonlight, and that's how come we ended up doing what we did there,' she said.

'Forgive me asking such a personal question, but did you love him? Was it that type of relationship? The coroner will want to know every last detail if he's going to accept the closed-doors approach,' I said.

'Good gracious, no. He was a very nice man and a dear friend too, but – if I may be brutally honest – he was also an immensely powerful man; a puller of strings. You can work the rest out for yourself,' she said.

I had to admire her candour.

As soon as we arrived at the police station, I got her seated beside a warm radiator in the front office then went into the sergeants' room and closed the door so that I could telephone the boss in private. A groggy Inspector Sumner answered.

'Good morning, sir,' I said. 'It's Steve Shearwater at the nick. I'm sorry to disturb you so early but I've got a very delicate situation down here that I really need your help with.'

'Tell me more,' he said.

It took me a few minutes to run through the sequence of events for him, though I omitted any mention of helping her to dress.

When I'd finished he said: 'Yes, alright. I know the woman. I have prosecuted several cases where she has defended. I'll be right there. Give me about quarter of an hour.'

I used the time to make Mrs Hemmingway a cup of tea.

'Yes,' she said, when I told her, 'I know Inspector Sumner. Does he know about everything that happened at the car park?' she asked.

'Everything except me dressing you. As I said, that will remain strictly between you and I.'

The look she gave me was inscrutable. It was as though she didn't know whether to believe me. But both she and I knew that a piece of police station gossip like that would catapult around the entire north of England legal arena like wildfire and would make her professional life very difficult. There was no good reason for me to be the cause of that.

When the boss arrived, I once again recounted the facts to him but this time in Cassandra's presence.

'Is what this officer has told me accurate?' he asked her when I'd finished.

'Yes, entirely,' she said.

'Well, Mrs Hemmingway,' said the Inspector. 'I have to say that I think you're fortunate that it is Constable Shearwater that's dealing with the matter. Many officers wouldn't have even thought about your predicament, let alone do anything to actually protect your interests. But you do realise, of course, that the purpose of what PC Shearwater has proposed is actually to protect Mrs Chatsworth-Dean from any further distress than that which she will imminently suffer, and not for *your* sake?'

'Yes.'

'Right, Steve,' he said, turning to me, 'I know you are on overtime but I would like you to stay on a little longer and take a full statement from Mrs Hemmingway. As soon as Taffy gets back I'll have a word with him. He's another trustworthy individual, Mrs Hemmingway,' he added, then back to me: 'I'll get him to inform the widow. My own immediate job will be to ask the two ambulancemen for their silence on the matter. I'll have a word with the doctor and the undertaker, too. Then at eight o'clock, I'll phone the coroner and put your request to him. I'm confident that he'll oblige but I don't want to risk annoying him by phoning any earlier than that.'

It took me an hour and a half to record Cassandra's statement in the thorough detail that was necessary. When it was completed and signed, I handed the statement to the Inspector, in his own office. By that stage he had spoken to Mr Magnusson, the coroner, and had obtained his apparently rather grudging permission for our proposed course of action.

'Just one other thing, Steve,' said Inspector Sumner. 'No matter how timid or vulnerable she might look now, don't ever underestimate Cassandra Hemmingway. Just remember when you eventually meet her face-to-face in court that the only difference between her and an angry Rottweiler is the lipstick.'

'Oh, I dunno, sir. I take your point, but I would have to admit that there might be one other significant difference: I've never really *fancied* a Rottweiler.'

Inspector Sumner smiled and shook his head at me. 'Now that would be a bit over-ambitious of you, young man,' he said.

With that, I went back down the stairs, booked off duty and gave Cassandra a lift back to her house in my own car. It was almost on my route home to Linthwaite; Lake Bank – an exclusive little estate of luxury bungalows high up, overlooking the town, and each with a stunning view over the Nethermere lake, far below.

'You are very welcome to come in for a coffee, if you wish, but I know that you'll be exhausted so I certainly won't be offended if you say no,' she said, as we drew up outside her house.

'Any other time and I would gladly have said yes, but you're right, I'm shattered. And you must be, too,' I said.

Cassandra reached out her right hand and rested it on my left hand, which was still holding the gear lever.

'Steve… thank you,' she said. 'I know this may sound empty but if *ever* there is anything I can do for you, then I shall.'

She got a business card from her purse and wrote on the back of it.

'There,' she said. 'Those are my home number and the number here at this house. And the office details are on the front, of course. Please don't forget what I've said.'

Her hand settled on mine for a couple of seconds more, then with a half-smile from her watery and now bloodshot eyes, she said her farewells and left the car.

My mother was being a typical mother when I arrived home. She had been waiting near the back door, on tenterhooks, and fussed over me to make sure I was alright. I went straight to bed and fell into it, and if I hadn't she would probably have frog-marched me there.

Chapter Sixteen

Something New

Twice during Christmas week I called to see Susan for a couple of hours before I went to work at 10pm, and I got to meet Andrew, too. He was a grand little chap; small for his age and maybe a bit timid, but as bright as a button. And it turned out he thought that it was exciting to sit on a policeman's knee, once he got over his shyness. But now I was going back there to party: It was New Year's Eve and the first of my two days off. And I was determined to enjoy it, too, seeing as I'd worked the last seven nights, right through Christmas. Susan had arranged for Andrew to stay at her mother's for the night and wanted me to collect her from there. It was further up, in the older part of Low Keld village.

'Ooh, do come *in*, Steven,' said Mrs Goss, who acted almost flirtatiously as though it were her I was calling for rather than her daughter. And as I left the house with Susan, a few minutes later, her mother took the chance to say: 'Don't forget you can always come here for a cuppa, too, you know.'

I took Susan up to Linthwaite, 12 miles away, just for an hour so we could have a couple of drinks with my friends in my own "local" and then we went back to Low Keld for the rest of the night. I parked the car on her little driveway and we walked, hand in hand, towards the Fisherman's Arms, beside the northern end of the bridge over the outflow at the foot of the lake, the start of the River Broom. The moon was full and its reflection carved a blaze of white across the water, cutting towards us from the far bank of the lake, glittering like an ice sheet. A few dead reeds, right beside the road, in only a few inches of water, swayed their feathery silhouettes at us, like dancers. We stopped and Susan turned to kiss me. A pair of ducks burst out of the reeds, startled by our arrival above their roosting place, and splashed noisily away across the lake surface, quacking loudly.

'I wish they wouldn't bloody *do* that,' she protested as she grabbed me, in her fright.

We kissed… a long, deep lingering kiss that seemed to send electricity to the very base of my spine and made me flinch. She only had on a short, party dress and a thin cardigan, and after a few minutes of kissing, the cold got the better of her and she started to shiver. I slipped my leather jacket off and wrapped it around her shoulders.

'But you'll freeze, Steve,' she said.

'No I won't. And anyway, it's only another couple of hundred yards.'

By that time, it was nearly nine o'clock and the pub was getting full. Susan seemed to know virtually everyone in there and the atmosphere was wonderful. I soon lost count of how many people she introduced to me, many of whom were her friends from school days.

She caught one man by the arm as he made to push past her.

'Tom, hiii,' she said, and then hugged him. 'Tom, this is Steve Shearwater. Steve, Tom Pearson.'

He was a burly chap, slightly shorter but quite a bit heavier than me. His curly, sandy-coloured hair severely needed washing. He just scowled at me.

'The Hawthwaite copper, eh? Well I don't like coppers so excuse me,' he said. And with that snarling dismissal, he turned and walked away.

'Oh, sorry Steve,' said Susan. 'He always has been a bit unpredictable but I thought that tonight of all nights he might have had the decency to be pleasant.'

'It's okay,' I said. 'You get used to it in my job.'

The drinking, laughter and jollity continued for the next couple of hours until the landlord's voice boomed out: 'Right! Shut up, the lot of you. It's nearly time for Big Ben.' And then he turned up the radio so we could all hear the famous London bell strike twelve and herald in another year.

There was much kissing all around as Big Ben rang out and then we all linked arms for "Auld Lang Syne." At the same moment, a tall, dark-haired chap, who had been in the bar all evening quickly slipped out of the door, largely unnoticed. He came back in just a few seconds later carrying a piece of coal that he threw on an already roaring, open fire to herald prosperity for the next twelve months; the Lakeland tradition of "first footing" the new year. And then we sang.

When we left the pub, about 1am, to walk back to Susan's house, I gave her my jacket again but the drink had made me impervious to the cold. As soon as we got into the house, she started tugging at the buttons on my shirt. She wanted me right there and then, in front of the fire in the living room. I wasn't going to argue. An hour later, we went upstairs to bed and it started again.

I was back at work on the 2pm-10pm shift, on the second of January. Sergeant Wyatt and Linda Hargreaves were both in the front office and even though the season was fading fast, we all wished each other Happy New Year.

'I've actually got a New Year's present for you, Steve,' said the sergeant.

I raised a sceptical eyebrow at him and he laughed.

'You used to be a cadet, didn't you?' he said.

'Yes, Sarge; when I was in Hull,' I said.

'Well we've just inherited a cadet from headquarters for the next six months,' he said. 'It's her first day with us, today, and I've put her on the two-to-ten shift with you for the rest of the week.'

'All *week*?'

Just in time to hear the protest in my comment, Samantha Stevens walked into the front office with us. In an instant, I remembered my own very first day as a cadet, when an old constable permanently shattered my teenage illusions – that all policemen were nice people – by looking me up and down and muttering: 'Oh shit, not another fucking cadet!'

'Sorry, love,' I said. I could feel my face going crimson as I spoke. 'That wasn't aimed at you, don't worry. I was just surprised, that's all.'

Linda burst out laughing. 'Now that's a sight I never expected to see! Come here Steve and let me warm my hands on your blush,' she said.

'Have you got any jobs on, Steve?' chipped in Andy Wyatt – himself barely able to hide his mirth.

'Yes, Sarge,' I said. 'There was a hit-and-run, damage-only R.T.A. on Christmas Eve and this week I want to try and trace the blue Mini van that caused it, now that all the bodyworks and repair garages will be getting back to normal, after the holidays.'

'Right ho,' he replied.

Then he turned to the cadet and said, 'Okay, lass, you go with Steve. Don't mind what he said; he was *once* known to be pleasant, you know. About ten minutes that lasted.'

Even I laughed at that comment, and said: 'Take no notice, Samantha. He's only kidding. Where have you worked prior to this?'

Samantha smiled shyly and said: 'Apart from my basic training I've done six months in Finance at headquarters, a six month attachment in Admin at Carlisle and another six months in

Prosecutions.'

'Dear God, three boring jobs in succession. Did you learn anything about the police?' I said.

'No,' she said, looking disappointed. 'It was really boring. I was the tea maker and apparently just the pretty face to keep the men happy. I got all the tedious chores to do.'

'So in all that time, you've never booked on duty with someone who's going out on patrol?' I said.

She shook her head.

'Right,' I said. 'Come with me into the muster room and I'll show you what we do.'

I picked up all the latest messages from the telex machine and separated them either into the station administration basket or the ring binder for those of us on patrols, then I showed Samantha the various things we had to check so we would know what to look for out on the beat. Like most first-timers, she was rather over-awed by what was actually a very basic system.

'Right, come on,' I said, when we had done the messages. 'It's time for your first investigation.'

Samantha's eighteen-year-old, green eyes lit up.

We walked out to the van, in the back yard, and I went through radio procedure with her. When she eventually picked up the radio handset to book us on the air with headquarters she tried her utmost to look calm but the excitement on her face was a picture.

We visited every garage and motor bodyworks in Hawthwaite and all the surrounding villages that afternoon, asking if they had come across a blue Mini van since Christmas, with substantial damage at the rear right-hand side. The answers were all disappointing and none of the people I spoke with seemed evasive, as though they might be covering for someone. By the time we had finished that task, it was time to go back into Hawthwaite for our refs, at 5pm.

As we sat, having our sandwiches, I said to Samantha: 'Well that's your first taste of a police enquiry. Most of it is just leg-work and tedium, but it's worth it when you get the result that you're after.'

'Is there anything else you can do about this one?' she asked me.

'Well,' I said. 'A lot of the lads would let a case like this just drop because they would see it as relatively trivial and a lot of work. But I really want to get this bugger. I hate people that do this sort of dirty trick. Anyway, all the repair garages will be shut for the night, now, so tomorrow when we come on duty we'll do some telephone enquiries around the outlying ones and around all of the tradesmen who might use vehicles with roof racks, like that Mini van had; people like window cleaners, electricians, plumbers and so on. We'll ask them not only if *they* have a blue van but also whether they know anyone else that does because, obviously, if we ring the van owner then he's likely to realise what we are up to and lie about it, and say he hasn't got that type of vehicle.'

Over the next two afternoons, we telephoned everyone we could think of within about a twenty-mile radius but with no luck at all.

'So is there anything else we can do about that damaged car?' asked Samantha, on the Friday afternoon.

'No, not much I'm afraid,' I said. But if ever he's silly enough to come back around here in his flamin' van I'll nail him if I possibly can.'

That evening, we visited the Ivinsons and told them the bad news about their damaged car. They had received estimates by then for the necessary repairs. As things stood, their brand new car would have to be written off and they wouldn't get a penny back.

The rest of the week of late shifts went very quietly; probably far too quietly for an enthusiastic young cadet but Samantha never seemed to be bored.

Susan had invited me around for dinner with her and Andrew on the following Wednesday, the first of my two days off, and she told me in advance that she hoped I would be staying for the night.

'It's alright, Andrew never wakes up through the night,' she said when I asked. 'And if you stay in bed while I get up and take him to school, he won't even know you stayed.'

'Mammy,' said Andrew, after we'd eaten, 'is Steve going to be my new daddy?'

'I don't know,' she replied. 'Nobody knows about things like that as soon as this, so why don't you just call him "Uncle Steve".'

That seemed to please the little chap. 'Will you read me my story, tonight, Uncle Steve?' he asked.

'Yes, of course I will,' I said.

About eight o'clock, when I had finished reading to him from a "Thomas the Tank Engine" story, I came downstairs and found that Susan had been in my overnight bag. She was curled up on the settee wearing one of my shirts. Nothing else, just a dark blue shirt. And it only had two of the lower buttons fastened. She was an enthusiastic lover and it was obviously going to be a busy night, but I certainly wasn't complaining. About 3am, though – two hours after we had eventually gone to bed, if not immediately to sleep – I heard the sound of little footsteps approaching.

'Mammy,' said a little voice in the dark. 'Who's that in bed with you Mam? Is it Uncle Steve?'

'Yes, it's Uncle Steve. Go on back to bed, Andrew, there's a good boy,' said Susan.

Without another word, the little chap padded back through to his own room. And before I could say anything to Susan, she was fast asleep again.

So much for Andrew never waking up through the night.

When I fell back to sleep, I must have gone out like a light and it was about ten past nine when Susan woke me up, just after she got back from taking Andrew to school. She was naked and just slid into bed with me. I had never met anyone like her; it was as though she was perpetually determined to break the bed, or maybe just my spine.

Chapter Seventeen

The Old and the Young

On the Friday morning, I left my parents' house shortly before half past five. That gave me plenty time to be at the nick fifteen minutes before my 6am starting time, as was required.

A magical site greeted me as I emerged from the warmth of the kitchen into the knife-sharp night air. There had been a heavy snowfall – not just on the tops of the mountains but coating the entire valley. Yet now the clouds had gone completely and the whole scene was lit by a blisteringly white moon. I stood for two minutes, loving the beauty of it all before I got into my car. Every surface was reflecting light, and shadows cast by the lunar spotlight seemed almost as well defined as those of a sunny day.

Across the valley from my home was the carved face of Linthwaite Pike, a long, steep, south-facing flank, split into five ridges by the four deep ghylls that gouged through it. I wondered whether water would still be flowing in the tumbling becks in each of the ghylls or whether the ice maiden had already nipped each stream to a standstill.

Unfortunately, despite my favourite William H. Davies' poem, I could stand and stare no longer. The roads would obviously be slippery so I had to leave now if I was to be on time getting to work to let the night-shift man get away home.

There were no early morning jobs waiting to be done at the police station, so I decided to go out on foot patrol in town rather than go out in the van, until my refs at 9am. For anyone that enjoys the crispness of a sharp, winter's day it was delightful to be out. Even the air itself seemed to be crackling with the frost.

I went back in to the office about ten minutes to nine. Andy Wyatt was already there, for his 9am-5pm shift, and Samantha Stevens came in just a couple of minutes later.

'Will you go with Steve, today, Samantha?' he asked, rhetorically.

'Yes, Sergeant,' she said, and turned to flash me a little smile.

'Steve, if you are going out of town at all remember you'll have to get Sam back here sometime between twelve and one, for her lunch,' said Sergeant Wyatt.

'Right oh, Sarge,' I said.

Just at that, the phone rang and Sergeant Wyatt answered it: 'Hawthwaite Police Station.' He paused to listen and I could see a frown spreading over his face as he jotted notes on the telephone message pad. 'I'm sorry to hear that, Mrs Taylor. What's your address, please? Yes, one of our officers will be there in just a few minutes. Goodbye.'

He put the phone down and turned to me. 'There goes your quiet morning, Steve. That was a Mrs Taylor. Her parents are Walter and Gladys Atkinson from number seven, Broom Street. It would appear that Walter has died in his sleep. The doctor hasn't arrived yet to certify death so you'll have to go up there and deal with it as a "sudden death", for the time being.' He turned to Samantha: 'What about you, love? Do you want to go with Steve? You don't have to if you don't want to.'

'Yes, I'll go. I have to learn,' said Samantha.

'That's mi' lass; that's the spirit,' said Andy, then he tore off the carbon copy of the phone message and gave it to me and he put the original in the station messages binder.

'Come on then, Sam,' I said to her. And once more we walked

out to the back yard to get the van. It only took two minutes to reach Broom Street. Two tiers, of five steep steps each, led down into the sunken garden of number seven. It was an end-of-terrace house and had a side door, at the right-hand end of the building. As we approached, the door opened and a woman who appeared to be in her sixties looked out.

'Hello,' she said. 'I'm Alice Taylor, it is my father who has…' She paused. 'Thank you for coming so quickly. Come in.'

As we went in, steep stairs lay directly ahead, before the start of which a door led off on either side of the tiny hallway. She turned right and took us into the kitchen.

'Mam's in the living room,' she said, indicating the other door. 'And if you don't mind I'll get back to her straight away, if I may.'

'Yes, of course,' I replied. 'I take it the doctor hasn't been yet?'

'No, not yet,' she said.

'Have you called an undertaker?' I asked.

'Yes,' she replied. 'Reg Tiplady is coming.'

'Right, that's fine,' I said. 'Were you here overnight by any chance, or just your parents?'

'No, just my parents. I live at Leatherside. Mam phoned me when she realised that Dad wasn't going to wake up.' Her words caught in her throat and she gave a little sob.

'It's alright, Mrs Taylor,' I said. 'Why don't you go and sit with your mam. We'll look after your dad carefully. Will she want to see him again before he goes?'

Alice Taylor was mopping a couple of tears with a tissue and just shook her head.

'Alright,' I continued, 'well in that case can I suggest that you draw the curtains to save her the distress of seeing your father being taken out. And also I would suggest that you keep the living room door closed for the same reason.'

'I will,' she said.

'Do you know whether your father has seen his doctor recently?' I asked.

'Not for years and years,' she said. 'He has just turned ninety and never ailed a thing. Mam says that she woke up this morning and that dad simply didn't.'

'Alright, well a bit later on I'll have to take a statement from your mother,' I said. 'I presume you'll be here with your mam for the rest of the day? It will be better if you are with her when I take the statement.'

'Yes, I'll be here,' she said.

'Right. Thank you,' I said. 'You go and sit with your mother now. We'll call you if we need you.'

Mrs Taylor left the kitchen and I said: 'Okay Samantha, let's go upstairs and see what's to do. Have you ever seen a dead body before?'

'No,' said Samantha.

'Well it's okay. The dead can't hurt you; it's the living that you've got to watch out for. Do you want to come up with me?'

She nodded but I added: 'If you want to come back down, don't worry about it, alright?'

'I'll be alright,' she said.

The stairs were very narrow and, to my dismay, doubled back on themselves three quarters of the way up. All the doors and skirting boards were such dark brown, heavily varnished wood that it almost looked black. The word "gloomy" didn't sum it up. It was a definite throw-back to the Victorian era. Two of the three doors off the landing were closed but the second of the two on the right was open a few inches. I looked in and there, lying as peaceful as a baby was the late Walter Atkinson. For all the world he looked just as though he was asleep but – unless the doctor could tell us otherwise when he arrived – that was clearly not the case.

'It's alright to come in, Samantha,' I said. 'There's nothing here to upset you.'

She came in, and looked. I went over and automatically tried to find the carotid pulse in the old chap's neck. Nothing. And he was a bit stiff to the touch, too.

'Is he cold?' Samantha asked.

'No, sweetheart. He's not very cold,' I said. 'The bed has kept him warm. Do you want to touch him? There's nothing to be afraid of.'

'I don't know whether I should,' she said. 'It seems disrespectful.'

'It's alright. Old Walter won't mind. And you have to get used to it sometime,' I said.

She walked across beside me, paused for a moment, then reached out and touched his forehead with the back of her hand.

'Good lass,' I said. 'Now, tell me, do you believe in people having souls?'

She nodded.

'Well I'll tell you what nurses do in hospitals and see if you want to do the same for old Walter, here. When someone dies in hospital, the nurses always open a window so that the spirit can fly free,' I said. Before I could ask whether she wanted to, Samantha crossed to the sash window and opened it.

'Will that be wide enough?' she said, timidly.

'I'm sure it will, sweetheart. You're doing fine,' I said.

Just at that, we heard a knock on the door, downstairs.

'Pop down and see if that's either the doctor or the undertaker, Sam, and if it is, bring them up here, please,' I said.

It turned out to be Doctor McDermott again. 'Hello, young Steven,' he said, as he entered the bedroom. 'We'll have to stop meeting like this. Slightly different circumstances this time though, eh?'

He checked for a heartbeat with his stethoscope and used his torch to test for pupil-dilation in Walter's eyes. Then he turned to us and said: 'No, nothing. This old chap's been dead for several hours.'

'Thank you doctor,' I said. 'As you can see, I have this young lady trainee with me today but I can't see any purpose in us checking the body for any suspicious marks so are you happy to say that there doesn't appear to be anything untoward here?'

'Yes,' he said. 'The pathologist will be looking closely anyway.'

Samantha looked at me and said: 'What would you be looking for?'

'Just the standard routine,' I said. 'It's the same for anyone who hasn't seen their doctor recently and had died unexpectedly. We just check for any signs of foul play.'

We all went down the stairs together and just as we got to the bottom Reg Tiplady, the undertaker, arrived and I immediately knew we had a slight problem. Reg, whom I'd never met before, looked as though he was about the same age as poor old Walter that had died.

'Are you on your own?' I asked Reg, as the doctor went in to see Gladys Atkinson and her daughter.

'Yes. I knew one of you police lads would be here and would give me a hand,' he said. 'My assistant has had to take the other hearse and go down to Birmingham this morning to collect a body from there.'

I took him into the kitchen, with Samantha, and closed the door to make sure that Mrs Atkinson and her daughter couldn't overhear our conversation.

'There's a very nasty u-turn on those stairs and we'll never get a box down there so do you think we should just bring it in here? I said to Reg. 'You can stay downstairs and make sure the two ladies don't come out of that room opposite, and Samantha and I can carry him down and we'll put him in the box in here. Then you and I can take him to the hearse.'

'That's fine by me, lad,' said Reg.

He and I then went out to bring the empty fibreglass shell from the hearse. We laid it on the kitchen floor then Samantha and I went back upstairs.

She looked apprehensive, so I said: 'Don't worry, love. Old Walter looks very light. Some elderly people lose a lot of their body weight over the years. I'll carry him down alone, in a fireman's lift, over my shoulder. All you'll need to do is watch where I'm stepping and make sure I'm not going to trip up over anything. Alright?'

She nodded. 'Yes, okay.'

I pulled the bedclothes back off the old chap and sat him up on the edge of the bed, ready to put him over my shoulder. But I had forgotten one thing. I had forgotten about the air that often remains in the lungs after someone has died. So as I eased him over my shoulder the air was forced out and Walter let out a wondrously loud moan.

I stood up, with him well balanced and secure, but when I turned around, Samantha had gone. She must have either disappeared in a puff of smoke or simply evaporated, because I'd never even heard her go.

When I got to the bottom of the stairs and helped Reg lower Walter gently into the shell, I said: 'Did you by any chance see my cadet leave the house?'

'See her?' he said. 'Aye, lad, but only just. I don't think she even *touched* those stairs on t' way down. She must have hit the ground doing about sixty miles an hour.'

We carried the shell to the hearse and Reg took old Walter away to the mortuary. I went back in, sat and talked to the two ladies for a few minutes, and then took the short statement that was needed.

It was about eleven o'clock when I got back to the nick. Linda Hargreaves was there, in the front office.

'Is Samantha here?' I asked.

'Yes, she is. What did you do to her, you big meannie?' said Linda.

For a moment, I fell for it: 'I didn't do *anything*,' I started to protest.

Linda gave a little laugh and I knew I'd been had.

'I know you didn't. She's through in the refs room, but she's still a bit upset,' she said.

I walked to the other end of the building and found Samantha sat at a table with her head in her hands.

'Hey, come on, lass. Cheer up,' I said. 'Most of us get a bit spooked by dead bodies the first few times. It's nothing to be ashamed of. There are even some experienced police *men* who still can't deal with it after a few years of service.'

I sat on the chair next to her and she turned her head towards me. Her face was pink and her eyes bloodshot with crying so much.

'It's okay, Sam; honest,' I said.

'I let *you* down,' she blurted, before dissolving into another flood of tears.

'What ever do you mean?' I said. 'You daft thing. You didn't let me down at all.'

I put my hands on her shoulders, and she looked up once more.

'You didn't let me down, love,' I said. 'If you hadn't happened to be on duty this morning I would automatically have gone to the job on my own anyway. So how could you have let me down?'

Her eyes flickered back and forth, focussing first on one of mine, and then the other.

'Come on. Why don't you come through with me to the front office and sit with Linda for a while,' I said. 'She has seen grown *men* cry; she'll tell you you're not alone.'

I got her settled with Linda then came back to the refs room to make the three of us a cup of tea, but while I was waiting for the kettle to boil, Linda came in.

'Is she alright now?' I asked.

'Steve, what do you think is wrong with her?' said Linda.

'She got upset at the sudden death and ran out...'

'You bloody men,' said Linda. 'You're all a bunch of blind tossers. She's not upset because the noise the body made frightened her, she's *dealt* with that. She's upset because she thinks she's fallen in *love* with you, ya daft pillock. You've become her *hero*. She's upset because she's convinced that you'll think she's pathetic.'

I stood there staring back at Linda, speechless.

'Come on, Romeo,' she said. 'Pick your chin up off the floor and bring those drinks through.'

Samantha was with me from 9am until 2pm on the Saturday, too. I just made a point of treating her exactly the same as I had been doing prior to her little upset, and we drove round and round the streets of Hawthwaite and the villages, looking for that damned blue Mini van, but we had no luck. It was very disconcerting that morning, though; each time she looked at me her eyes would keep flickering from one to the other of mine, and then down to my mouth, and then back to my eyes. It wasn't that I didn't fancy her; she was a lovely young woman. Nor did I think her too young for me, either. Only four years separated us. Eight years separated my own parents and they had a wonderful relationship. But there were two problems: firstly, I already had a girlfriend and I wasn't a believer in two-timing, and secondly – even without that girlfriend – I could have no way of knowing how far a eighteen-year-old's emotions might get in the way of us both doing a proper day's work, together. It simply wasn't a desirable situation.

It was Samantha's day-off on the Sunday. I had a bit of a headache on my early shift from having had a few pints with my mates in the Birch Hill Arms and then the Drovers Inn, at Linthwaite the night before. I had some civvy clothes with me because Susan had invited me to a late Sunday lunch as soon as I finished work.

I spent the first couple of hours writing various reports but just after 8am there was a rather quiet knocking on the outside door. When I opened up, I found an elderly lady waiting, with an ancient golden retriever dog on the end of a bit of string.

'I found it up the street,' she said, handing me the string. And she turned to walk away.

'Can I just make a note of your details before you go, please?' I said.

'No, thank you. But you can keep the string,' she said. And with that the old dear, who was obviously not one for bureaucracy, had gone.

We had a kennel for stray dogs, out in the back yard, but it was freezing out there and this rather stately old gentleman of a pooch looked far too ancient to be left outdoors. So I named him "Fred" and sat him by the heater in the front office with me whilst I got on with my reports. The only problem was that the old boy kept coming and sitting beside me and pushing his nose under my elbow to flick my arm up, to persuade me to scratch his head.

'What's up, old chap? Are you hungry?' I said.

I knew there were some dog biscuits in a cupboard out in the kennels, but Fred really didn't look as though he would take too kindly to such common fare. I went and got one of my sandwiches from my own refs and gave him that. He quite obviously approved of the brand of corned beef that my mother had put in the sandwiches because the whole thing disappeared down his throat in one uncouth, swift gulp. And then he got all excited and started prancing about, bouncing his front paws off the floor. I could only assume that it was a sort of dance to the God of Fray Bentos. He liked corned beef, did Fred!

'Alright, alright, you can have another,' I said. 'But please use your manners and eat it nicely. If you go and choke yourself to death, I'll have more paperwork to do, *and* no sandwiches left.'

I might as well have talked to the wall, for all the good it did. The second sandwich went down the long red tunnel even faster. And then his excitement seemed to increase. It wasn't long until all six of my butties were gone. He ate the lot! And he didn't even show any gratitude, either. He just kept nudging my arm, doing his corned beef dance and occasionally getting completely carried away and doing the quietest little "woof" I think I've ever heard. It seemed like the equivalent of a big male, Serengeti lion going "miaow". Then he ate my three biscuits, too. It looked like I would have go and buy myself some chocolate at refs time; none of the pie shops were open on a Sunday.

Just before 9am, Andy Wyatt came on duty.

'Oh, the Brigadier's dog's been on the rampage again, has it?' he said as soon as he spotted the retriever. 'Hello, Rex.'

'Ah, so you're a Rex, not a Fred, eh?' I said to the owner of the thumping tail. It was mildly absurd, really; two grown men talking to a dog as though it were likely to answer.

'It belongs to Brigadier Allday,' said the sergeant. 'His number's in the phone book. He lives on Sorrel Drive, in one of those dream houses.'

I found the number and rang.

'Who the deuce is phoning at *this* hour on a Sunday?' was the gravelly reply. And if I'd thought that Lord Nethermere had had an aristocratic sounding voice at the police ball then even that was no match for the Brigadier's.

'Good morning, sir. It's the police station. I think you'll find that your golden retriever has gone for a walk without you,' I said

'He has? Well, the blighter,' said the Brigadier. 'I'll be there shortly. Is he alright?'

'Yes, he's fine,' I said. I wanted to add: *As he should be, seeing he ate all my sandwiches,* but I didn't know if the Brigadier had a sense of humour so I kept quiet about it.

If the Brigadier's voice conveyed upper-class authority then it was as nothing compared to his appearance. He came in to the police station wearing a tweed shooting jacket with a matching deerstalker hat and a monocle. A pair of "plus four" knee breeches, long beige socks and a pair of brogues completed his aristocratic ensemble. His curled-up, handlebar moustache and the curved pipe he was smoking, rounded off the image. Sherlock Holmes would have been thoroughly proud of him.

He walked into the front office. The man must have been 6'5" and he had no stoop, despite his advancing years – talk about an imposing figure.

'Now, Rex, you little blighter, you're for it this time, mi' boy,' said the Brigadier.

The dog alternately looked up at him then looked down at the floor as though it knew it was being chastised. And it kept licking its lips as though the fright of its reprimand was making its mouth go dry.

'What did I tell you, eh?' continued the Brigadier. 'Didn't I tell you that such insubordination would not be tolerated again, eh? Didn't I tell you that if you went AWOL again you'd be for the chop?'

The dog, head held low, actually whimpered.

'Well, old boy; I meant it. When we leave here I'm going to march you to the veterinary surgeon and you'll get the needle. It's the big kennel in the sky for you, old chap. Better than the firing squad though, what?' said the old man.

At that, the dog slid to the floor, lay flat out, put its right paw fully over the top of its head and gave a sort of low, conversational howl of which the cartoon character Scooby Doo would have been envious.

If I hadn't seen it with my own eyes, I simply wouldn't have believed it. Maybe the sergeant and I had not been so foolish talking to Rex earlier after all, for if ever a dog seemed to understand human speech then this one did.

'Thank you, chaps,' the Brigadier announced to us, a few moments later. 'Come on, Rex. You have an appointment with a needle.'

And off they marched.

'Surely he's not really going to have that dog put to sleep, Sarge?' I said.

'Nooo. He goes through that same bloody pantomime every time he comes for the dog. The Brigadier would re-fight the Boer War single-handed before he would let anyone harm Rex,' said Sergeant Wyatt. 'It should be on the stage, that animal.'

I left the nick bang on the stroke of two o'clock. I was looking forward to my meal with Susan and Andrew. Once again, we'd been blessed with some winter sunshine and even though a lot of the snow had gone, it still made for some wonderful views as I drove along the side of Low Water on my way to Low Keld. The fringes of the lake were covered in ice – some white, and some clear – but the deeper water was free from it. At one point, a raft of ducks were all swimming, about a hundred feet from the shore. They were mostly pochard, "tufties" and mallard, but I briefly spotted the striped crowns of a couple of drake wigeon amongst them; the low sunlight made their yellow bands gleam.

To my surprise, there was no answer when I got to Susan's house. I knocked a couple of times at the front door, then tried again at the back door but it was obvious that there was nobody in. Her garage had no windows in it so I couldn't see whether her car was there or not. There seemed little choice but to go to her mother's house, about half a mile up the road.

At her mother's, I knocked and was greeted by Mary Goss.

'Come on in, Steven,' she said. 'Susan was hoping to be back by now: Something about having to go and help a friend. But come on in; Andrew's here, and I've kept you a bit of roast beef just in case Susan didn't make it back in time. Just as well I did, eh?'

'Thanks, Mary; you're a pal,' I said.

Just at that, little Andrew came hurtling through into the kitchen from the living room.

'Uncle Steve, Uncle Steve!' he yelled.

I bent down and he flung himself happily into my arms.

'Grandma,' he said, turning his head to Mrs Goss, 'Uncle Steve slept with my Mammy one night last week.'

I very nearly let him fall from my arms, in my shock. From the mouths of babes and infants…! If ever there was a moment in my life when I would have actually liked for the ground to open up and swallow me then this was it. Mary Goss just stared at me. After a few moments, I put Andrew back down on the floor and said: 'Why don't you go back through there and play?'

As soon as he was gone, Mary Goss – to my utter astonishment – burst out laughing and said: 'I bet *you* learned a thing or two!'

I didn't know where to put myself. I was dumbstruck; thoroughly gob-smacked. And what a thing for a mother to say about her own daughter!

'Come on,' she said. 'It's no good standing there looking like a wet week. Sit yourself down at the table and I'll get you your lunch. What happened between you and our Susan wouldn't do either of you any harm although I'm not too happy that Andrew found out. Anyway, I'm going to say no more about that. Just enjoy your food.'

Enjoy my food? After *that*? I sat in embarrassed silence as I ate.

About twenty minutes later, just before three o'clock, Susan came hurrying in as I was finishing my meal.

'I'm so sorry, Steve,' she said, but then she saw the expression on my face and added: 'Whatever is the matter?'

Her mother burst out laughing. 'He's still waiting for me to stab him, or something, I think. Little Andrew spilled your night-time secrets and it fair put Steven off his food.' She chuckled again and then went through to the living room, leaving the two of us alone.

'Oh God, Steven; what did he tell her?' said Susan.

'That we spent the night in bed together, last week,' I said.

'Oooops. Sorry,' she said, quietly.

'Where on earth have you been, sweetheart?' I asked.

'Oh, yes, sorry. One of my girlfriends from Whitehaven called me this morning and asked me to go and be with her for a couple of hours because her father's dying,' said Susan. 'There's only him and her; her mother died when she was little, and she just needed someone to talk to. I hope you don't mind but I felt that I had to go. I thought I would have been back in time but she was too upset.'

'Oh, dear. Well never mind. What would you like to do this

afternoon, then?' I said.

'Could we take Andrew for a walk on the beach at Allonby or somewhere?' she said. 'I know it'll be dark in an hour and a half but we could maybe get a little walk in before that.'

'Gladly. Let's get going then,' I said.

What was left of the afternoon was a bit subdued. Susan seemed to be pre-occupied by her friend's predicament.

From the beach at Allonby we could see right over the Solway Firth to the solitary mountain of Criffel, in Dumfriesshire.

'That's Scotland over there, Andrew, where that big mountain is,' I said. 'Have you ever been to Scotland?'

'No.'

'Well you have been once, when you were a baby, Andrew,' said Susan. 'But you were far too young to remember.'

'Will you take us there, Uncle Steve?' he said to me.

'Yes. We can go there some day,' I told him.

I looked up at Susan, as I crouched to pick Andrew up in my arms and she beamed at me. It was the only proper smile I got out of her that day.

That evening, after the little boy had gone to bed, she told me that she had a blinding migraine so we just sat and cuddled in front of the television. I went home around 1am; we were fully agreed that we didn't want any more of Andrew's "news flashes" to reach his grandmother.

Chapter Eighteen

Iron Curtain, Rock Wall

All was quiet and routine at work the next morning – until 11:52am.

The red "999" telephone rang but Linda, who was nearest to it, deliberately let me pick it up; she was experienced enough to know that a police officer would sometimes be better placed to swiftly assess an emergency call than would a civilian.

'Police, emergency,' I answered.

It was a young woman. 'There's been a terrible accident at Farm Crag. A climber has fallen. He's probably dead. He'd finished a climb and was at the top having a sandwich and then he walked back to the edge to look down. And he slipped. Oh, Jesus, it was awful. He screamed, then he…'

'It's alright,' I said. 'Try to calm down. If you can give me the details I need, we'll have the mountain rescue team on their way in minutes. Was he with anyone else?'

'No. I don't think so. No, he definitely wasn't; he'd just soloed the route,' she said.

'Which route was he on, or near? I said. 'That's important.'

'He was on the one called "Exorcise",' she said. 'My boyfriend and I were climbing "Steeple Ridge," about fifty yards away, when the man fell. I was only about thirty feet up so my boyfriend lowered me off and told me to run to the phone. He said he was going to abseil down and try to help the guy.'

'Where are you phoning from?' I asked.

'I don't know,' she said. 'Somebody picked me up and gave me a lift here.'

'Is it a public phone box?' I asked.

'Yes.'

'There'll be a notice just in front of you, on the wall of the box, that says where you are,' I said.

'Hang on. Oh, here it is. It says that I'm outside High Foss Post Office,' she said.

'Alright,' I said. 'So you are not too far away from the crag then. In a moment, I want you to set off and walk back along the road until you are below where the accident happened; it should only be about half a mile. I'm going to come up there in the police van so when you see my van, flag me down. I want you to show me exactly where he fell, alright? I know the climbing routes you named but I want to be certain.'

'Yes, I will,' she said.

'The last thing I need from you, before you put the phone down, is your name and your home address,' I said.

'Janet Burton. 241 Conningsby Way, Oxford.'

'Alright, Janet, thank you for calling,' I said. 'Set off to walk back now. If by any chance you see the police van parked when you get there then I've arrived first and gone up to the crag.'

'Okay,' she said, and she put the phone down.

'Right, Linda,' I said. 'I'm sure you got the gist of all that.'

I handed her the telephone message that I had written whilst I'd been talking.

'I'm going to go to the scene because it sounds likely to be a fatal,' I said. 'Commence the Mountain rescue call-out, please, and then either get one of the sergeants or the inspector to come in to co-ordinate it.'

'Yep, I will,' she said. 'I know the drill.'

'When you commence the incident log, show me as en-route at eleven fifty seven hours,' I said.

With that I left the building, jogged to my own car to get my climbing boots from their semi-permanent home in the boot, then I trotted back to the police van and jumped in.

'Zulu-Three-One to BB; over,' I said on the radio.

'Zulu-Three-One, go ahead.'

'Zulu-Three-One: Mobile from Hawthwaite to the scene of a serious rock-climbing accident at Farm Crag, in Overdale. Possible "Foxtrot". Hawthwaite police station have commenced the rescue team call-out. I will almost certainly be out of radio contact when I reach the scene; over.'

'Roger, Zulu-Three-One noted; over.'

'Zulu-Three-One out,' I said.

Prior to moving to Hawthwaite from the force headquarters, I had been a member of the Penrith Mountain Rescue team. They were a relatively small team with not too many call-outs each year by comparison with the bigger Lakeland teams. Any call-out, including this one – for me – certainly got the adrenalin flowing. It also made me realise that I really must get something done about transferring to the Hawthwaite rescue team.

Sure enough, by the time I got up the Overdale Valley as far as Farm Crag, the surrounding mountains had blocked the radio signals and even though I could still hear the transmissions from BB, they could certainly not pick up the much less powerful signals from my van radio. I checked my watch for the sake of the report I would later have to make. It had taken me just seven minutes – driving with blue lights and two-tone horns – to get there. A girl in her late teens came towards the van as I parked.

'Are you Janet Burton?' I asked, as I started pulling on my

climbing boots.

'Yes.'

'Okay, Janet, show me where he fell,' I said, as I fastened the final lace.

She gabbled a bit at me as we climbed up through the boulder-strewn woods – repeating what she had told me on the phone. It had clearly shaken her up very badly.

'It's okay, love. I know you're upset,' I said. 'You don't have to talk to me unless you want to. Just save your breath for this hillside. It's steep.'

I knew Farm Crag intimately and had climbed on it maybe forty or more times, although I wanted her to show me the way to the victim just in case she had got the name of the route wrong. But she hadn't.

As we approached the bottom of the cliff, and the route called Exorcise, a youngish man called to her from behind a twisted yew tree: 'I'm here, Janet. You stay there; you shouldn't see this.'

She sat down on the lip of a huge rock and turned her back on the scene. I carried on the last few yards, to where the man was standing. The victim, lying half-hidden under low fronds of the yew tree that he had fallen through, had massive head injuries. That the incident might be a "Foxtrot" was now beyond even the remotest doubt. I covered his head with my waterproof jacket.

'Let's go and sit with Janet,' I said. 'There's nothing we can do for him now.'

We sat in a circle, on the rocks. I was close enough to the body to stop any unwitting walkers or climbers from stumbling across it if they were traversing along the foot of the crag. It was a good opportunity for me to jot everything down in my notebook. I got Janet to repeat her details for me and also wrote down the name and address of her boyfriend, Gary Winterton.

'Are the pair of you on holiday?' I asked.

'Sort of,' said Gary.

'Well, not really,' said Janet.

'Would you care to explain that, Janet?' I said.

We are both meant to be in class at our uni's but I was fed up so we've skived off for a few days to come climbing,' she said.

'Alright, well that's irrelevant to anything I need to know so don't worry about it. Where are you staying?' I said.

'At Hawthwaite Youth Hostel,' said Janet.

'Yep. And that poor sod was, too,' added Gary, thumbing backwards over his shoulder to where the dead man was lying.

'Was he?' said Janet.

And I said: 'Are you sure?'

'Yep; definitely,' said Gary. 'He finished his breakfast before we got ours this morning but I saw him as he was leaving.'

'Excellent,' I said. 'That will help me a lot. Will you be at the youth hostel this evening?'

As I spoke, we heard the sound of a two-tone siren, approaching up the valley. Apparently, the first rescue team Landrover was here.

'I'm not sure, after this,' said Gary. 'What do you think, Janet?'

I interrupted them. 'It would help us if you were there tonight because one of us will have to take statements from you in the very near future. And I'm sure you'll realise that it will be much easier to do it here in Cumbria than to have officers visit you at your homes or your universities.'

'Okay. We'll stay, then,' he said.

'Great. If you want to go down now, and go back to the youth hostel, please feel free to do so,' I said. 'If you see the rescue team guys coming up then you can tell them that a police officer is here. One of my colleagues will come to the youth hostel to interview you properly either late this afternoon or during the evening. Thank you for what you did when it happened. It was exactly right.'

As they set off down the rough hillside, I went back to the body and started searching his pockets for identification. What I found surprised me a little. He was not exactly local. He had a passport in the button-down, breast pocket of his shirt. It was Australian. His name seemed to be Eastern European: Pietr Malinowski. But in between the pages of his passport was a student identity card – from Harvard University in America. I took possession of them, plus his wallet, his watch, a signet ring, and all the other bits and pieces he was carrying. This looked as though it was going to be a complicated can of worms.

The noise of boots on the rocks below me got my attention. Nine members of the rescue team were tramping up to where I was waiting. As was to be expected, two of the men were carrying their respective halves of a collapsible MacInnes stretcher on their backs, like rucksacks.

'How d'you do,' said the woman at the front of them. 'Is he dead?'

'How do. Yes, well and truly, I'm afraid,' I said.

I removed my jacket from over the dead climber.

'Oh, yuck,' she said, as she busied herself with a camera, taking photographs that could be shown to the coroner at the inevitable inquest, and – no doubt – shown at Mountain Rescue Team training sessions too.'

I turned to one of the men, as they assembled the stretcher, and asked: 'Is one of you the team leader?'

Yes. I am. Mike Edmondson at your service,' said one of them. And he shook my hand.

'Steve. Steve Shearwater,' I said.

'He only likes to *think* he's the boss,' the woman commented, without looking up from her grisly task.

'That's true,' said Mike, sarcastically. 'That's my wife, Sally!'

'I have two favours to ask of you, please Mike,' I said.

'By all means,' he replied.

'Well firstly, this chap apparently soloed this route, sat and had a rest at the top, then came back to the lip to look down and slipped off,' I said. 'I've only got my boots and no other gear, so I wonder if a couple of your team could go to the top with a camera and take a lot of shots of that area, then collect any of his property – after it's been photographed *in situ* – and ab' back down the route to check whether any items are stuck on ledges or anything, please.'

'Yes. Fred and I will do that, as soon as Sally lets me have my camera back,' said Mike. 'I've got some spare film. Second request?'

'My second request is to ask whether or not you have any vacancies on the team,' I said. 'I'm a member of the Penrith team but now that I've been transferred to Hawthwaite police I'd like to transfer teams, as well, if I can.'

'Now that *is* a damned silly question. We always have room for new people, especially if they have a track record with another rescue team,' said Mike. 'Do you climb, or just fellwalk?'

I lead up to "Hard V.S." I'm not up to leading "Extreme," yet. And I do a lot of fellwalking too,' I said.

'Brilliant,' said Mike. 'And have you done much rescue training or real rescues?'

'Three years of training, interrupted by a bit of injury, and I've been on maybe a dozen call-outs,' I said.

By now, the other members of the team were securing the dead climber into the stretcher and covering him over. Four walkers had stopped about 30 yards away obviously stunned by what they were seeing.

'Great,' Mike said to me, unabashed. 'Write your name and phone number down for me and we'll ring you when we have our next training night. Do you know where our team hut's at?'

'Yes,' I said.

'Great. Well we always meet there then resume to the public bar of the "Leg and Gaiter" pub, afterwards.'

'Alright,' I said. 'I'll look forward to that.'

I scribbled my details on a slip of paper for him.

'I'd best be heading back now, seeing as there's nothing else I can do here,' I said. 'If you find any of this chap's possessions at all, could you drop them off at the nick, please?'

'We certainly will,' said Mike.

Back at the nick, Sergeant Wyatt had come in early to co-ordinate the rescue, although in purely rescue terms it had turned out to be very straightforward. He should have been on a 5pm-1am shift.

'Ah, it's Chris Bonnington, back from Mount Everest,' he said in good humoured sarcasm, as I walked in at ten minutes to two. 'Perfect timing, too; just in time to go home.'

'When you see what I've got landed with, you won't be letting me go home for a *month*!' I said.

I showed him the passport and identity card, and told him what had happened. He said he would get the statements from Messrs Burton and Winterton himself, that afternoon.

Dick Price came wandering in at 1.55pm for his 2pm-10pm shift. Throughout the force we were always meant to report for duty fifteen minutes before our shift so we could do all the preparatory tasks. I could see that Sergeant Wyatt wasn't very pleased with Dick but in front of myself and Linda, who was working away quietly at her desk, he said nothing.

'Notify the coroner, before you go home, Steve, and start the ball rolling for the Home Office pathologist to do the post mortem,' said the sergeant. 'Until we can prove beyond doubt that he either slipped or jumped, we'll have to treat this as though he may have been pushed. Other than that there's not a lot you can do until we have gathered together all his possessions from the scene and from the Youth Hostel so we can see what other info there is, in amongst it. Tomorrow morning, once it gets to about nine o'clock, you may have to phone the American Embassy in London to get the address and telex number for the police force that covers Harvard, in the USA. If my geographical knowledge serves me right, it will be Boston, but find out for definite. Once you've found that info, you'll have to draft out a forwarding report, asking our divisional chief superintendent that the relevant American police force be contacted by telex and requested to obtain the dead man's home address so that we can notify his next of kin, presumably in Australia. Happy with that?'

'Absolutely, Sarge'. I'll see to it,' I said.

'Okay, and don't forget that you'll have to attend the post mortem to identify the body and relate the circumstances to the pathologist. I'll see if I can find out, later this afternoon, when that's going to happen,' said Sergeant Wyatt.

I did the two tasks I'd been given, then booked off duty, but before I could head off home to Linthwaite, Dick said: 'Hang on, Steve. Sarge, have you got a minute? I've got something to show the pair of you, out in the car park.'

We followed him out and there, sat gleaming in the corner, was a brand new MGB GT sports car, in British Racing Green.

Andy Wyatt gave a low whistle. 'Very nice, Dick; I take it it's yours?'

'It certainly is, Sarge. I just collected it this morning.'

'Oh, well I might just forgive you for coming to work late, then,' said Andy with a stern look on his face. Then he eased off a bit and added: 'I'm pleased for you, Dick. It's very nice.'

It was obvious that Dick was as proud as Punch so I chipped in with: 'Yes, it *is* nice, Dick. You must have been saving for *years* to get one of these little babies, brand new.'

And then I went home for a late lunch.

By the next morning, nothing else had been found giving us any more details about Mr Malinowski. The statements that Andy Wyatt had obtained from the two witnesses merely confirmed what they had told me; there was no significant additional detail in them. The items recovered by the rescue team from the top of the route, and the rest of his possessions from the youth hostel, told us nothing, either. I was therefore given the job of tracing him.

'Good morning. United States Embassy. How can I help you?' was the cheery response to my first phone call.

'This is Police Constable 8-6-8 Shearwater of the Cumbria Constabulary. Could I speak to somebody who could give me the details of one of your police forces in the USA, please?'

'One moment, Officer; I'm putting you through.'

The lady to whom I spoke next was also cheerful, and very helpful. She told me that although Harvard was in the area covered by the Cambridge Police Department, Massachusetts, the university had its own campus police, and she gave me their contact details.

I dictated a forwarding report to Linda, who jotted it down in shorthand and had it typed before 10am:

Sir,

I have to report that at 1204 hours on Monday 14th inst., I attended the scene of what currently appears to be an accidental, fatal rock climbing incident, at Farm Crag, Overdale, Cumbria, England.

Through the recovery of an Australian passport and a student identity card, we now know the deceased to be a Pietr Malinowski, aged 26 years, who was apparently alone at the time of the incident. It would appear that Malinowski either is or recently was a registered student at Harvard University, Massachusetts, U.S.A.

As no other form of identification or document giving any address for the deceased was found, either at the scene or at the youth hostel at which he stayed on the previous night, it would appear to me to be necessary for us to make the relevant enquiries at Harvard, initially, in an attempt to establish an address for his next of kin.

Should the results of such be negative or unobtainable, I propose to pursue a second line of enquiry via the Australian Embassy in London. In this context, however, I am of the belief that any available university records of the deceased's home address may be markedly more up to date than those at the Australian passport office as the passport in question was issued eight years ago.

I therefore respectfully request that a copy of this report – or a telex transcript thereof – be forwarded to:

> *The Chief of Police,*
> *Harvard University Police Department,*
> *29, Garden Street,*
> *Cambridge, MA 02138,*
> *U.S.A.*

I further respectfully request that the said chief officer allow an officer to attend the student records department at Harvard University with a view to obtaining the aforesaid home address, and any other useful information about the late Pietr Malinowski.
Submitted for your consideration,
Steven Shearwater,
Constable 868.

As soon as it was typed, I took it up to the inspector's office, where the boss was wading through his usual huge pile of paperwork. He quickly scanned through it and counter-signed it.

'Yes, that's fine, Steve. Give headquarters a ring and see if there's a traffic car that can take this report through to Penrith this afternoon. Failing that, you'll have to get it away in the ordinary internal mail but that would create a day's delay.'

He paused as he re-read the report, then said: 'My only concern is the Australian authorities. They may get a bit irate if we don't notify them immediately so what I'll do is send a letter from here, just to inform the embassy in London that we are investigating the matter. We needn't bugger-about going via headquarters for this one. If we give the Aussies his name and passport number now, they won't be able to grumble afterwards. I'll write that one for you, so when you go down, ask Linda to pop up here and I'll dictate it.'

That evening, at home, the phone rang. Dad answered it.

'It's for you,' he said, holding the handset towards me.

'Hello, Steve?' said a woman's voice.

'Yes.'

'It's Sally Edmondson from the mountain rescue, yesterday. You asked Mike about coming to a meeting, I believe?' she said.

'Yes, I did.'

'Well I'm sorry, he was concentrating so much on the job in

hand and I was so engrossed with doing the photos that both of us were being a bit dim. There's a meeting tomorrow night, at the hut, at seven thirty. Will you be able to come along?'

'Yes, gladly,' I said.

'Good. Have you by any chance got any "magic boots;" you know, the smooth soled ones?' she asked.

'Yes, I've got a pair of E.B. Super Grattons.'

'Right. You have to bring them with you. We'll explain when you get there,' she said.

'Okay. I'll look forward to it,' I said.

'See you tomorrow night then. Bye.'

Chapter Nineteen

The Tale of the Runaway Coffin

Samantha was on earlies with me on the Wednesday – my last shift before my four-day weekend off. I had done all the paperwork I could in respect of Mr Malinowski, so by ten past six we were out on foot patrol in the town.

The first couple of hours went quietly but just before half past eight we came across a large, dark blue Mercedes car parked fully on the prohibitory zig-zag markings of a pedestrian crossing. The driver was almost certainly in the newsagent's shop, adjacent to where the car was parked.

'I'm not having this,' I said to Samantha. 'Those zig-zags are there to prevent people getting killed. This one is going in the book.'

Just at that, a white-haired, refined looking man emerged from the shop, in a classy pin-stripe suit.

'Excuse me, sir; is this your car?' I said to him.

'Of course. Do I look as though I need to borrow other people's cars?' he answered snappily.

'Were you aware that you had parked on the zig-zag markings on the approach to the zebra crossing, sir?'

'No, constable; I wasn't!' he said, impatiently. 'Look here; I just had to pick up a Financial Times. I'm due at an urgent meeting in

Whitehaven shortly. Can I be on my way?'

'No sir, I'm afraid not, but as your car is still causing danger to the schoolchildren that – as you can see – are crossing here, I require you to move your car around this corner into the side street and park safely, there, so that I may talk to you,' I said.

The look of contempt on his face was dazzling.

'You'll regret this, constable,' he growled.

'Sir, you have committed an offence of failing to comply with a legal traffic sign. You are not obliged to say anything unless you wish to do so but what you say may be put into writing and given in evidence. I must warn you that if you do not follow my instructions and stop, around the corner, for me to talk to you in safety then I will most definitely have you stopped again on your way to Whitehaven, and reported for obstructing a police officer in the execution of his duty, in addition to the offence I've already mentioned. Now, kindly move your car.' I said.

He opened the car door and unceremoniously flung his *Financial Times* into the passenger seat then climbed in and set off around the corner.

'What an obnoxious shit-bag,' said Samantha. It was the first time I'd heard her swear.

'It isn't over yet, love,' I said. 'Just watch and say absolutely nothing.'

In the side street, the driver got back out of his car and came to stand with us on the pavement.

'Could I have your full name, please, sir?' I said.

'I'm Sir Giles Pemberton-Pennington. Have you never *heard* of me? It's fair to say that I'm one of the country's top industrialists,' he said.

Mischief got the better of me.

'Well, good morning, Sir Giles. Actually, I haven't heard of you, I'm afraid, but I'm Constable Shearwater and I'm pleased to meet you.'

I deliberately held out my hand to shake hands.

'You impudent runt!' he said.

'Being offensive isn't going to help you, sir. Now, as you should know from something as basic as the Highway Code, parking close to pedestrian crossings is not allowed because it blocks the view for approaching drivers – especially of children that may be crossing – and naturally it also blocks the pedestrians' view of approaching vehicles; a double jeopardy. That is why the zig-zag warning marks are there. Do you have any lawful reason for parking on them, this morning?' I said.

'I hope your chief constable is in the Lodge, young man. I'm going to have your hide for this,' he said.

When I asked him for his documents, he was only carrying his driver's license so I gave him a form HO/RT1, obliging him to produce his certificate of insurance within seven days at his own choice of police stations. He nominated one in Chelsea, close to the London home address that he gave me.

'Sir Giles, you will be reported for the consideration of the question of prosecuting you for failing to comply with a legal traffic sign, namely the zig-zag markings at a zebra pedestrian crossing. Do you wish to say anything? You are not obliged to say anything unless you wish to do so, but whatever you say will be taken down in writing and may be given in evidence,' I said, by the book.

'Just you *wait*,' he said. Then he turned to Samantha. 'Don't take any example from this whelp, young lady. He won't last five minutes.'

She started to protest but I caught her arm and shook my head at her.

'It's not worth it,' I said, as he drove off, far too quickly for safety. 'But I want you to remember exactly what was said because I rather think that there'll be a Section 49 about this.'

She looked blankly at me.

'Sorry: Section 49 of the Police Act, 1964. That just means an official complaint,' I explained. 'But more importantly, do you understand what I was saying when I told him that he would be reported for the consideration of the question of prosecuting him for that particular offence?'

She looked at me, shaking her head a little, and said: 'I know I should remember it, from training, but I don't really.'

'That's alright, it's a lot to take in. There are some traffic offences which, by law, require something called a Notice of Intended Prosecutions – which we just call N.I.P. These have to be sent out by mail within 14 days of the offence but just in case they aren't sent out in time because of admin-holdups, its good practice to give one verbally at the time and this is done by stating it accurately before the formal caution. That's why the last thing I said to him was such a long-winded mouth-full. It was the N.I.P. and the formal caution. So,' I joked, 'your mission if you choose to accept it is to spend the next week learning the short caution, the formal caution and the N.I.P., absolutely word-perfect, and I'm going to test you on them.'

Samantha laughed.

'Oh, and one other thing,' I said. 'Don't ever talk about reading anyone their rights. That's purely American and it's a nonsense if that phrase is used in Britain.'

We went back in to the nick at nine o'clock for our sandwiches, and after that I told Inspector Sumner about our industrialist friend. He had a quick word with Sam' to confirm what had been said and then the pair of us were back out on patrol again.

About eleven o'clock we bumped into Joe Stuart, outside his chapel of rest.

'Hello, Steve,' he said. 'By heck, lad; your police lady-friend's a damned sight better lookin' than you are!'

'Morning, Joe,' I said. 'I'm glad you think that. I'd be worried about you if you didn't.'

'Come on in and have a cup of tea, and get warm, the pair of you,' he said.

Samantha looked a bit alarmed.

'It's alright, young lady. We have a separate office. We won't be sitting with any of the – erm – customers,' said Joe.

The main door led into a smartly furnished reception area, with a small desk and leather armchairs. A door on the left was standing open and revealed a beautifully appointed room which then led through to the chapel of rest. Joe led us through another door, behind the receptionist's desk, into a private office where a woman was busy with paperwork.

'Come in, you two,' said Joe. 'This is my wife, Ivy – Ivy, this is the young man who got me to bring that big chap in; Mr Chatsworth-Dean, just after Christmas.'

'How ever did you get on with him, Joe?' I asked. 'Bringing him back here in the front seat like you did.'

Samantha looked a bit startled again.

'You take no notice of them, love,' said Ivy to Samantha. 'Undertakers and policemen all have the same sick sense of humour. Doctors and nurses and firemen do, too. It's the only way they can keep their sanity with some of the jobs they have to deal with.'

Joe carried on, unabashed: 'Well, it was funniest when we were coming back into town because people were up and about by then. A lot of them waved to me but I think they were all a bit puzzled by who the big chap sat next to me was, nodding to them all.'

I couldn't stop my chuckle completely but I did my best not to laugh out loud, for my cadet's sake.

'Don't worry about it, love,' Joe said to Samantha. 'There's some very strange things happen in this job. You know where Dalzell Street is, down the bottom end of the Main Street?'

Sam nodded.

'Well,' said Joe. 'Me and a policewoman had to remove a body from a house right up at the top of the steep hill on Dalzell Street, one winter morning. Flossy was her nickname – the policewoman that is, not the client. Anyway, I was carrying the head end of the shell and she was carrying the feet end – it was only a little chap that had died. So we got out onto the street and Flossy slipped and fell, and we dropped the shell. Well! It set off, foot first, down that sheet ice and right towards the main road and all the traffic. I was panic-stricken. As luck had it, though, it shot right across Main Street without being hit by any cars. It went right across the far pavement and hit the double doors of Boots chemists shop – burst through them and collided with the pharmacy counter. The impact flung it up on end and the lid fell off. And the chap inside said to a startled young chemist: "Have you got anything to stop this coffin?"... Aye, it was a queer do, was that.'

'You daft bugger, Joe,' I said, between laughs. 'You even had *me* believing you, then! Anything to stop this coffin, indeed.'

It had taken a few moments for Sam to get the joke but then she started giggling, too.

Then Joe seemed to get quietly serious again.

'Actually, Flossy and I *did* drop the coffin on the ice but it hit a parked car and stopped,' he said to Sam. 'You see, love, it's like this. Death is a taboo to most people and it's always surrounded by somebody's great sadness. But for all we need to laugh about it sometimes, for our own sakes, the main thing is always to treat the deceased person with total respect. That's the secret for all of us that have to work with death. It's nothing to be frightened of; it just has to be dealt with the right way. Then afterwards, you can have a stiff drink.'

It was Ivy's turn: '*Joseph*, you're incorrigible. This poor lass won't know what to make of you. Take no notice of him, love – stiff drink, indeed. If ever you need any advice on anything to help you with your work, you just phone me. Not *that* daft baboon,' she said, looking at Joe.

Meanwhile, Joe had got the kettle and made us all the cup of tea we'd been promised.

'So how are you settling in at Hawthwaite then, Steve?' he asked, after a while.

'Great, thanks,' I said. 'It's a bit like coming home, really.'

'Are you local?' asked Ivy.

'He's Bob and Isabella Shearwater's son, from Linthwaite,' chipped in Joe, before I could answer.

'Ohhh, yes. I know your mam and dad. Well fancy that,' said Ivy.

'Aren't you the one that does a lot of climbing, Steve?' asked Joe. 'Went to Africa and climbed Kilimanjaro, or something?'

'Yes, that was me, but it was Mount Kenya,' I said. 'And now, I'm swapping over from being on the Penrith Mountain Rescue Team to the one here in Hawthwaite. Actually, I'm going to my first meeting with them tonight. It sounds as though it'll be a ten minute meeting followed by a couple of hours hard drinking in the Leg and Gaiter.'

'That wouldn't surprise me,' said Ivy. 'By all accounts they sink a lot of beer, them lot. They're a proper bunch of "crag rats," but they do a wonderful job.'

When we came out of the undertakers, a few minutes later, Joe said: 'Don't forget, you're both always welcome here for a cuppa and a chat. If nobody answers at the reception, just lie on the floor with your eyes closed and shout "shop"!'

As we walked away, Samantha seemed all excited about something.

'Will you take me to the rescue team meeting with you, please, Steve?' she eventually said.

I was taken aback. 'Have you ever *done* any mountaineering?' I said.

'Not much,' said Sam. 'But there must be other things I could do to help out. I would really like to.'

'Well,' I said, as I tried to work out what to do for the best, 'it's not for me to say you can't go. But it will be up to them as to whether they think you are suitable, not me.'

'That's okay,' she said. 'I don't mind that.'

'Do you want me to pick you up, on my way there?' I said.

'Yes, please. That would be nice,' said Sam. 'I live on Woodlands Rise, number seventeen.'

'With relatives, or with a landlady? Your parents live at Carlisle, don't they?' I asked.

'A landlady. Inspector Sumner arranged it for me when I was moved here.'

'Oh, I know just how that is. I was in digs myself for three years, when I was a cadet in Hull.'

'Will you tell me about that, sometime? You know; when you were a cadet.' she said.

'Yes, of course, if you're interested.'

When I picked Samantha up, at twenty past seven that evening, I had to do a double take. She came out of the house as soon as I stopped the car. She was wearing jeans that looked as though they had been painted on her, a pale blue blouse, a tan leather jacket and matching long, tight, tan leather boots, worn over the top of her jeans. It all showed off her figure in a way that a police uniform never could.

'Hiya,' she said, as she got into the car. And then she leaned across to kiss me.

'Damn, Sam!' I said, as I pulled back. 'As gorgeous as you look, you *know* I've got a girlfriend. And I don't do two-timing. Are you sure you want to go to help the rescue team tonight? If it's just to be with me, love, then it really isn't wise. I don't want to hurt your feelings.'

'It's okay,' she said, without losing the smile off her face. 'I was only being friendly. Yes I really do want to help so I would still like to go, please.'

This didn't seem at all like the shy little girl who had cried only a few days earlier when she thought she'd let me down.

As soon as we arrived at the MRT building, on the edge of one of the town centre car parks, Mike and Sally Edmondson came over to say hello.

'Is this your girlfriend?' said Sally.

'No, this is Samantha,' I said. 'She's a cadet at the police station and wants to see if there's anything she can do to help the team. She hasn't done much climbing.'

There were about 25 people gathered for the meeting, only five of whom, including Sam, were women. The rest were a fairly hard-looking assortment of burly guys, several with beards. And I knew for a fact that, women definitely included, they were the salt of the earth; it was the nature of why they were there.

'Can everybody listen,' bellowed Sally – Mike was right, I thought, she really *is* the boss – 'Everyone *listen*. This is Steve Shearwater. He's a policeman here in town but I suppose he can't help that.'

She had to pause to allow time for the inevitable, but good-humoured booing and hissing when my job was mentioned.

'He's been a member of the Penrith rescue team...'

'Part-timers!' shouted someone from the back. More laughter.

'He's been moved to Hawthwaite and hopes to transfer onto our team,' continued Sally.

'We'll only have him if we can practice mouth-to-mouth resuscitation on his girlfriend,' another man shouted.

'Okay, okay, let's get on with the meeting then you won't all be grumbling about being kept from the pub.' This time it was Mike that spoke.

Samantha was standing pressed quite close against me. She obviously hadn't allowed for the fact that the so-called hut was only a big garage where the two team Land Rovers had to be parked outside to make room for people to meet, inside. Her leather jacket and jeans were no match for the unheated chill of a January evening.

'Here's my car keys,' I whispered to her, to avoid interrupting the talk. 'Look in the boot; you'll find my down climbing jacket. If you put that on it'll keep you warm.'

She smiled and slipped away. She was back a couple of minutes later, deeply wrapped in what was for her a rather outsized, very thick, duvet jacket.

The talk was about stretcher lowering techniques and lasted about half an hour. Then Mike spoke to me across the crowd: 'Steve, you have two tests to complete tonight. The first one is quite obvious. We all want to know that you can be trusted for rope work so come and show us some knots.'

I stood there in front of everyone and went through a whole repertoire, on demand. Then they blindfolded me and made me do the main ones again as though we were on a night rescue and had no light.

'Right, Steve, very good,' announced Mike. 'Your second test is later. Bring your magic boots to the pub.'

Everyone laughed.

Once we got into the Leg and Gaiter, all of the team came across and were very friendly. Questions were fired at me, thick and fast:

What grade did I lead to?

'Hard V.S.'

Who did I climb with?

'When I was a police cadet in Hull, I climbed with the Hull & East Yorkshire Mountaineering Club. Here in Cumbria my usual climbing partner is a Kendal Fireman called Tim.'

Had I climbed in the Alps? '

Yes, mostly around Chamonix.'

The Himalayas?

'No, but I'd love to.'

The Andes?

'If only!'

Best climb, abroad?

'Mount Kenya, without doubt.'

Next climbing goal?

'El Capitan, Yosemite, in the States.'

And all the time these questions kept coming, so did the beer. It was as though they *all* wanted to buy me a pint. I quickly realised that I would be getting a taxi home, for Samantha and I, and then I could collect my car the following day. After a couple of hours of what – for me – was very hard drinking, Mike shouted for order. Even the locals who were in the pub but had nothing to do with the team went quiet, because they apparently knew what was coming next.

'Right, everyone; we've heard that Steve wants to join our exclusive and merry little band of drunkards. We've watched the big-head tie flawless knots while he was blindfolded. And we've sat here and listened to him boasting about Chamonix, the Old Man of Hoy, and Mount Kenya; Mount-bloody-Kenya, I ask you! When was the last time we had a new recruit bragging about something as glamorous as Mount-bloody-Kenya?'

He paused for the laughter, as I shouted: 'Well you did ask!'

Then Mike continued: 'Well Steve, now you've got to put your feet where your mouth is. It's time for your second test.'

I had forgotten all about this second test, with all the beer and chat. But I had a good idea of what was to come.

'Get your fancy Ellis Brigham Super Gratton boots on, Steve,' shouted Mike to the crowd. 'You're going *climbing*. Twice, in recorded history – *nay*, twice since Adam and Eve were nobbut kids – famed and courageous mountaineers have managed to traverse the entire perimeter walls inside this room without touching the floor, touching anything covered with upholstery, or using their knees. The one-armed-bandit can be treated as a rock outcrop, and anything that's actually fastened to the wall, but tables and chairs are forbidden – instant death. Get your boots on and start by the door where we came in. You're going anti-clockwise.'

I knelt down to put the smooth-soled rock boots on, sniggering to myself through an alcoholic haze. How bloody silly – but good for a laugh. I casually wondered if I could break the record for falling off sooner than anyone else had ever done. I might have managed a bowline, blindfolded, earlier but my bootlaces – after maybe ten pints of bitter – were another matter entirely. And Mike announced *that* to the crowd, too. After the minor success of tying the laces, I stood up, swaying.

'Come on, Mister-Mount-bloody-Kenya, this is where you start,' shouted somebody near the door.

The back wall of the bar was entirely made out of rough slate blocks, making it very easy indeed to climb across – apart from the beer that I had drank. As soon as my feet were above ground level, everyone in the bar started yelling banter or encouragement, however the mood took them. Through it all I could clearly hear the voice of a teenage girl – a girl who had wisely been drinking fruit juices and Cokes all evening because she knew she couldn't keep up: 'Come on, Steve! You show them. Mind you don't fall.'

A third of the way along that wall was a long fireplace with a long smooth slate mantelpiece, so that bit was easy. Then it was more of the slate blocks. I got to the end of that without incident then used two windowsills on the end wall to find myself half way around the route. Then there were two doors, side by side, and they had round, metal knobs rather than handles. And polished brass would be a challenge even for "magic boots" to grip. I got my fingers on the thin upper edge of the doorframe and stepped through with my right foot onto the first doorknob. I had to get into a crouching position because the distance between the top of the doorframe and the ceiling was only a matter of inches. I had kept my left foot free so that I could move leftwards and step onto the next doorknob but, as I did so, my right boot lost its grip on the first bit of brass and my foot shot off, into mid-air. A cheer went up as I struggled to hold my weight with my fingertips on the frame, but somehow I managed and got both feet back onto their respective perches. After the doors came the one-armed-bandit, which was bracketed to the wall so getting across the front of it, with one foot in the prize-money tray, was easy. Then came the actual bar. I had to get my feet on the bar – that much was obvious – and a wooden beam ran along the ceiling above the front edge of the bar. After a bit of experimenting to get enough purchase and get my balance, I got my feet onto the bar and my hands under the beam. I did a weird version of what climbers call a "lay back", using my own body weight to pull on my hands and give them enough grip to let me temporarily defeat the laws of gravity. The upper part of my body was almost horizontal, my chest and face brushing along the ceiling; my feet inched along the bar, and my hands clung on for grim death. Had I been able to look behind, I would have seen some of the bigger guys standing behind me, ready to catch me if I let go. But all I could hear, still, was Samantha's voice: 'Go on, Steve. You can do it. Oooh, be *care*ful!'

At the far end of the bar, things looked quite easy. There was a dado rail running along the wall about three feet above the ground and a picture rail about a foot below the ceiling; more crouching and shuffling and I would be at the final short wall, with two more windowsills to make it easy. Maybe I'd cracked it.

But both of the rails were rounded; I could get no grip with my fingers, and after maybe three feet of successful sideways movement I could feel my fingers slipping off. There wasn't a blind thing I could do about it either. In climbing parlance, I "peeled off backwards". But my newly-found friends were there, ready to catch me. And they set me down on my feet.

'Good on ya, Steve. You got a bloody-sight further than most manage to go,' seemed to be the shouted consensus.

And then the drinking began again.

Chapter Twenty

Fried Bacon, Poached Venison

As the trials and tribulations of my hangover wore off, around Thursday lunchtime, I decided that some icy, fresh air would do me good. I would walk to Hawthwaite to collect my car.

After I got well wrapped up against the cold, I walked a mile or so across to the north side of the valley then turned up Calva Lane that led north-westwards to West End Farm. From there, a cart track led downhill and crossed over Great Lingy Beck, a lovely, fast-flowing little torrent; too small to be called a river and yet too big to be just a stream. The bridge was just a few yards upstream from where the beck joined the River Bure, churning down towards Hawthwaite. The rough road I was on climbed at an angle up the far side of the ghyll and led out onto the tree-covered flanks of Rudd Howe, which still had plenty snow lying because of the altitude. The rest of my walk was a two-mile, gentle downhill stroll.

It was only when I got to the car park and saw that my car had been moved onto a free space which was reserved for team members that I remembered one of the women asking for my car keys, the night before, so she could move it to prevent me being fined for parking without a ticket. It *must* have been a good night, I thought, if there were bits I couldn't properly remember. I drove the car to the police station car park, left it there and walked up Main Street. There was something I'd seen in a travel agent's window that I wanted to go in and ask about.

Half an hour later, I went back to my car again and drove to Low Keld. To my delight, Susan was at home for my unplanned visit. As soon as I got in the door, she slipped her arms around my waist and kissed me.

'God, I'm glad to see you,' she purred. 'Coffee? Or bed?'

'Wait,' I said, laughing. 'I have something to ask you.'

'If it isn't about making love, it'll have to wait,' she said.

'Well it may be, indirectly. What are you and Andrew planning to do, this weekend?'

'Nothing, why?' she said, clearly puzzled.

'So you don't have to be at home?' I said.

'No. *Why?*'

'So I could take you away for the weekend?' I teased.

'Yes. But *where?*' she said.

'Well you know what Andrew said, up at Allonby, about Scotland?' I said. 'Would you let me take the two of you to Edinburgh for a couple of nights? I've got an option at a hotel with two adjoining rooms. It's right on Prince's Street, in the city centre, and there's lots we could do that Andrew would enjoy. And it's your birthday in three weeks' time and this is my last weekend off until after that, so it's our last chance, really. We can go up by train.'

She had listened with her mouth open and was obviously a bit taken aback.

'Steve,' she said quietly, 'I would *adore* that.'

I used her phone to confirm my reservation with the travel agents I'd just been to, and then we did go to bed.

We had fun, that weekend: Susan dragged Andrew and I around the House of Fraser department store on Prince's Street; Andrew and I dragged Susan around the reptile house at Edinburgh Zoo; and we all enjoyed the castle. Once Andrew was asleep each night, Susan came through the linking door from their room to mine and stayed until we were too tired to move.

The hotel breakfasts were excellent, especially the porridge. Say what they like, no-one makes "poddish" like the Scots!

Perhaps most of all, though, little Andrew adored the main line express train that we caught from Cumbria to Scotland's capital and back. When we went over Beattock Moor, I told him to listen to the "clickety-clack" rhythm of the wheels while I entertained him with the first verse of W. H. Auden's evocative railway poem:

This is the Night Mail crossing the border,
Bringing the cheque and the postal order,
Letters for the rich, letters for the poor,
The shop at the corner and the girl next door;
Pulling up Beattock, a steady climb,
And the gradient's against her but she's on time....

I didn't know any more of the verses but later, when we were clattering over all the points and track-joints on the approach to Waverley Station in Edinburgh, he really got the gist of the poem's tempo. He sat there going "clickety-clack" in time with the wheels and yet another recitation of that one verse that he demanded from me, over and over. Even *I* was getting weary of it by then so heaven only knows what the other passengers sitting around us must have thought.

On the Monday, I started another week of night shifts. I'd only been at work for twenty minutes when I got a phone call from a man called Kit Reynolds.

'How-do! I'm the chief gamekeeper on Lord Nethermere's estate. I've come across some deer poachers in Blackcock Wood, at Leatherside, but unfortunately my damned under-keeper is away on his bloody holidays. Judging by their van, I'm sure I've had dealings with this gang before. They are from West Cumberland and they're violent. Is there any chance of you giving me a hand to lock them up if we can catch them in possession of game, please?'

'Yes, of course,' I said. 'Do you know how many of the poachers there are?'

'This time, I think there's only three but last time there were four of them,' he said. 'They're using a grey Ford Transit van, DHH 978M. It's parked up a forest track so I would suggest that I meet you outside the Lord Leathes pub if that's alright and I'll show you where their van's at. Our best bet's probably to wait near the van and nab them when they come back to it. How many of the lads can you bring with you?'

'Sorry, Mr Reynolds,' I said. 'At this stage it will only be me, myself and my shadow but I'll phone headquarters and see if I can get a dog van to attend, too.'

'You better had, lad,' said Kit Reynolds. 'Or you and me are gonna get some rare punishment.'

As soon as Mr Reynolds was off the phone, I rang the control room at headquarters and told the duty inspector what was about to happen.

'One thing, sir,' I said to him. 'As you'll know, it's quite possible that I'll be out of radio contact in parts of Leathermere valley. Leatherside itself is alright, I've transmitted from the village several times before, but other parts of the valley can be dubious.'

'Right ho, son,' said the inspector. 'The dog handler is tied up with a stolen vehicle near Penrith at present but he should be clear in a few minutes, and as soon as he, is I'll get him on his way to you.

'Unfortunately, the traffic car is involved in the same incident and they have made an arrest so I can't see them reaching you in time. I'll put out an observations message for that Transit van you mentioned, for all surrounding areas, just in case it moves off before you get there. All I can suggest is that if you find that you *are* out of radio contact, leave the police van at the entrance to the relevant forest track and you go up in the gamekeeper's vehicle, if you can. That way, the dog man can at least find your van and head towards you, so don't block the lane. Whatever vehicle the gamekeeper's driving is bound to be more suitable for those type of roads anyway.'

By the time I went out to the van and booked on the air, my adrenalin was flowing. I drove to Leatherdale, and the Lord Leathes pub, as quickly as I could. A burly chap in a Barbour jacket and flat cap came over to the van as soon as I pulled up. I opened the door and he thrust his hand in, to shake mine.

'Kit Reynolds,' he said.

'Steve Shearwater. What's the latest?'

'Well they were still in Blackcock Wood about ten minutes ago,' said Kit, 'so I don't think they'll have left yet.'

'Alright, well the boss at Penrith is hoping to get a dog van to us. He's suggested that if I can't get through from that part of the valley on my radio, I should leave my van by the main road to show the dog handler which track to turn up. Frankly, I think that'll be a good idea anyway, so when we turn off this road I'll jump in with you, okay?' I said. 'If you tell me which is Blackcock Wood now, I'll try and pass that bit of info to them from here. The radio usually works here.'

That part of the plan went well so at least any back-up would now know the approximate location of the wood. At the turn off, I swapped my police boots for my own climbing boots, which I had brought especially from my car when I set off. They would be much more suitable in a rough wood. And I took two torches: the big, heavy, square rechargeable one from the van, and in my jacket pocket a nine-inch long, rubber-covered flashlight of my own.

There was enough moonlight filtering through the Sitka spruces and larches to let Kit drive his Land Rover without lights, very slowly up the track for about half a mile. And there, part hidden where it had turned in amongst the trees, was the Transit van. Kit carefully reversed, then turned the Land Rover sideways about a hundred yards back down the forest track in order to block the route. Then he hid the keys under a small log nearby.

'There,' he whispered. 'If I have to leg it into the woods after one of the bastards you know where the Land Rover keys are if you need them.'

It was obvious that he'd played this game before, I thought. Probably a lot more times than he could remember, and definitely more times than me.

'Alright,' I said, as quietly as I could. 'This is your shout. How do you want us to handle it?'

'Well there's no telling when they'll get back but maybe it won't be long because the van's been here for at least an hour,' said Kit. 'They'll not want to stay in one place too much longer. We'll go on foot, up close to their van. When they come back, wait until you are sure they are all there so there's less chance of one of them getting around behind us. I'll shout summat like "gemmkeepers and police, stand still" and they'll either leg it or they'll try to outfight us. Knowing this lot it'll probably be the fighting. If it comes to that, lad, don't start pissing about trying to do things properly; there are no "Judges' Rules" out here. You just clobber the bastards and you hit them with everything you've got. If you don't put *them* out cold then you can rest assured that they'll do it to you. Fight dirty, or you'll lose.'

With that, he picked up what looked like the bottom twenty inches of a pickaxe handle that he'd laid on the bonnet of his Land Rover, and we walked very slowly and very quietly up the edge of the track towards the Transit, keeping our boots off the gravel.

'Only two of you?'... 'That's bad odds!'... Two different voices, behind us, and both had spoken just as two more figures stepped out of the trees ahead of us.

One of the men in front of us said: 'Just give us the keys to your Land Rover and keep out of the way and you won't get hurt. Your other option is hospital.'

Even though he was fractionally behind my shoulder, I could sense Kit slowly turning around to face the two, behind us. It was clear what we had to do; he was going to tackle the rear-guard and the two in front would be mine.

As silent as a ghost, he whispered 'Ready!' so that only I could possibly hear it. Then after a couple of seconds: '*Now!*'

Both of us switched our torches on simultaneously. I managed to get one of my pair right in the eyes with the powerful beam of my big, rechargeable torch and it was dazzling enough to make him cry out. The other turned his head, a fraction of a second before I could get the light onto his face. He had to be my first target for a punch up, while his friend was still unable to see. Both he and I lunged at each other but now I switched the torch off again so that it wasn't a homing beacon for the poacher. Behind me there was a steady glow and I realised that Kit's torch must already have been knocked from his hands and was lying on the ground. My torch was in my left hand. I collided with the poacher and we each managed to land one punch. The poachers' words were fixed in my mind, and so were Kit's: "*Fight dirty! – Your other option is hospital.*'

As the man lunged towards me again, I quickly swapped hands with the huge torch and swung it down as hard as I could, right on top of his head. Down he went, but so did the torch, broken. Immediately, another one of them grabbed me around the neck from behind with what must have been his left arm and started punching me on the back of the head with his other fist. At least three hard punches landed home on me before I was able to back-elbow him in the belly and knock him away, winded. He was doubled over so it gave me a perfect chance to bring my right fist up and slam it into his face. He fell back against a tree, and almost without thinking, I whipped my handcuffs off my belt and fastened his arms around the tree. *He* was going nowhere.

As I turned around to get back to Kit, I met another bit of tree coming the other way – fast. It was later established that the only other man still on his feet at that stage had picked up a bit of branch that was maybe three feet long and about three inches thick and whacked me right in the face with it, as I turned.

The light hurt my eyes. 'Steve? Steve? Jesus Christ, Steve, can you hear me? Are you alright? It's me; Ken, the dog handler.' He was shining his torch on me.

'Yeah,' I said. 'Turn that bloody light off.'

'What a mess your face is,' said Ken. 'Listen, mate, I take it the guy in the waxed jacket is the gamekeeper. He's out cold, lying on top of one of the poachers. There are two more of them here; one's hugging a tree and the other's lying about fifteen feet away. Are there any more of them?'

'Yeah. One more. He must have legged it,' I said.

'Right, let me check the game keeper's breathing and get him into the recovery position, then I'll get the dog,' said Ken. 'Can you stand up?'

'Get the dog. I'll try,' I said.

I used a tree to help pull myself up. My own torch was still in my pocket so I used it to check the time. It was still less than twenty-five minutes since I'd met Kit outside the pub, so the fourth man probably wasn't very far away at all.

Ken arrived back with his dog, Spartan, on a short leash and I told him the good news about the time factor. He must have arrived only a minute or two after I'd been clobbered.

'I've managed to get through on the radio, Steve,' said Ken. 'I've asked for urgent back up and a couple of ambulances, so you'll be okay.'

'Be okay?' I said. 'I'll be bloody okay when I get that bastard who dropped Kit and me. That's when I'll be okay.'

'Right,' said Ken. 'So which side of the track did they first appear from, before the fight? Can you remember?

'This side. The same side of the road as their van is on,' I said. 'Definitely.'

'Okay. Let's just hope he's run in the opposite direction then, so that the dog doesn't pick up all the earlier trails. Let's just handcuff the other two buggers together first,' said Ken.

He dragged the one lying alone on the track over to the Transit van and then did the same to the one Kit had been lying on top of, and handcuffed the two poachers to each other through behind the bumper bar of the van. Now *they* wouldn't be going anywhere either.

He checked Kit one more time, then turned back to the trees. Spartan got on a trail in seconds. I remember keeping my left hand pressed hard against my face but I was determined to go with Ken, whatever.

'You sure you're up to it?' he asked me.

'Too bloody right I am,' I said.

It was a fast trail. Spartan never slowed once and we had to run hard. Ken wanted the poacher to know the dog was after him. A scared man does silly things and gives himself away.

'Speak to him, Spartan,' he cried. 'Speak lad, speeek!'

The woods seemed to shake to the barking of that huge Alsatian. The depth of his bark summed him up perfectly; he was as hard as a bag of bricks. The trail led out of the trees and across two fields, still at full run. It took us straight to a farm. A cur dog was already barking in one of the sheds.

'Go and tell the farmer what's happening while I start to search the buildings, Steve,' shouted Ken.

It was the farmer's wife that opened the door. 'Good *grief*,' she said. What on earth has happened to you? Tommy? Tommy, come here. There's a young policeman and he's been hurt.'

'It's alright, honest,' I was saying, as her husband came to the door.

'What's to do, lad?' he said.

'We've had a fight with poachers. The one who did my face is probably hiding in your buildings. Our dog handler is searching now.

I hope you don't mind.'

'Mind? I'll come and help you. I'd bring my bloody *gun* if I had *my* bloody way.' said the farmer.

And it was Tommy the farmer who found the poacher, hiding behind a large drum in an outhouse.

'Here he is, boys,' Tommy shouted to us. 'Come and get him.' But Tommy was already using his own fists to good effect.

Ken caught my arm as I tried to push past him and Tommy.

'No, Steve. He's done enough to you. You already need a doctor. And anyway,' said Ken, as he bent down to unfasten the leash, 'Spartan hasn't bitten anyone for a few weeks.'

As Tommy and I left Ken and Spartan to it, the last thing I heard from that direction was Ken saying: 'Get your arm out of my dog's mouth!' with what sounded like genuine indignation.

The farmer took me in his old Volvo estate car, down their lane and along the road, then back up the forestry track, to where two ambulances and the traffic car were now standing in a line at Kit's Land Rover.

'Oh, bloody hell,' said one of the ambulancemen as he saw my face in their lights.   'Let's have a look at you, son.'

'You can, as soon as I've moved that thing out of the way,' I said.

Then I got the keys from under the stone and drove Kit's Land Rover to the side of the track.

One of the traffic lads came over to me. I knew his face but not his name. 'What's to do, mate?' he said.

'The three poachers here are all my prisoners – assaults and any other offences that come to light. Ken, the dog handler, is bringing another one back from the next farm,' I said.

'Well two of these lads are still unconscious, and so is your gamekeeper friend. One of us will have to go with the two unconscious prisoners to Carlisle Infirmary but one of us can take the one who's handcuffed to the tree into Hawthwaite nick, if you like, then carry on to Carlisle. That one will only need the local G.P.

197

to see to him in the cells; he's not badly hurt. And I presume that Ken will take the other prisoner in for you. Is that okay? What are *you* going to do?' he said.

'I suppose I'd better drive to Hawthwaite hospital and get this cut sorted out,' I said, wiping away some blood.

'Will you be alright to drive?' the traffic lad said.

'Yes. I'll be okay,' I said. 'But as soon as you can, will you radio H.Q. and ask them to get one of the sergeants or the inspector turned out at Hawthwaite, to receive the prisoners, please?'

'Yeah, certainly; we'll do that straight away,' he said.

I walked back to the nearest of the ambulances: 'One of the traffic bobbies is going to come with the two poachers to Carlisle Infirmary with you,' I said to the nearest ambulanceman. 'I take it both ambulances will be going there?'

'Yes, lad. But what about you?' he said.

'I'm going to drive to Hawthwaite hospital and get patched up there,' I said. 'Listen; when you get to the C.I.C. will you remember to tell the nursing staff to keep Kit separate from those two shits. It wouldn't do for the gamekeeper to wake up in a bed next to two of his poachers. It's debatable which one would kill the other one first.'

'Aye, we'll see to it lad. Don't worry,' he said. 'Let's be having a look at you... Oh, aye. You'll be needing a stitch or two in your cheek but it's not too bad, just the blood that makes it look worse than it is. But are you sure you'll be alright to drive?'

'Yes,' I said. 'It's nowt to fash about.'

I heard Ken, in the background, putting his prisoner into the back of the dog van. He came over to me, laughing.

'What's up?' I said.

'Spartan played a blinder,' he said. 'Matey-boy tried to get away from us while we were walking back along the road and the stupid clot wrapped his arms up around his own neck because he thought that police dogs would only go for an arm. And good old Spartan here caught him, sank his teeth into the daft bugger's arse and gave it a good savaging. He'd already given the fool's arm a bit of a nibble.

Anyway, it'll be a month or three before the bastard will be sitting down again. I'll take him to C.I.C. myself then I presume I'll bring him back to the cells at Hawthwaite before the night's out. I can't see how else we can do it. We can't put him in the same ambulance as the keeper and we wouldn't have a spare man to travel as escort even if we could.'

'That sounds good to me,' I said.

Ken gave me a lift back down the track to my own van. His dog van was partitioned into two, in the back. In one half was Spartan – dog of the very sharp teeth; and in the other half, separated only by chain-link wire, was the poacher – man of the very sore arse.

I swapped vehicles and set off back to Hawthwaite. For all the world it looked like a miniature United Nations convoy: three police vehicles and two ambulances, all in a line. It struck me that Leathermere had probably never seen its likes before.

I walked into Hawthwaite hospital about ten minutes later. The only nurse near the reception had her back to me. She turned when she heard me coming. It pleased me greatly that it was Elizabeth.

'Steve? What in God's name have you been doing to yourself? Let me have a look at your face,' she said. Then she led me through into an examination cubicle.

'Take both your jackets off, and your tie, and lie on the couch,' she said.

I threw my waterproof outer jacket down on the floor, in the corner. It was filthy from when I'd been knocked down. Then I hung my tunic on the back of a seat. By the time I lay down, Elizabeth had got a bowl of hot water and rather a lot of cotton wool. She set about cleaning up my face – concentrating hard and working in silence.

'Right,' she said, after a few minutes, 'I'll get Gillian to ring for the duty doctor to come and put a couple of stitches in this and I'll clean the actual wound out while we are waiting for him. Just hang on.' She went into a nearby ward and I could hear her chatting to one of her colleagues.

'He'll soon be coming,' she said, when she came back.

'There's an awful lot of muck in this wound. What on earth caused it?'

'One of the men I was arresting tried to make me eat a tree,' I said, with a silly grin on my face. But the silly grin made it sting like hell.

'What do you mean?' she said.

'I got a smack in the mouth with a big bit of wood.'

'No wonder it's such a mess. It's going to take some cleaning,' she said.

'Feel free. It's got to be done,' I told her.

When the doctor arrived, about twenty minutes later, Elizabeth was just finishing her wound-cleaning session. And she'd made me wince a few times, into the bargain, even though I was trying hard not to. This time, it was Doctor Gilbert, not Jim McDermott. He looked at the gash and said: 'What I'm going to do is put four tiny stitches in this, rather than two or three normal-sized ones. That way, it will reduce the chance or size of any scar. Okay?'

'Yes, fine,' I said.

'Do you want an anaesthetic for the pain?' he asked me.

'No, just do it. If it gets too bad, I'll tell you,' I said.

I can't say that I really noticed his needlework; Elizabeth was hovering around him, helping – wiping the occasional dribble of blood from my cheek. And all I could think was that I had been right; she was easily the loveliest creature I had ever laid eyes on. Fifteen minutes later, he was finished.

'Right, Constable,' he said, 'I want you to come back here later today when the radiology department is open, and have your cheekbone x-rayed. I've got a sneaking suspicion that it may be fractured.'

'I will,' I said.

'I'm just going to make a cup of coffee, doctor,' said Elizabeth.

'Would you like one before you go?'

'No thank you, Nurse Hodgson. I've got to go to the police station now to patch up a chap whom I suspect is one of this officer's reciprocal victims,' he said, grinning. Then he added, 'And you can rest assured that if *he* needs stitches, he'll be getting the biggest and roughest I can do. Maybe I should use a knitting needle.' And, with that, he left.

'Well, I'm sure *you* could use a hot drink, Steve,' said Elizabeth. 'In fact I think I'll make that an instruction. It is my medical advice that you must have a cup of hot coffee, right now.'

Whether Elizabeth realised it or not, there was absolutely no chance that I would have refused.

It was bang on three o'clock in the morning when I got back to the nick. Sergeant Clarke was sitting in the front office, in the middle of a telephone conversation. She looked up as I walked in.

'Oh, here he is now. Yes, I must admit he does *look* as though he's still alive, but I'll double-check.' She laughed at something that she was told. 'Yes, very good, sir. I'll tell him.' And she put the phone down.

Then she said to me: 'The inspector in force control room says that people are going to start refusing to work with you, Steve, because everyone that does ends up in the Cumberland Infirmary with their head caved in. The bad news is that Kit Reynolds does have a fractured skull. He's already been transferred to Newcastle – the specialist head injuries place – but the good news is that I've talked to the consultant who attended him at the C.I.C. and he's saying that he considers it to be a precaution. That it doesn't look *too* bad.'

'Oh not another one,' I said. 'Has anyone notified Kit's wife?'

'No,' said Sergeant Clark. 'Unfortunately, we are way off the mark with that. There's nobody in the area that could do it and I couldn't leave here while there's a prisoner in the cells. I'm going to go and do it now. I want you to stay in, now, and I'm sure you'll want to do your report so that we can get at least some of these four turds charged.'

I stayed on duty until almost 10am to give me some daylight time go back to the scene of the incident and search it, with Taffy Williams, who was on the early shift. In the back of the poachers' Transit van were two lurcher dogs and, underneath what was effectively a false floor, was a dead roe deer hind. It had been cut from throat to groin and cleaned out – grolloched as Kit would have said if he'd been conscious – venison is ruined very quickly unless that is done straight away. But it was also easy to see the much rougher wounds around its throat and one back leg where presumably the two lurchers had grabbed it and dragged it down until the poachers could catch up and slit its throat. Clearly, the gang had put the carcass in their van at some point before Kit and I had driven up the track. They'd seemingly heard us approaching and had time to get ready for us.

Taffy drove the police van back to the nick and I drove the poachers' Ford Transit, which was then impounded as evidence. I was then able to give the sergeant full details of all the offences that the four poachers should be charged with. Top of the list now was the offence of attempted murder in respect of Kit's fractured skull, but as was always the case, this had to be listed with the alternative offence of assault occasioning grievous bodily harm – known in the legal world as just G.B.H.

As I was about to go home, Carol Clarke stopped me and said: 'I rang the inspector, at home, earlier and he said I've got to tell you to have at least the next couple of nights off work, sick. We'll get someone else to cover your nights. Let us know the results from your x-ray. If you need more days off, you know you'll only need to say so.'

Of course, my poor mother nearly threw a fit when I got home with my face in the state it was. Huge bruises were sprouting all down the left side, and the stitches – as neat and tiny as they were – were still very visible.

'Why couldn't you have been a banker or an accountant,' she teased. 'Something less dangerous!'

'But that's far more dangerous than being in this job,' I replied, as sternly as I could make myself sound.

'How on earth do you come to that conclusion?' she asked.

'Easy,' I said. 'If I hadn't died of boredom by now, I'd have thrown myself off a tall building to make it end!' And I laughed.

'Oh, stop it!' she scolded.

But she was forgetting that I knew just how proud she was of my choice of career.

Chapter Twenty-One

Down, and Out

I went back to the hospital in pain on the Tuesday afternoon and got my face x-rayed. My left cheekbone was cracked, as the doctor had predicted. There wasn't anything they could do about it, they said. "Just stay off work until you feel well enough to go back."

I rang the nick and told them I'd be off for a few days, probably until my rest days, the following week.

That evening, we were all sat in the living room at home and heard a knock at the kitchen door. Dad went through then came back after a few seconds: 'Steven, it's for you.'

I went through, puzzled, and there, standing just inside the door, was Samantha.

'I hope you don't mind me coming to see you,' she said, a bit nervously, 'but I heard that you'd broken your cheekbone and I wanted to come and say hi and see how you are.'

'Come and sit down, Sam,' was the best I could manage.

I couldn't think what on earth to say to her. It was very flattering to have a pretty young lady chasing after me but I was already courting.

My parents' house was a former quarry workers' cottage – small rooms, three-up, two-down – so the kitchen doubled as our dining room. I pulled out one of the chairs from one side of the dining table. Then I pulled out one for myself, around the corner to her left.

'Does it hurt a lot?' she asked.

'You know the old saying: "only when I laugh."'

'I was so upset when I found out you'd been hurt,' she said, as her eyes brimmed with tears.

Just at that point, my mother came through from the living room. 'I'm just going to make a cup of…' she started saying, but then she saw Sam's glistening eyes. 'Oh, well maybe I'll come back in a few minutes,' said Mam. And she turned and went again.

'Sam, sweetheart, listen,' I said. 'If I wasn't seeing someone then I would like to go out with you. You are a lovely girl. But what would you think of me if I two-timed my girlfriend so that I could see *you*? Apart from anything else, you would never be able to trust *me* after that, now would you?'

The tears began to drip silently from her cheeks onto the legs of her jeans. 'No, I suppose not. I'm sorry; I just can't help it. I've never felt like this before,' she said.

I felt awful. I reached out with my right hand and cupped the left side of her face. She tilted her head over into my palm. With my thumb, I wiped away yet another big tear that was starting to roll down her cheek. We sat like that, in silence for a couple of minutes, then she said: 'I'd better be going.'

It was at least three or four minutes after she left that I realised that I hadn't asked her how on earth she had come up to Linthwaite from Hawthwaite, or how she was getting home but I did know that she couldn't drive.

'I'd better go and check,' I told my parents. If she had come by bus, it was over a mile to the bus stop, right across the far side of the valley. It was black dark and freezing cold outside. I got my car drove all the way over there, even though I knew she couldn't possibly have walked all that way in such a short time, but she was nowhere to be seen. I was left hoping that a friend might have brought her to my house then home again.

I phoned Susan that night and told her a little bit about my fight with the poachers.

'Oh, baby, I'm sorry,' she said. She sounded really quite upset. 'If you want to, you can always come and stop here for a night or two.'

By the time the Friday evening came around, I was bored beyond words just sitting at home. At eight o'clock, I decided to go to Susan's, as she'd suggested, so I grabbed a few things, threw them in a bag, said my farewells and set off. It took me just over quarter of an hour to get there. But when Susan opened the door she seemed a bit subdued. We hugged and kissed but she was so cool with me that I said: 'What's the matter?'

'Oh, I'm sorry,' she mumbled. 'That friend I was telling you about, at Whitehaven, well her dad's just died.'

'I'm sorry to hear that,' I said.

'It's just one of those things, I suppose, but it's taken the wind out of my kite a bit. Anyway, come and sit down,' she said. 'Your face *is* a bit of a mess, isn't it?'

About nine o'clock, Susan's phone rang and she went out into the hallway to answer it. She didn't fully close the door and I heard a few snatches of her conversation: 'What do you want?...I told you, it was just once...No. No you can't...I've got company...Don't be silly, what do you mean, get rid...No...*No!*...Hello?...*Hello?*...'

I heard her put the phone down but several minutes went past and she didn't come back into the room. In the end, I quietly went to see where she was. Susan was sat on a small chair, beside the telephone table, trembling and crying.

'Whatever is the matter?' I asked, as I took her hands to lead her back through into the living room.

I sat her next to me on the settee, facing each other, her hands in mine. She cried for several more minutes before my repeated pleas for her to tell me what was happening finally got through.

'Steve, I am about to lose somebody who is second only to my son in importance to me,' she said.

'What do you mean?'

'You, baby. You! I can't do anything but tell you. I'm so, *so* sorry. Steve, I've been unfaithful to you.'

I was dumbstruck. I felt as though every ounce of strength had gone from my body at that moment. My fingers uncurled, seemingly of their own will, and her hands fell from mine.

'What do you mean?' I said.

'It was Monday... Monday... I decided to go for a lunchtime drink at the Fisherman's Arms, where you and I went for New Year,' she said. 'Well, Tom Pearson was there. I used to go out with him when we were still at school. He was my first... Well, you know – my first.'

'You mean that nasty git who was rude to us on New Year's Eve?' I said.

'Yes. Well he was just a bit jealous that night he saw you and I together, that's all. He always *has* been jealous of me with other men. He wanted me to marry him years ago before I married Adrian. I think he must have stitched my drinks with Vodka, or something, because I got totally legless. I was there in my car so he said he'd drive me home because I was in such a state. Anyway, he drove me to that car park, up in the woods, overlooking the lake... And we sort of did it; in the car,' she said, very quietly.

'Sort of? *Sort of?* Did you or didn't you?' I said, trying not to yell.

She nodded, and the tears came again. Then, ever so quietly, she added: 'That isn't all.'

'What? You mean it gets *worse?*' I said.

'Yes,' she said. 'Much.'

'Tell me,' I said. I felt like running out into the garden to vomit.

'While it was happening – at the car park – one of your mates appeared,' she said.

'What do you mean, one of my mates?'

'One of the other policemen, in the van you sometimes come here in. One of the men that was at the police ball,' she said.

'*And?*

'And on Tuesday, he turned up here and asked to come in and talk to me,' she said. 'I was scared. I knew it was him that had caught Tom and me. I thought he was maybe going to tell me that he would say nothing to you if I could tell him it was a one-off or something. But that wasn't it.'

'Well?'

'He told me that he knew I was screwing around behind your back. Those were some of his words; he said much worse stuff than that. And he asked me whether I wanted him to come straight to see you that afternoon and tell you what he'd seen. Steve, I was already gutted at what I'd done; I was so, so ashamed. I knew it wasn't going to happen again. I *knew* Tom had got me plastered just so he could do what he did. I was desperate for you not to find out. I was desperate to keep you. *I love you.*' She broke down and sobbed. 'Steve, I *love* you.'

'So what happened?' I said.

'He got hold of me. I was really frightened. He pushed his hand inside my blouse and groped me. And he said that if I'd let him have sex, just this once, he would forget all about what he'd seen. I was *petrified*, I didn't know what to *do*,' she said, sobbing.

'Jesus Christ, you mean *he*...? Him too...? Ohh Jeeesus,' I said.

Susan was crying inconsolably now.

'Which of them was it, Susan? Which policeman?' I said.

'Dick Price. He didn't even tell me that you'd been hurt until after he'd finished. And that was him on the phone just now; leering and laughing at me. He said he's coming here just after ten o'clock tonight to have sex with me again. He told me that he couldn't care if I did have company; I had to "get rid" of them. He obviously didn't realise it was you I was talking about,' she said.

My mind was racing. Wave after wave of fury, and nausea and sheer, indescribable... – I couldn't even think of the words – I felt as though I was drowning. After what seemed like an eternity, I checked my watch. It was ten o'clock. I only had a few minutes; Price would be setting off from Hawthwaite nick at any moment now. I presumed that he'd been put onto nights in place of me and would be driving to Susan's in the police van.

'Right,' I said to Susan, 'This is what we are going to do. I'm going to park my car in around the corner so he doesn't see it when he arrives, then I'm going to come back here and hide. When he comes, you let him in but I want you to argue with him, to protest. Tell him that he forced you to have sex last time, if that's the truth, and tell him you're not going to let him do it again. I want to clearly be able to hear him say that if you don't let him have sex with you he will do something to hurt you – that he'll tell me about it, or that he'll do something else to hurt you, or whatever – do you understand?'

'What are you going to do?' she said. 'And what do you *mean*, "if that that's the truth"? Of *course* it's the truth. Why else do you think I told you?'

'I'll work out what I'm going to do as it happens,' I said. 'We'll have to talk about the rest later.'

By six minutes past ten, my car was hidden and I was lying on the floor between the back of the three-seater settee and the wall of the living room. I'd taken the precaution of taking a rolling pin with me from Susan's kitchen drawer. Dick Price would have his truncheon and I wanted a matching weapon in case it was needed. At eleven minutes past ten, I heard a vehicle draw up, outside. It sounded like it could be the police van. Moments later, there was a knock at the door. I heard it being opened and heard them both come into the living room. My heart was racing.

'Well, come on then,' he said. 'I haven't got long. I'll make it nice for you.'

My hand gripped the rolling pin so hard that it my knuckles hurt.

'No, I don't want to,' said Susan. 'You frightened me into letting you have sex on Tuesday. It was a filthy trick. I'm not doing it again.'

'Suit yourself,' snarled Price. 'But if you don't – right now – then lover boy Steven will know exactly what you've been up to, before tonight is out. And I'll make sure that all the kids at your little boy's school get to hear that his mommy screwed three men in a week – and just after her husband died, too! Which of us do you think Steve will believe?'

That was too much. I jumped up, keeping the rolling pin out of sight.

'Lover boy Steven already knows the answer, Dick.' I said.

'What the fuck…? How…?' he gasped.

I stepped out from behind the couch. Price was totally mesmerised. Apart from his eyes following me, he didn't move a muscle. I kept my left shoulder towards him, keeping my right arm clear in case I needed it if we came to blows.

'Turn around and face the wall,' I said, with a voice so cold it startled even me.

'What do you mean?' he said.

'I mean,' I bellowed, 'turn around and face the bloody *WALL!*'

As I grabbed him and started to turn him with my left hand, I raised the rolling pin high over my head in my right. He was petrified at the sight. I pinned him to the wall by his neck – all the while keeping the rolling pin held high and ready. I was within a breath of putting him in a box and me in a prison.

'Susan,' I commanded, 'find his handcuffs. They'll be on the left hand side of his belt.'

'They're on the right; they're on the right,' Price bleated, as though he realised he might not come through this alive.

She found them.

'Put your hands behind your back, Price, you disgusting twat.'

My thumb was in the right hand side of his neck and my fingers in the left-hand side. My knuckles were white with the pressure. Susan put the cuffs on him and the ratchets clicked shut. I let go of his neck and squeezed the cuffs tighter on his wrists. Once tightened like that, they wouldn't slacken until he was released with a key. And it hurt him. It was meant to.

'Turn around,' I said.

He did. He was trembling and shuddering.

'Apologise to Mrs Watson.' I said.

'I'm sorry.'

I brought my right knee up as hard as I could, right into his groin. If he could have drawn breath he would have screamed, but he just dropped to the floor gasping for air – desperate for air.

'Constable Richard Price of Hawthwaite Police Station, you disgraceful, disgusting bastard,' I said, 'I am arresting you on suspicion of rape and attempted rape. If you can't remember the wording of the short caution, tell me now and I'll remind you what it is.'

I hauled him to his feet by his hair and searched his trouser pockets with my free hand until I found the ignition keys for the van and his handcuff key.

That was when we heard a frightened little voice calling from upstairs: 'Mammy?'

'Leave the front door open and go and see to Andrew,' I said to Susan, as I pushed Price out. 'I'm coming back in a second.'

I locked Price in the back of the police van and walked back to her. She had Andrew in her arms but she put him down and ushered him into the living room and closed the door as I approached.

'I'm sorry, Susan,' I said. 'You must realise that you and I are beyond repair; it's no good pretending otherwise. The only thing I can do for you now is try to make sure this bastard goes to prison. Making a woman have sex through fear or intimidation is rape in the eyes of the law, and for a policeman to do it is utterly evil,' I said. Then I added, rather officiously, 'Anyway, I simply wanted to say goodbye, that's all.'

We looked at each other for a couple of seconds. She was beside herself; her mouth was moving but no sound came out. Then I turned and left.

As soon as I got in the van, Dick started pleading with me to come to some sort of deal. It was when he said I could have his new MG that I stopped the van and turned around to scream at him through the wire mesh: 'Don't you *dare*, you little shite. Don't you try and measure that woman against your miserable, little car. You are nailed, you bastard. Make *no* mistake about it – you are nailed.'

To hammer the point home to Price, I immediately got on the force radio to the headquarters control room and requested that either Inspector Sumner or an officer of even higher rank be asked to attend Hawthwaite Police Station immediately to deal with a prisoner in a highly sensitive case.

It was another long night.

The following morning, my parents' phone rang at nine o'clock. It was the Divisional Chief Superintendent.

'Listen, Shearwater,' he said. 'I don't doubt that you acted in good faith last night when you arrested Price, but you shot from the hip, boy. I'll tell you right now that he has been released from custody and he will not be going to court on any of these rape allegations.'

'Pardon?' I was incredulous.

'I'm coming down to Hawthwaite this morning to try and sort this mess out,' he said. 'I want you to be there – not in uniform, I know you are technically off, sick – at ten o'clock. Will you do that?'

'Yes, sir. Of course, but…'

'I'll talk to you about it then, not before,' he said. 'Alright?'

'Yes, sir,' I said.

By the time I'd been in the Inspector's Office with Brian Sumner and the chief superintendent for ten minutes, my head was spinning. I knew the bosses were right. I knew I'd cocked it up completely.

'Steven, it's like this,' said the Chief Superintendent. 'First of all, your own evidence would be seen as unreliable, simply because you were so emotionally involved with the victim. Secondly, even if it *did* come to court – which I must tell you once again, that I'm afraid it won't – then it would be seen by the newspaper-reading public as nothing but a cat fight between two policemen. The press would have a field day with it and make you *both* look thoroughly immoral, not just Price. And finally – and most crushingly – Inspector Sumner, here, has been to see Mrs Watson already this morning and she has said that if it goes to court the whole thing is bound to come out in the press. She says that for the sake of her son she cannot face that. As a result, she is refusing to make a statement. The only consolation is that the inspector did persuade her to answer some questions for use in a Section Forty Nine complaint against Price. There are only two things I can guarantee you about this, young man. One is that your own distress and emotionally misguided reaction will certainly *not* be held against you on your personal record. What Price undoubtedly did do was evil and in the heat of the moment I would guess that any of us would probably have done the same as you. And secondly, I will promise you that Price will be kicked out of the force before the end of this coming week. He need not know that Mrs Watson doesn't want a court case, at that stage. He will be told that he has the choice of resigning or being put on trial. I will be doing that interview myself. Believe *me*, he is going. Can you live with that?'

'Yes, sir,' I said. 'I'm just sad that I got it wrong and I apologise to you. Price deserves to be put behind bars for such a vile abuse of the job and I've unintentionally stopped that from being possible'

'Well, you know what they say about hindsight, Steve,' said Brian Sumner, quietly. 'It's a perfect science.'

'True, sir,' I said. 'But there is one other thing I want to ask you both about because this rape incident might not have been the only offence Price was involved in. May I tell you my concerns?'

'Of course, lad,' said the Chief Super'.

I put my thoughts to them over the next few minutes. They both listened intently, with raised eyebrows. When I'd finished, the big boss promised he would have an investigation carried out, and then my interview was at an end.

I waited for ten minutes until I saw the chief superintendent come downstairs to the front office, then I popped back up for a quick word with Inspector Sumner.

'Yes, Steve. What is it, son?' he asked.

'Well, one way and another, sir, I've rather depleted our manpower this week, and as I'm just sitting at home, bored, I want to know if you'll let me come back in on nights, as normal; as from tonight? I need something to try to focus on.'

'What about your fracture?' said Brian.

'Oh, the bones aren't out of line, just cracked. So there's nothing that can be done about it,' I said. 'I'll just have to make sure that if I got another clout off anyone they'll have to hit me on the other cheek.'

'Well,' said Brian, 'I have to admit that you being back would help me greatly. We have one man on earlies, nobody on lates or nights, and one man on rest days, so if you were able to do that, the sergeants could cover the two-to-ten shift today and tomorrow.'

'Right, I'll be in tonight then,' I said.

'Thanks, lad,' said Brian. 'And I'm sorry what's happened.'

'No, sir,' I said. 'There was nothing the boss said that I could disagree with. It's just hard to accept. Is it right what he said, though, about Susan not wanting it to go to court?'

'Yes; absolutely,' said Brian. 'She's more upset about losing you than about what happened with that scum-bag, Price. But Steve, I have a confession to make, son. I would never have said a word to you without this happening because you're old enough and smart enough to work things out for yourself and make your own decisions. The fact is, I'm afraid, I've known about Susan for many years. She has always been a bit too friendly with the men. I know for a fact that she was unfaithful to her late husband and that was seemingly the catalyst for much of the trouble between them. Despite the distress you suffered last night, son, it may be a blessing in disguise. I hope it goes without saying that I wish to God now that I had told you earlier; I'm sorry. I thought I was doing right by you.'

'It's okay, sir,' I said. 'It's been very unpleasant but I'll just have to put it behind me.'

Back downstairs, I went to the ref's room to make myself, Linda and Brian a cup of coffee apiece. I hadn't realised that Samantha was on duty and was already in there, rinsing some cups.

'Oh, hello,' I said, surprised. 'Listen, I was thoughtless the other night. How on earth did you get home?'

'Hiya,' she breezed. 'On my bike.'

'On a pedal bike?' I said. 'You must be mad. It was like the arctic out there.'

'Oooh! So what happened to Mister Big Hard Mountain Climber then?' she teased. 'I didn't think you would be bothered by a little bit of cold. *I* certainly wasn't. And anyway, when are you going to take me out fellwalking? You know we've both got Monday and Tuesday off, next week, don't you?'

I finished pouring the coffees. 'We'll see,' I said, with a little laugh. She deserved full marks for perseverance.

I worked the next two nights, as I'd said I would. The only thing of interest that happened was a reply that arrived – via the telex at Divisional Headquarters and then our internal mail – from the police in the United States. It stated that according to the records at Harvard University, the late Mr Malinowski's home address was shown as being in Wollongong, Australia. I submitted a second forwarding report to the boss, asking that the police in New South Wales be contacted and asked to make enquiries at the Wollongong address with a view to obtaining the names – and, if necessary, obtaining a further address – for Mr Malinowski's next of kin. Until they had been found and been able to make arrangements for his funeral, the hapless climber was destined to remain in Hawthwaite mortuary.

Chapter Twenty-Two

Frozen Hills

I got up at noon on the Monday. I hated staying in bed all day after my final night shift, it just meant that one of my two rest days was wasted. My face was still feeling sore but the sharper pains had eased off.

After thinking about it all weekend, I had decided to phone Samantha and see if she really did want to come out fell-walking with me. I knew it was a silly question, though, because I knew she would probably fall all over herself to do so. I had to admit to myself that it was all very flattering; I had never before had a young lady pursue me quite the way she was. But there was also the solid certainty in the back of my mind that I mustn't just use her to bury my own pain from the Low Keld fiasco.

First, though, I phoned the Lake District National Park offices for a mountain-top weather forecast for the next day: "Bitterly cold above two thousand feet; 10-12 degrees below freezing. Snow lying above the level of one thousand feet; expected to be cloudless and very sunny." Well *that* couldn't be much better for a spectacular walk.

Next, I rang my brother Chris and his wife, Felicity. They were both keen mountaineers and Felicity was about the same size as

Samantha. I asked "Fliss" whether my friend could borrow some of her gear if we decided to go out, tomorrow. Her "yes" was a foregone conclusion, she's a very kind-hearted girl, but her jokes about what would or wouldn't be possible with a girlfriend on top of a mountain, in sub-zero temperatures were teasingly uncouth, to say the least!

Then I phoned Sam.

'Hello?'

'Hello. Is Samantha there please?' I said.

'Steve? Is that *you*?' Her voice seemed to leap an octave.

'Oh, hello Sam! I'm sorry,' I said. 'I expected it to be your landlady answering. I didn't realise it was you. Listen, would you still like to go up on the fells tomorrow? I can get you all the gear if you would, but it will be very hard work. It's going to be desperately cold.'

'Yes. Yes, of *course*,' she said. 'If you can get me the gear. I know you'll look after me. Ohh, yesss.'

I was amazed at how elated I felt when she said yes, and it was rather obvious that I wasn't the only one to feel that way.

'Good,' I said, smiling to myself. 'I'm pleased. Are you doing anything tonight? Because if you're not I'll need to take you to my brother and sister-in-law's house so we can kit you out with her stuff.'

'I'm not doing anything at all tonight. Or at least I wasn't, until now,' said Sam.

'May I pick you up at six?'

'Yes, I'll be ready,' she said.

The biggest relief that evening was when Fliss's boots fit Samantha well. Sam had shown me the pair that she owned when I picked her up from her lodgings and they were too lightweight for serious winter walking. If she'd had to wear them we would have had to stay well away from any steep ground.

Felicity took Sam into the utility room from where, every now and then, Chris and I could hear them both giggling. By the time they came back, fifteen minutes later, Sam looked more like Sirdar Tensing than a teenage cadet. She had Fliss's Helly Hansen cagoule, woolen balaclava, gloves, snow goggles, over-trousers, gaiters, boots, instep crampons, rucksack, Silva compass, and survival gear.

We stayed for a coffee then set off to drive back towards Hawthwaite. As we left the house, Fliss gave me a swift prod in the ribs and very silly wink, while Sam wasn't looking.

'Do you need to go straight back to your digs, Sam, or would you like to go for a drink, first?' I said.

'Nooo. Let's go for a drink somewhere cosy,' she said.

I drove us to the Lord Leathes, at Leatherside, where I bought a pint of lager shandy for myself, and a Britvic Orange and lemonade for Sam. Despite being eighteen, she apparently wasn't interested in alcohol. We sat side by side on a comfy bench seat, close to a blazing log fire. She sat very close to me, all sort of curled in my direction. It was very distracting but I couldn't deny it was also very pleasant. I'd brought a one-inch to one-mile Ordnance Survey map of the Lake District into the pub with me, from the car.

'Would you like to see where I was thinking of us going, tomorrow?' I said.

'Yes. Of course,' said Sam.

We moved our drinks aside and spread the map out.

'I'll drive us to the head of Haweswater and park there – we'll go via Penrith to get there – then we can walk south-westwards, up Nan Bield Pass, past Small Water,' I said, tracing the route for her on the map, with the retracted tip of my pen. 'That brings us out onto a bit of a hause, at the top of the pass, then we'll swing up to the right, to the summit of Mardale Ill Bell. They're lovely names, aren't they? Nan Bield Pass and Mardale Ill Bell? That area seems to have more than its fair share of evocative names.'

Sam was nodding, as I spoke.

'Depending on the time,' I continued, 'we may have our lunch there. Then, as long as the conditions are alright, we'll continue north-westwards onto High Street. Do you know how it got its name?'

'Nope,' she said.

'Well,' I said, 'until a few hundred years ago, the Lake District was still very heavily wooded and a lot of the valley-bottoms were almost impassable swamp, so the experts say. When the Romans were here, in the first three centuries A.D., they looked for the easiest, straightest and safest routes for their roads. Logical, I suppose. That particular summit – High Street – is a long, fairly level ridge, as you can see from the contour lines on the map, so the Romans' main north-to-south road through the Lake District, in part, followed that ridge, up above the trees and the swamps. Maybe High *Road* would be more accurate, but that's where the name came from. Part of it is known as Racecourse Hill and it's not that long since they used to do just that – bring horses all the way up from the valleys to race there. Seems like unnecessarily hard work, if you ask me.'

'Can you still see the proper Roman road, then?' Sam asked.

'Not in any detail, and definitely not under the two or three feet of snow that'll be up there at the moment, but in summer you can get a much better impression. Anyway, if it goes well tomorrow, we'll turn east, just north of the summit of High Street, and come back down to the valley via Long Stile ridge. It brings us down over Caspel Gate and the tops of Eagle Crag, Heron Crag, and Swine Crag, down onto The Rigg. That's this wooded promontory that sticks out into Haweswater reservoir,' I said, pointing at the map. 'Then we almost double back on ourselves, south-westwards along the lake shore, under the steep slopes at Dudderwick, back round the head of the lake, and back to the car.'

'Sounds great. I can't wait,' said Sam.

'It should be good, but I meant what I said about it being hard work and you'll get a hell of a shock at the temperature difference between the valley bottom and the summits, even though we are only going up to about two thousand seven hundred feet,' I said.

I put the map away then. We chatted for another hour and it became even more relaxed and pleasant.

'Listen, Sam,' I said as we finished our drinks, to leave. 'If you didn't already know, I'm not seeing anyone else now. But if you hadn't heard, the end of my relationship was dramatically unpleasant, to say the least. Everyone that knows us both will warn you about me being on the rebound and I want you to *listen* to them. I like to think that I am very level-headed, Sam, but I *am* stunned by what happened to me and I'm desperate that you don't end up getting hurt. If our friendship does develop then please, for God's sake, be wary. You don't need something to happen that you might regret for years.'

Samantha simply nodded. And, for a few moments, she looked like a little girl lost.

When I dropped her off, I told her how much food to bring, and to carry two flasks of hot drinks. I arranged to pick her up at 7.30am.

Sam was beaming her face off when she came out to the car, the next morning, despite the savage frost.

'I've been awake since four o'clock,' she said. 'I'm really looking forward to this.'

It took us just over an hour to reach the head of Haweswater. The last half of the journey – to Bampton and beyond – was on unsalted roads and some parts were very slippery. Only the east-facing upper slopes of the fells over on the far, west side of the lake were in sunlight; the rest of the valley was lying in its own deep shade.

Only one other car was there and the couple from it got out and, like us, started to get their winter gear on.

'Wonderful morning!' the man said to me.

'Yes, it's brilliant! Are you going up Nan Bield?' I said.

'No. We're going out to the left; up Gatescarth Pass, then down

Mosedale to Swindale Head and back over by Rowantreethwaite Well. We've decided to stay lower today, the tops are a bit out of our league in these conditions,' he said.

The couple finished getting ready and set off first, but before Sam and I left my car I put a large note on the dashboard. Anybody looking through the windscreen could read the full details of our intended route and all potential escape route options should conditions let us down. I knew from my mountain rescue experience and frequent newspaper reports that many lives had been lost on our seemingly humble little mountains because rescue teams didn't know where to start looking when someone was badly overdue.

At last, we were off. Initially, we kept our ice axes and crampons fastened to our rucksacks. The arduous pull up Nan Bield Pass was all on a rocky path where many rocks were showing through the snow and crampons would have been as much a hindrance as a help. After the first few minutes, chattering, we soon started to walk in breath-hungry silence. The air itself was wickedly cold, and spiked at one's throat and lungs. Seven hundred feet higher, and just under a mile further on, we reached the side of Small Water, a dramatic little tarn set in a steep sided, rocky corrie. It looked a bit grim, today, because it was frozen solid – a deep shade of battleship grey.

I pointed south westwards, over the tarn, and said to Sam: 'That's another of those good place-names. That shallow gully thing, below Harter Fell, is called Black John Hole.'

'Where did the name come from?' she gasped, still panting from the climb.

'I don't know. But Harter Fell comes from the old Norse name for a red deer stag – hjarter I think – a hart.' I paused for a moment. 'Do you want a drink or anything, or shall we bash on and get up into the sunshine?'

'The sunshine, please,' she said.

I laughed. 'If you think it's going to be any warmer, up there in the sun, you're in for a rude awakening. But come on, I'll let you find out for yourself,' I said.

The sun hit us in the face seven hundred even-steeper feet later, as we reached the top of the pass. And so did an unremitting wind that felt as though it had come straight-necked from the Arctic, even though we were facing south.

'Oh, my Goddd,' exploded Sam.

'*That* has put paid to your dreams of sun bathing, *hasn't* it!' I chortled. 'Let's drop back about twenty feet down the slope and we'll get sorted out.'

Back down in the lee of the hillcrest and some rocks, we both took our rucksacks off and sat down. Up until then, we had both been wearing our climbing balaclavas rolled up, like ordinary wooly hats but now was definitely the time to pull them down to cover our lower faces and throats, too. Just a slot was left clear for the eyes. I knew that Sam was wearing just one pair of gloves, my sister-in-law's, alpine-standard mitts, but I was deliberately wearing two pairs: my ordinary police leather gloves underneath a thin pair of wind- and waterproof mitts. That combination meant I could slip the mitts off and have the dexterity of using my fingers for fiddly jobs and to take photographs without losing all my protection from the cold.

'Don't take your gloves off, Sam,' I said. 'It will hurt you if you do. I'll get all the other bits you need. We're going to put our crampons on, now, too.'

I dug out our snow goggles from their respective stowage places. I leaned close to Samantha and was about to slip the elastic over her head when she got hold of the chin of her hat and pulled it down, clear of her mouth, and then she did the same to mine and used it to pull me towards her. We kissed. A long, deep kiss. It was easy to feel how inexperienced she was and yet it was still so natural. After two or three minutes of silent enjoyment, I said to her: 'If we're not careful, we'll freeze together at the mouth.'

She re-adjusted her balaclava and I slipped the goggles over her head. It took me a few minutes to fasten both our sets of crampons on. Sam had little, four-point crampons that fitted under the instep of her boots but I had the much bigger, jointed, twelve-point "lobster-claws" that could also be used for climbing vertical ice on frozen waterfalls. We re-emerged into the sun and the razor wind, and then swung right, up towards Mardale Ill Bell. On a smooth, rock-free and safe little section of hill, I showed Sam how to use her ice axe in the event of a fall. Ice axe practice was always brilliant fun – just like sledging without the sledge – so we stayed there, playing and laughing, for quite some time.

A few minutes later, just after we had passed the summit of the fell, I caught a glimpse of something momentarily flash – very brightly – far below us and to our left, in the head of the Kentmere valley. Wings! There was immediately a quickly growing, whistling sound and then all hell seemed to explode at our feet. With a colossal roar, a red and white Jet Provost, one of the RAF's training planes, catapulted up from Kentmere, over our heads, and immediately dived to his right, over the ridge, down towards Blea Water and Haweswater.

Samantha grabbed me, in fright at the incredible noise.

'You *lucky, lucky bugger*!' I shouted after the plane, at the top of my voice. Then I remembered who I was with and said: 'Oh, I'm sorry, Sam, but that was magnificent. I just got carried away.'

I needn't have worried about offended feelings, though. She was too busy laughing at me.

'You don't mind them making all that noise on your mountains, then?' she said.

'No, not at all. On the contrary, I get bloody annoyed at those people who *do* complain. Most of the grumblers are offcomers – not locals – and they would soon twine on the other side of their faces if ever Britain was forced into war again and we needed the military to protect us. We were caught with our trousers down before World War 2 and paid a heavy price for it, all because of the do-gooder, disarmament people,' I said.

A few minutes later, we found some rocks on the slope overlooking Blea Water and were able to tuck down out of the wind, but still in the sunshine, to have our sandwiches. We ate in near silence but a lot of little smiles were exchanged.

Near the course of the old Roman road, on High Street, a dry-stone wall had been coated in wind-blown snow that had frozen onto it in the most amazing sculptures. Only the cap stones along the very top of the wall were partially clear of the white cladding. For about the twentieth time that day, I dug out my camera from the warm depths inside my jacket and took several photographs. Changing films was a swine of a job though, because even my police gloves were far too clumsy for that so I had to remove those as well and change the film as quickly as I could, even though film gets brittle at those temperatures and I had to be careful not to damage it. By the time I could get my gloves back on, the cold was really hurting my hands.

At the summit of High Street, we stopped at the trigonometry point to scan around the distant mountains. Away to the south, the gleaming waters of Morecambe Bay reflected the light of the low, winter sun. And beyond them, only just visible in the far distance and silhouetted in a strange, pinkish haze that coated the entire southern skyline, was Blackpool Tower. From south west to north west was a breathtaking panorama of all the main Lakeland peaks, all wearing their pristine white hats and dazzling the gods.

A short distance north of the summit we turned right, to start our descent of Long Stile, a steep-sided ridge that led all the way back down to the lakeside. Our crampons became vital now, and cracked and crunched through the nearly rock-solid top layers of snow and ice to gain purchase. The particles that broke free were whipped away by the now rising wind that was still coming from the south. An attempted descent of the ridge that day, without crampons would have been suicide. Several times, Samantha was a bit apprehensive so for part of the descent I roped us together and to give her some confidence I showed her how I would stop her if she did slip. Once away from the dangerous crags, I removed the rope and simply held her hand. When we were almost down to the forestry, near the lakeshore, she obviously decided that she liked the hand-holding because she didn't let go. When we were only a few yards into the trees – out of the sun and out of the wind – we stopped, spontaneously. Both balaclavas were unceremoniously pulled off and dropped on the ground, and we kissed for an age.

By the time we emerged from the forestry, with rolled-up hats reinstated, it was after three o'clock and the light was fading quite quickly. We walked back along the shoreline, underneath the steep flanks of Dudderwick and back around the head of the lake towards the car. I told her all about the village of Mardale, somewhere down in the depths to our left, which had been submerged when the dam had been built and the valley flooded to create the Haweswater reservoir. I still didn't know her well enough to know whether she was genuinely interested or she was just being polite when we chatted about it.

We got back to the car and threw all our gear in the boot. The other car, from the morning, had gone and we were all alone. I started the engine and soon the heater was bringing life back into our chilled limbs. We turned to each other and kissed again. I reached over Sam to the little wheel on the far edge of her seat and started to recline it. She didn't protest at all. Then I did the same to my seat. We kissed more deeply and when the car had warmed up, I reached into her clothing, under her bra, and cupped her firm, left breast in the palm of my right hand. She sighed, pushed herself towards me, and kissed me deeper.

'I've never let anyone touch me like that before, Steve. You can do it all, if you want to. I trust you, Steve,' she said.

'Are you a virgin, then?' I asked.

She nodded. 'You don't mind, do you?'

'No, sweetheart, I think that's wonderful. But I'm not going to go any further. Not here; not now. No matter how much I want you,' I said.

'Well I want you, Steve. I really do,' said Sam.

We kissed again, and then I sat up, straightened my seat, and got the car moving before anything else could happen.

We rang my parents and Sam's landlady from a telephone kiosk in Bampton, just to say we were down safely off the fells, and then we drove to the Stoneybeck Inn, just north of Penrith for a bar meal. It was just after 8pm when I dropped Samantha off at her lodgings. I'd had to. It had become stunningly obvious as the day had worn on that us having sex was too likely. Of course, I physically wanted to but after the disastrous events of recent days, I simply wasn't prepared to do it and risk hurting Samantha.

Chapter Twenty-Three

Of Dogs and Drunks

'Was it a good day, up there, Steven?' my dad asked me, when I got in the house.

'Wonderful, absolutely wonderful,' I said.

'You could have brought Samantha home for tea, you know,' added my mother. 'I baked a big meat and potato pie just in case, *and* made a big rice pudding too.' Poor Mam was a bit indignant.

'Well, I don't want to spoil your evening,' chipped in Dad, again, 'but the police station have been on the phone. They say that Taffy went off sick yesterday so would you work nights tomorrow, instead of lates. Just that one night, apparently.'

And so it was that at ten past ten the following night, I was driving the police van down Main Street when I saw an old chap kneeling next to what looked like a bundle of rags on the pedestrian crossing. I parked, with the blue lights flashing and walked across towards him.

'What are you doing? What's the matter?' I said.

'It's my dog,' the man almost whispered. 'It's been run over.'

And then he looked up.

'Max...?' I said. It was. It was my dad's mate, Max Knight, and Tess. 'What happened?'

'Well when we git doon this end o' t' street of a night, I generally let the lass off her lead. She *allus* sits and waits for me here, at t' crossing, but thoo didn't tonight, did thoo, lass,' he said to her.

Tess, laying there in a pool of blood, managed two little flicks of her tail at the old man's voice.

'Right Max,' I said, 'this is what I think we should do. I'll radio our control room and get them to call the vet out at the surgery at the bottom of Gale Hill. You and I will take Tess up there and I bet that by the time we are there, the vet will have arrived. Alright?'

'I nobbut have mi' pension, lad,' he said. 'I could nivver afford a vet's bill.'

'Max, don't worry about that. I'll help you with that if needs be. Just don't worry about it,' I said.

I made the radio call then got a folded "Police – Accident" sign out of the back of the van and removed the flexible plastic part to use as a stretcher. It wasn't too difficult sliding the little dog gently onto it but she whimpered when we moved her. It really didn't look good for the poor old girl.

The old man sat beside me with the makeshift stretcher on his lap as we drove to the vet's – his hands comforting Tess. Sure enough, as we got there, the fluorescent strip lights inside the building were just flickering into life. Between us, Max and I carried the sign and its precious little cargo in and set it on an examination table that the vet pointed us to. Max stroked his pet on the head. She licked his hand, flicked her tail once more, and died.

A minute or two later, I got the vet on his own and asked him to send any bill to me at the nick.

'Don't be daft, Steve,' replied Simon Farrington. 'There won't be a bill.'

It was only then that I looked at him to see how he knew me. He was one of the four mountain rescue team members who had caught me during my inebriated tumble from the pub wall, a few days previously.

'What do I do, Vet?' asked Max when we re-joined him, beside the dead border collie. 'Do I take her home to bury her?'

'It's alright, Mr Knight,' said Simon. 'Not unless you want to. I can take care of Tess for you. You don't have to worry, I'll be very gentle and careful with her.'

I set off to drive Max back to his house. It wasn't until we were nearly there that I realised he was silently breaking his heart. Tears were flowing hard and fast.

'It's okay, Max. At least she didn't suffer for long,' I said, rather weakly. 'She must have been a good age so maybe this was better than a long, drawn out carry on with illness or something.'

'No, it's not that, lad,' he said. 'You don't understand. My only brother was killed in the war, my only child was killed in a car crash when he was just seventeen, and last year my wife died. That little dog was all I had left.'

I had no answer for him. All I could do was ask if he'd seen the car that had hit Tess.

'It waz some drunken old sod in a big white Rover,' said Max. 'I didn't get the number. He waz all over the road, but then I suppose it wazn't all his fault, Tess did run oot in front o' him.'

Just before he got out of my van, Max turned to me and said: 'Do me a favour, son. Dun't tell your dad that you saw me cry. Please dun't. Him and me were in t'Second World War togither. I dun't want him to know I cried.'

'Don't worry, Max,' I said. 'I won't say a word about that to anyone – *ever*. And for what it's worth, I don't blame you for being upset.'

When I went back into the nick at one o'clock for my sandwiches, I entered details of the pedestrian crossing incident in the Station Occurrence Book, as what was legally classed as a minor Road Traffic Accident. And that was the end of poor old Tess.

Just after two o'clock, I was back out on patrol, driving up Coleridge Street – a one-way street – and so I was more than a bit surprised to see the headlights of a slow-moving car coming towards me. I stopped my van in the middle of the street, turned my headlights down to sidelights so the oncoming driver wouldn't be dazzled, and then I switched the blue flashing roof light on. I watched in amazement as the oncoming car – seemingly in slow motion – bounced its wheels first off one kerb, and then off the other one. I stayed inside the van for safety's sake; a slow-speed collision had to be a better option that to risk getting run over. But just before it reached me, the car – a white Rover 2000 – mounted its left-hand kerb and crunched to a standstill against a shop wall. I radioed in to Headquarters: 'Zulu-Three-One, out of the vehicle at the scene of a one-vehicle RTA, Coleridge Street, Hawthwaite. I believe there's no injury. No assistance required at this stage. Will update; over.'

'Received, Zulu-Three-One; BB out.'

I walked over to the Rover and opened the driver's door. The extremely fat driver was so drunk that he literally rolled out of the driver's seat onto the ground at my feet, giggling.

'Oh muck pee, it's the folleece!' he laughed, seemingly delighted with his triple Spoonerism.

'Did you know this was a one-way street, sir?' I said.

His laughter hit new heights: 'I was only *going* one ferkin' way!'

'Are you hurt in any way?' I asked him.

Now it was a mock serious voice: 'No, but I require you to arrest that wall, immediately,' he said. 'It's dangerous – ramming my car like that.'

Unless somebody else drove the wrong way down the same street, he was in no danger, sitting on the road, so I left him there whilst I got a breathalyser kit from the van. But I knew fine well that he would never manage to inflate it.

When I gave him the full instructions for giving me a sample of breath and gave him two chances to do it, he just came back at me both times with: 'You want me to blow that up? Are we having a party?'

I arrested him for failing to supply a specimen of breath and with difficulty I managed to get him into the back of the police van. I then locked his car up and put a couple of cones and flashing amber lights beside it to discourage anyone else from running into it. There was enough room for people to drive past it safely. I radioed control room again and asked that a supervisory officer be called out at Hawthwaite to receive a drunk for second-stage breath testing.

It was only through searching the man, at the nick, that we established he was called Titus Martindale. Mr Martindale, it seemed, had won five hundred pounds on an "accumulator" at the betting office, earlier in the day and had spent the time since then successfully introducing his bladder to his winnings. I had never seen anyone so drunk who was still conscious.

I had the Rover towed away to a garage, later that night, but first, using the powerful rechargeable flashlight from the van, I checked the bumper and the wings. Sure enough, I found some strands of black hair and splashes of blood; Tess would be avenged.

Apart from eventually being reported for failing to supply a specimen of breath and subsequently refusing to supply either a sample of urine or blood, Mr Martindale was also reported for failing to stop at the scene of a reportable Road Traffic Accident and failing to later report such. What aggravated me most was that he said he didn't even know he'd hit anything. Thank God it hadn't been old Max on that crossing, instead of the dog.

The following day, I was on my proper 2pm-10pm shift, a little bleary-eyed from the "quick turnaround". Samantha was on 9am-5pm but the first I heard from her was only a minute or so after two o'clock when her voice came timidly over the short-range UHF radio: 'Can somebody please help me at the dog kennel? I've been cornered.'

I hurried out to the kennels, in the police station yard, only to find Sam in the back corner of the run with a bowl of dog food in her hand and a hungry but quite affable looking boxer right up to her. His little stumpy tail was jiggling away quite merrily but he'd got so close to her that she was thoroughly intimidated by him. I let myself in then went across and took the bowl from her and set it down at the other side of the run. Good old "Bongo" – his real name wasn't known – pounced on it with delight. We came out of the run and Sam clasped my shoulders and rested her head on my chest. 'Thank heavens you came; I was scared stiff,' she said.

'How long has he been here, Sam?' I asked. I knew a cadet would inevitably have had the job of feeding any strays we had in so she would know the answer.

'Six or seven days, I think,' she said.

'Wonderful. I think we've just found him a home,' I said. 'Get your hat; we're going to take him for a short drive.'

On the way to Max's house, I briefed Sam to back me up on whatever I told him. But as soon as the old chap saw us on his doorstep he cottoned-on immediately.

'I'm not having another dog, even if he *is* a stray,' Max protested.

Sam jumped swiftly into the fray.

'Oh nooo, *please!* He's been with us a week so the RSPCA are coming for him at three o'clock and he's going to be put down. There's nobody else we can *ask*,' she pleaded. She deserved an Oscar for that bit of acting, even if I said so myself.

'It'll probably only be for a day or two, Max; until the real owners claim him,' I lied. 'But Sam's right, if he's not out of the kennels within the hour he'll get a needle in his backside and that'll be that.'

'But he's only *young*,' said Max. And I knew we'd won.

I saw Max at least once or twice each week for a couple of years after that. Not once, though, was he taking the boxer for a walk. It was always the other way around, but Max was always smiling.

Chapter Twenty-Four

Up Against Cassandra

The Magistrates Court in Hawthwaite was held each Wednesday. I had been "warned for court" for the thirteenth of February, a couple of weeks in advance. Sir Giles Pemberton-Pennington, of Chelsea, was pleading not guilty to failing to comply with the zig-zag markings at a "zebra" pedestrian crossing. And his defending solicitor was Cassandra Hemmingway. She passed me as she went through the foyer where witnesses wait to be called. Her smile to me was warm but very discreet.

A few minutes passed whilst the case was introduced to the magistrates then the usher came to the door and called: 'Constable 8-6-8 Shearwater.'

I went straight to the witness box and, as we all did, I went straight into the oath without waiting to be asked. I held the bible high, in my right hand and, without needing the prompt card, looked straight at the three magistrates and said: 'I swear by Almighty God that the evidence I shall give will be the truth, the whole truth and nothing but the truth. Your Worships, I am Constable 8-6-8 Steven Shearwater, stationed here at Hawthwaite.'

Inspector Sumner, acting as prosecutor, stood for a moment and said: 'Constable, would you kindly give your evidence in relation to the alleged incident involving the defendant – Sir Giles Pemberton-Pennington.'

Lord Nethermere was chairing the bench so I addressed my next question directly to him, out of courtesy: 'Your Worships, I made notes about the incident immediately after it happened. May I have the court's permission to refer to those notes?'

Lord Nethermere was just turning to the magistrate on his left, a retired lady doctor, for the inevitable cursory nod to permit such when Cassandra – rather predictably – jumped to her feet, like a jack-in-the-box.

'If it please your worships, I wish to question the officer in connection with these alleged notes,' she said. She was obviously out to impress her client and would have to go through the whole ritual of challenging everything.

'Very good,' said Lord Nethermere, wearily.

'Constable,' she said, with solid eye-contact on me, and a face like stone, 'you say your notes were made immediately after the event. Rather vague, isn't it? Ten seconds later? Ten minutes later? Ten hours later? When?'

'Your Worships,' I replied – for I had been taught early in my career always to address my answers directly to the magistrates or the judge, not the lawyer – 'at the location where I actually reported Sir Giles, there is a vacant shop. Within about fifteen seconds of his eventual departure from the scene, I stepped back into the doorway of that shop and wrote all of the notes to which I now wish to refer.'

Cassandra muttered 'Very well,' and sat down again.

I took my notebook from its home in the left, breast-pocket of my tunic and opened it at a pre-marked page. With the book opened, I said: 'Your Worships, at 8.26am on the morning of Wednesday 16th January this year, I was on foot patrol towards the western end of Main Street, here in Hawthwaite, accompanied by Police Cadet Samantha Stevens. At that time, we saw...'

Up bounced Cassandra. 'Objection, Your Worships.' This time she didn't even wait for their nod of approval. 'Constable you say "we" saw. Is this girl cadet giving evidence to this court today?'

'Not to my knowledge, Your Worships, no,' I said.

'Well in that case, Constable,' said Cassandra, 'would you kindly confine your evidence to what *you* saw and not speak on behalf of others.'

Damn! "Fifteen–Love" to Cassandra. And it was elementary, too. I could have kicked myself.

'My apologies for that grammatical error, Your Worships,' I said. 'At that time *I* saw a blue Mercedes saloon, registered number "GPP 1" parked facing west, fully on the zig-zag-controlled zone, on the approach-side of the crossing. It is also relevant to mention that this location is directly outside Greenup's newsagents shop.'

Up she bounced, again. 'Constable, it is for the court to decide what is and is not relevant, is it not?'

This time it was me that didn't wait for the magistrates to speak. 'Your Worships, given that the accused emerged from that newsagents shop with a copy of the Financial Times, may I say – with respect – that it escapes me how that fact could not be relevant to the case,' I said.

'Yes, *quite!*' growled Lord Nethermere. 'Mrs Hemmingway, in rural courts we may have more time available than in your average city court but we do not have time for frivolous, time-wasting tactics. Kindly keep your *own* comments and questions relevant.'

Fifteen All.

I continued: 'Moments after I arrived beside the Mercedes, I saw a smartly dressed gentleman – the defendant here today – emerge from the newsagent's as I have just mentioned, carrying a copy of the *Financial Times.* As he approached the car, I asked him whether or not it was his car. He replied: "Of course. Do I look as though I need to borrow other people's cars?" I then said…'

Up came Cassandra. 'Constable, is it not true that you actually said, and I quote, "Oy, you! What the hell do you think you're playing at in your big, posh car?" Is that not a more accurate rendition of your words?'

'Your Worships, I never said anything even remotely like that and frankly I'm amazed by the allegation,' I said.

'You deny being insolent to my client, then, Constable?' said Cassandra.

'I certainly *do*, Your Worships,' I said. But this looked like "Thirty–Fifteen" to her, on the basis that she seemed to have something devious up her sleeve.

However, it was Inspector Sumner who was next to his feet: 'Your Worships, with respect, the defence solicitor is actually flouting courtroom rules here. The officer has not even been able to give his evidence-in-chief yet. It is surely for the defence to cross-examine him *after* he has done so,' said Brian, and he then sat down.

The Magistrates Clerk – himself, by requirement, a highly experienced solicitor – rose from his seat directly in front of, but below the level of the Magistrates' Bench, and turned to whisper to them. There was a moment of collective head-nodding and then Lord Netheremere spoke: 'The Inspector is quite right, of course. Except for any *legitimate* objections, the defence will remain seated and silent until the officer has completed his evidence-in-chief. Carry on, Constable Shearwater.'

Thirty All.

'Your Worships,' I said, 'I then asked the defendant whether he realised that he had parked the vehicle on the zig-zags on the approach to the crossing, and he replied "No". He then told me that he had just been to collect a copy of the *Financial Times* and that he was on his way to an urgent meeting at Whitehaven. I told the defendant that because his car was still presenting a danger to pedestrians who wished to use the crossing, because it was blocking the view of oncoming drivers, I required him to move his car around the corner so that the danger element would be removed whilst I spoke to him. Your Worships, the accused's reply surprised me. He said, and I quote verbatim: "You'll regret this, Constable." . . .'

This time, it was Sir Giles himself who leapt to his feet. 'I said *no* such thing. This man is a *liar*,' he barked.

Lord Netheremere's usual, placid exterior hardened in an instant. He went red with annoyance. His voice took on a note of quiet ferocity. 'You, *sir*, will sit down and be *quiet!* You are not in your boardroom now! One more outburst like that and, "Sir" or no "Sir", I will have the police put you in the cells to calm down. Mrs Hemmingway, do I make myself fully understood to your client?'

Cassandra had already tugged Sir Giles' jacket tails to get him to sit down and now frantically whispered in his ear. She then stood and addressed the bench: 'Yes, Your Worships. My client understands and apologises to the Court.'

Thirty–Forty.

Lord Netheremere looked too cross to speak. He simply nodded at me to continue.

'Your Worships, because of Sir Giles' demeanour, I believed it possible that he might just get in his car and simply drive away. I therefore told him the precise nature of the offence that he had committed and gave him the short caution. He made no reply at that point. He then drove his car around the corner to the place I had asked him to park. It was after he had moved the vehicle that I asked him his full name and he replied: "I'm Sir Giles Pemberton-Pennington. Have you never heard of me? I'm one of the country's top industrialists." I then pointed out to him once again why it was that parking on the zig-zags was illegal, because of the danger to pedestrians who could not be seen by approaching drivers. I then issued him with a form "H.O.R.T–One" for the production of his insurance at Chelsea Police Station, London. I then gave him verbal notice of intended prosecution and a formal caution to which, Your Worships, he replied "Just you wait." The defendant then drove off, rather quickly, westwards, out of town.'

I looked at Inspector Sumner to indicate that I'd finished giving my evidence.

He then stood, and said to the magistrates: 'I have no questions, Your Worships,' and sat down again.

Cassandra now stood again, slowly this time, playing out the amateur theatricals so beloved by lawyers in court. It was her chance to cross-examine my evidence.

'Constable,' she said. 'You used your notebook whilst giving your evidence. May I now see those notes please?'

This was a rare but perfectly valid request. As always, though, I had already fastened all irrelevant pages securely closed, with rubber bands, in front of and behind the pages referring to Sir Giles. Not even a lawyer had the right to see a police officer's notes about any unrelated incidents. As I once more removed the notebook from the left breast-pocket of my tunic and opened it at the appropriate page, I glanced to the magistrates for their direction on the matter. Lord Netheremere gave me an almost imperceptible nod of approval. I handed the notebook to the usher who then passed it to Cassandra. If she was surprised at the things I had left unsaid – her client's wielding of the Masonic threat, or the unpleasant names that he'd called me – she certainly didn't show it. But then that was her job. She glanced quickly through the notes then handed the book back to the usher, without comment and it was soon back in my pocket.

'Right, Constable,' said Cassandra. 'You have told the court that you gave Sir Giles a verbal notice of intended prosecution, and the formal caution. My client will tell the court that you told him no such thing. What *are* the verbal notice of intended prosecution and the formal caution, officer? Kindly tell them to the court, now, without referring to any prompts.'

This was a relatively common trick that solicitors use. If one made a mess of the precise wording, because of courtroom nerves, then they would argue that the evidence must effectively be a lie because the officer didn't even know the correct wording and therefore could not have done what was claimed.

'Yes, Your Worships,' I said. 'What I specifically said to the defendant was: "You will be reported for the consideration of the question of prosecuting you for failing to comply with a legal traffic sign, namely the zig-zag markings at a zebra pedestrian crossing. Do you wish to say anything? You are not obliged to say anything unless you wish to do so, but whatever you say will be taken down in writing and may be given in evidence." I think the defence solicitor will find those to be the correct terms.'

'One last question, Constable,' said Cassandra. 'You state that the car was parked fully within the confines of the controlled area – the zig-zags. Is it not actually the case that only part of the car was within that area?'

'No, Your Worships,' I said. 'The whole vehicle was not only fully within the controlled area, but it was *well* within the controlled area. Of that, there is no doubt.'

'No doubt, Constable?' said Cassandra. 'Is that not for the Court to decide?'

She rattled me a bit with that smart-Alec remark and I responded a bit more vigorously than I ought to have done: 'When *I* was at the scene, Your Worships, the Mercedes car was parked, unattended, fully within the controlled area. And I'm sure that the defence solicitor is aware that the offence would in any event have been just the same had only a few inches of the vehicle been over the zig-zag markings.' I said.

'Constable!' rumbled Lord Nethermere. It was not for witnesses to try to teach defence lawyers the law. And I knew it.

Damn! Deuce.

Cassandra presumably thought my mild reprimand to be a good moment to sit down, because she said 'No further questions.' But, as she did so, her client got very agitated.

'What do you *mean*: "No further questions"?' Sir Giles growled at Cassandra. 'This young upstart is a damned *liar*! Get back up and *do* something.'

Cassandra whispered quickly and crossly at Sir Giles, but he was clearly having none of it. After a few moments he leapt to his feet: 'You're sacked,' he half yelled at her. 'I'll do the damned job myself.' He looked up at Lord Nethermere, almost as though trying to defy him. 'D'you hear that? I'm running my own defence now.'

The Magistrates Clerk was the first to speak: 'Sir Giles, you are of course entitled to do that but I have to ask you whether you think it wise to dismiss an experienced lawyer.'

'I've told you once; I'll do it myself, damnit!' said Sir Giles.

'Very good,' said Lord Nethermere, 'but you will refrain from any further "damnits" or curses unless you wish to be fined for Contempt of Court. Do I make myself *clear*? Mrs Hemmingway, you are at liberty to leave the court if you so wish, or you may listen from the back.'

Cassandra went to sit in the public benches, presumably to hear the outcome before she invoiced her now-former client. And her dismissal had ruined my mental tennis match, too.

'One last thing, Sir Giles,' said Lord Nethermere. 'You will keep your questions pertinent otherwise they will be disallowed.'

'Constable,' said Sir Giles to me, in a comically patronising voice. 'Firstly may I ask why you are claiming that all of my car was on the zig-zags when in fact only a few inches of it were overhanging the marks and not even one wheel was on it?'

'Because, Your Worships,' I said to the bench, 'all of the car *was* well inside the boundary of the controlled area, as were both the front and rear wheels, and not just a few inches of the vehicle.'

'So you say, Constable,' said Sir Giles. 'But that's a lie. Now, you've recounted your tale from that little book of fairy stories in your pocket...'

'Sir Giles!' barked Lord Nethermere.

'What?' he impertinently replied.

'You are not here to pour scorn on British policing methods, *that* is what. Now, kindly stick to factual questions. You will have your chance to rebut any of the officer's comments afterwards. This is not a head-to-head battle,' said Lord Nethermere.

'Constable Shearman, you haven't told the court everything that was said when we met, have you?' said Sir Giles.

'It's Shearwater, sir. No, Your Worships, more things were said than I have recounted.'

'And why would that be, Constable? Is it that you are wishing to hide my protests that you were being unfair?'

'You made no such protests, sir,' I said. 'Your Worships, the only items I omitted from my recount were either just personal abuse that the defendant made against me or outright threats. It was not my intention to seek to crucify him in front of the magistrates by repeating it all.'

'Another lie, Constable! I neither abused you nor threatened you,' said Sir Giles. He then turned to the bench. 'I have no further questions for this man. He is nothing but a liar.'

'Right. Well in that case, Sir Giles, sit down for a minute,' instructed Lord Nethermere. Then, turning to me, he said: 'Constable, will you please read out to the Court the *full* account of the incident from your notebook so that we are left in no doubt as to your full side of the story.'

'Hang on,' shouted Sir Giles, as he leapt to his feet again.

'Sit *down*!' said Lord Nethermere. 'That is your final warning. You will not command us to hang on, and you will not interrupt me again. Be quiet. Carry on, Constable.'

I read quickly through the full account that I had in my book: Sir Giles' references to me being an impudent runt and a whelp, and his comment that if the Chief Constable was in the Lodge I would be "nailed".

At the end of it, I was told that I could step down from the witness box but that I must remain available in case required again. I went to the back of the court and sat close to Cassandra. In a way that nobody else could see, she immediately passed me a note that took my attention away from Sir Giles' protestations to the Bench now that he, himself, was in the witness box, giving his own evidence.

<u>CONFIDENTIAL</u>

Dear Steve,

I am so sorry about that fiasco. Suffice it to say one has to pander to important clients; please forgive me.

In any event I was hoping to speak to you after court, today, because I would like to dine this evening at Sharrow Bay and I am hoping greatly that you might wish to accompany me as my guest. Shall we call it a small "thank you" for the kind way you treated me when we first met?

If we don't get the chance to speak after court and I merely have to hand you this note in the corridor then please telephone me before 6pm to let me know, either way.

> *Yours,*
> *Cassandra.*

XXX

I wrote on the back of the note I'd love to come, thank you, and surreptitiously passed it back to her.

The next note to me read: 'Good, then that's settled. Give me your address and I'll collect you at seven o'clock.' I wrote it in the small notepad that she had passed to me then handed it back.

When my attention eventually returned to the court case, Sir Giles Pemberton-Pennington was in the process of summing up: '...and, do you know, when I asked him if he knew who I was, and then told him, he had the audacity to say, "Good morning. No, I haven't heard of you, but I'm Constable Shearwater and I'm pleased to meet you." Can you credit *that?*'

Several people in court, magistrates included, seemed to be fighting back little chuckles but Sir Giles kept hammering on: 'One last thing. If you find me not guilty, I'll not hold a grudge against the young constable. He's over-zealous no doubt and made a big mistake, but then we all make mistakes. But I'm sure you magistrates, being shrewd people, will have noticed that I am wearing the tie of the Institute of Advanced Motorists. I am proud to have worn it for over twenty years with ne'er a blot to my driver's record or safety. If you *believe* that young man and actually find me *guilty* then I shall remove this cherished tie and I shall never blacken the name of the I.A.M. by wearing it ever again.'

'Inspector, do you wish to cross-examine the defendant,' boomed Lord Nethermere.

'Frankly, Your Worships, I see no merit in so doing,' said Brian Sumner. 'Everything seems to have been covered adequately.'

The magistrates retired to consider their verdict and for what they would no doubt feel to be a long-overdue cup of tea.

Half an hour later, they re-emerged.

'Stand up for the verdict, Sir Giles, said the magistrates' clerk.

'Sir Giles,' said Lord Nethermere. 'We find you guilty. I'm sure you'll be able to afford the maximum penalty for this offence although I wish we could fine you more. And lastly of course, take your tie off.'.

Chapter Twenty-Five

Manna from Heaven

Virtually everyone in Cumbria had heard of Sharrow Bay – voted the top restaurant in Britain by Egon Ronay and holder of Michelin stars – its reputation was second to none.

My mother had been a bit bemused when I said that a lady solicitor was taking me to dinner.

'What about Samantha?' she asked.

'Well, I'm not sure, Mam, but this is just a one-off meal tonight,' I said. 'I did Cassandra a big favour and she wants to say thank you, that's all.'

'Oh, aye? What sort of favour?' asked my father, in all sincerity.

'Just at work, Dad,' I said. 'Just a technical matter. Perfectly straightforward.'

Whatever her views, my mother busied herself pressing my suit whilst I polished my shoes.

'Listen,' she said. 'If you are going to Sharrow Bay, you'd better have part of your birthday present a few days early. Dad and I had got you a new shirt for a week tomorrow, so you can have it now and wear it tonight.'

I thanked them both, and kissed Mam. She busied herself like a mother hen. At one stage, I thought she was going to want to check my finger nails and behind my ears.

'Mam, calm *down,*' I said. 'It's a solicitor I'm going out with, not Princess Anne.'

We were all a bit surprised when Cassandra knocked at the door, about five past seven. We hadn't heard her car arrive. My surprise disappeared when I went outside with her though; Daimlers aren't noted for being noisy.

'Oh, this is *nice,*' I said. Then I kicked myself; I must have sounded like a right prat.

'Good,' she said. 'I'm glad you like it because you are driving us there.'

'Me? Driving *this?*' Oh, God, I was at it again.

'I thought you might like that idea, so yes, you,' she said.

After a few miles getting used to the dream of all of the power coming from what I presumed was a turbo-charged 4.2 litre engine, I wasn't even sure I still wanted to go for dinner. A couple of hundred more miles driving the Daimler would do nicely as an alternative. I drove us to Penrith then turned south at Kemplay roundabout, adjacent to the Police Headquarters, down the steep hill and over the hump-back bridge in Eamont Bridge – a former border between the recently merged counties of Cumberland and Westmorland. Two hundred yards later, by the Crown Hotel, I turned right and drove us out, past Yanwath, through Tirril, and into Pooley Bridge, at the foot of Ullswater. I turned off left, towards Howtown, and after a few miles of narrow, twisty road, pulled into the car park of the famous Sharrow Bay. I quickly got out and went around to help Cassandra get out.

'You're not here as the chauffeur,' she laughingly chastised.

'No, I'm not. But I am very aware that I'm here with very special lady,' I said.

'What, me? The Rottweiler with the lipstick? Don't worry, I know my reputation!'

As soon as we went inside, a man whom I took to be a manager approached.

'Good evening, sir. Good evening, madam. Your name, please?' he said.

'Hemmingway,' Cassandra answered.

'Would you care to take a seat?' he said, while leading us towards several luxurious-looking leather settees. Cassandra was on my right and, as we sat, I was convinced that we might be lost without trace. To say that we sank a long way into that particular sofa is an understatement.

'May I bring you a drink whilst you read the menu?' said our host.

'Have what you want,' Cassandra said to me. 'You won't be driving later.'

'A dry sherry, please,' I said to the man.

'Tío Pepe Fino, sir, or perhaps La Gitana Manzanilla En Rama?'

I only knew the Tío Pepe name but Cassandra saw my expression and said, 'Actually, do you have a well-aged Jalifa VORS?'

'Indeed we do, madam.'

'Then we shall both have that,' said Cassandra, and then, turning to me, she added: 'I think you might find it rather special by comparison. Wine snobs call it "complex"!'

It was only now that we were indoors and settled that I really noticed what my companion was wearing. It was a long, midnight blue dress – just above ankle length, with a single side-split on the right hand side, to just above the knee. It was sleeveless and had a large teardrop shaped hole below the throat line which showed off Cassandra's distinct cleavage to nice effect. She had brought in a tiny matching jacket, but merely carried it. Her bobbed, black hair was shining; not a single strand out of place. And her shoes, bracelet, dress ring, watch and delicate necklace all appeared to be precisely the same shade of gold. There were no rings at all on her left hand.

'Oh, you've noticed already,' she said with a smile when she noticed me glance at her hand. 'Well don't worry. You aren't having dinner with a married woman. After what happened at Christmas, I thought it was time for a re-appraisal. I suggested to Rupert, my husband, that we go our separate ways and he agreed without hesitation. At a guess, I would say that he has been having an affair, too. Our decree nisi was granted on Monday and the decree absolute will follow in a few weeks' time.'

'So tonight is…?' I was genuinely curious.

'Ours,' she said, coyly. She paused for quite a few seconds, then added: 'Among other things, it is a chance to say a genuine thank you and to enjoy your company. *And*, of course, a salacious attempt to plead for your forgiveness after that debacle today.' She hugged my arm for a few seconds and grinned at me. 'There are times when doing one's job can be thoroughly tedious.'

A minute or two before eight o'clock, several immaculately attired waiters and waitresses gathered quietly at the end of the room away from all the settees. And on the hour, the deep note of a gong sounded from the adjacent hall. One member of the waiting staff went to each couple, picked up their drinks and invited them to follow through to the dining room. I had literally never seen service like it. And with Cassandra's three-inch stiletto heels bringing her up to about six feet tall, just two inches short of me, and her undeniable beauty, I don't think I'd ever felt either self-consciousness or pride quite like it as we went through to the dining room.

'Would you like to choose the wine?' said Cassandra, as she passed me the wine list. I took one quick skim through it, agog at how many of the bottles were well into three figures, and handed it back.

'Sorry, now that I've seen those prices I feel faint,' I joked.

'You *are* silly,' she laughed. 'We certainly haven't come here to drink Blue Nun. You can have whatever you like. Do you prefer white or red?'

'White, by preference, but I'm happy with whatever you like best.'

'Well let's have white. Do you like dry?'

'Yes, please,' I said.

She ordered a rather special bottle of Chablis. Even I could tell it was rather special because it cost about the same as one of my month's wages.

'Actually,' she said. 'Most people have Chablis with fish but that's just stuff and nonsense. I love it with anything.'

Not that I could be surprised, but the meal that followed was absolutely excellent. Cassandra chose quail; I decided to try the guinea fowl. For most of the seven courses there were several items on the menu that I had never even heard of before. And then there were courses between courses, amazing little titbits and treats that we didn't order but were placed in front of us at strategic moments.

We chatted throughout the meal. At one stage I told her that if ever I were to be sentenced to death for some heinous offence she was not to save me until the last minute.

'Why ever not?' she laughed.

'Because if ever I got the chance for a last request, it would be another meal at this place,' I said.

'Oh?' she said. 'And is there any reason whatsoever that I can't bring you here again... repeatedly?'

I had no answer for that. It was quite clear that she was serious. I sat there wondering what on earth was happening to me. I sometimes went months without a girlfriend and yet here, in a space of just a few weeks, I'd had three very attractive women just about throwing themselves at me. You can't win, Steve, I thought. It's either a feast or a bloody famine!

After the meal, we had coffees – and even *they* were particularly nice – and then we went back through to the lounge for liqueurs.

'I don't mean to be a bore, Cassandra,' I said, after she'd ordered a large Remy Martin X.O. cognac for herself and a Quinta do Noval vintage port for me, 'but are you sure you ought to drive?'

'Of course not,' she said. 'But then I didn't say I *was* driving; I only said that you weren't. I occasionally employ a part-time driver at Hawthwaite and if things have gone to plan his wife should be arriving here with him anytime around now. She'll drop him off here, then *he* will drive us back to my house.'

Well *that* was obviously decided, then. We were going back to Cassandra's "house on the hill".

'What shift are you on, tomorrow, out of curiosity?' she said.

'I'm not. Today was the last of my earlies. Tomorrow is my rest day,' I said.

The wicked little smile that spread across her face had to be seen to be believed. And I, for one, was not going to argue with any plans she had for the rest of the night. We walked out to the car park a few minutes later and the Daimler had been moved close to the door. Her driver had obviously got his own set of keys. I didn't know him by sight; she referred to him just as Jennings, and he to her as "Ma'am". Although it had never really been in doubt, it was now very clear that Cassandra was indeed from a very privileged background.

Jennings opened the rear, passenger-side door for Cassandra and I went around to the other side and sat on her right. As soon as he got into the driver's seat, Cassandra said: 'I'm sure you can manage with just the external mirrors tonight, Jennings.'

He took the hint and immediately tipped the internal mirror up towards the roof so that he couldn't see into the back seat. Then she had him put some rock music on, by Queen, quite loud. Now Jennings could neither see nor hear anything he shouldn't. I learned more about kissing in the next half hour than I had ever done before. My right hand ended up on top of Cassandra's left thigh, and through her thin dress I could feel suspenders. She felt my excited response and lifted both her legs and draped them over mine. The invitation was unmistakable and too thrilling to ignore. I put my left hand on the outside of her left calf then slowly started to slide it up her leg – forcing myself to take my time. Up towards her knee, resting there a while, then slowly on, up her thigh until my hand slid past the top of her stocking onto bare flesh.

'I'm sure you won't mind if I tell Jennings we don't need him anymore, tonight,' she whispered to me, 'because you're going nowhere!'

And who was I to argue.

By the time we got back to her house, I was nearly beside myself with lust. Jennings parked the Daimler by the front door, immediately said his goodnights and walked back down the drive to where his wife was waiting for him in their own car.

Cassandra and I made love against the wall in the hallway, in semi-darkness, with her dress up around her waist. And then we went to bed.

Chapter Twenty-Six

Fighting in the Dark

My night shifts, the following week, started very quietly. The Monday, Tuesday and Wednesday were dead, and I was bored. I took the chance to look back through various bits of unfinished business. The only thing that was frustrating me was that damned Mini van from the fail-to-stop collision on Christmas Eve. I had long since told the Ivinsons that there was no longer any chance of finding it but that didn't stop the situation from aggravating me greatly.

I welcomed the quiet solitude of those first three nights, though, because it also gave me the chance to spend lots of time wondering what to do about Samantha and Cassandra. Elizabeth Hodgson was in my thoughts too, but she was courting and had turned me down so I tried not to linger on that topic. Samantha was young, vulnerable and besotted. If I turned to her it had to be in the hope of a long-term relationship but would the novelty wear off for her? Would she want new experiences, new excitement and new boyfriends like some teenagers seemed to do? And what of Cassandra: classy, elegant, beautiful; sometimes lacking in morals – that couldn't be denied – but a dream if ever there was one. Making love to her was like something on a different wavelength. I was at a total loss. They represented opposite extremes. In some ways, I wanted both but very clearly I knew that couldn't happen.

On the Thursday night, when I went in for duty, all hell had broken loose in Hawthwaite Police Station. Sergeant Wyatt was there on 5pm-1am anyway, but the Inspector was there and C.I.D., from Penrith. And it quickly became evident that a dog handler was in town, too.

'What's up? Have the Russians invaded?' I asked.

'Ah, Steve,' said Inspector Sumner. 'Get all your bits together as quickly as you can. We've had a robbery at the garage on Broom Levels, about an hour ago. The cashier got a smack over the back of his head with a crow bar, and they broke his arm too. The suspects are two youths or young men dressed in parka jackets and black hoods or Balaclavas with eye slits – both thought to be about 5'8" tall, and medium build. It's thought that they got away with about three hundred pounds from the petrol takings. I want you to go down and start doing door-to-door enquiries, around the corner in Scarbank Road, at any house that's still got any lights on. While you are up Scarbank Road, call at the hospital, too, and see if anyone's been in with glass wounds or any other unusual injuries. The C.I.D. are doing the houses on Broom Levels so you don't need to worry about that area.'

I got no useful information at all from any of my enquiries and everyone else drew a blank too. The C.I.D. learned nothing – or so they told us – and the police dog hadn't found a track. It was a bit dispiriting; even my subconscious hope of seeing Elizabeth Hodgson on duty at the hospital was dashed when I called there. There were two other nurses on nights. And no, they hadn't seen anyone with suspicious injuries, either.

There was only so much that could be done so late at night but apparently, the next day, the nick was crawling with half of Penrith C.I.D., all here for a day out and to see if they could get an arrest from it. Once again, however, nothing turned up.

On the Friday evening, when I turned in for duty, a couple of detective constables were swanning around and when I asked if there was anything I could do to help, I was just met with a dismissive: 'It's alright, mate, we've got it under control.' It was possible they knew something they weren't letting on about but equally possible that they were just bluffing.

When I checked my tray, however, there was some important news waiting for me: A reply from the New South Wales Police, in Australia. Their telexed report stated that one of their men had visited the address that we had supplied in relation to Mr Malinowski, in Wollongong, and that it was a rented flat which had now been re-let. Enquiries with the landlord, however, had revealed a note of Mr Malinowski's parents' address in the town of Bydgoszcz, Poland. This was excellent news; now at last we might be able to let the unfortunate climber's family know of his sad fate and get him back to them and his homeland.

My first job, though, was to get out into town on foot patrol. All was quiet until half an hour after "last orders" in all the pubs but then, about half past eleven, pandemonium broke loose in the archway and alley that led to the Silver Stag pub. I heard the ruckus from well down the street and called the nick on my radio. The noise of the fighting suggested that this was going to be much more than one man could handle. Sergeant Wyatt was on 5pm-1am again, so he replied that he was on his way, with the van. It was only afterwards that he told me that he'd asked the two C.I.D. lads to assist but that they'd claimed they were too busy, but they were "sure we could handle it".

By the time I was almost at the archway, Andy Wyatt was already coming up Main Street behind me, full pelt, in the van. He jumped out and came to me then we walked around the corner into the alley together, to be met with what seemed like a riot. Somewhere between thirty and forty men and youths were having a pitched battle. There was nothing we could do except break up the opposing gangs and hopefully each manage to arrest one.

'Police!' bellowed Andy Wyatt.

'Stand still or we'll release the dogs,' I shouted. That one often worked for breaking up fights, and it did this time, too. They scattered. Most went away from us, down the alley and ran away along side streets, but a few tried to break through between us. There wasn't time to be selective. I grabbed the nearest one and whacked him face-first against the wall of the alley. I pinned him there by the neck and said: 'If you so much as move, your face'll become *part* of that wall. Understand?' With difficulty, he nodded. 'Put your hands behind your back.' I said. He'd had enough, so he did what I had told him. I handcuffed him and made him lie face down, on the ground.

When I turned around, Sergeant Wyatt was on the ground, pinned down by a big guy who was kneeling on his shoulders and punching him in the face. I did something that I'd normally never dream of. I ran the four or five paces to where they were and swung a hard kick up into the yob's face and sent him flying backwards. He landed, stunned, with blood oozing from the sides of his mouth.

'Thanks, Steve,' said Andy as I helped him up. 'I was getting the worst of that.'

'Yes, I can see,' I said. 'Your face is a bit of a mess, Sarge.'

'Well, I got this one down,' he said, pointing to another one of them, lying handcuffed, that I hadn't even noticed until then. 'Then that big git came running at you from behind with a bottle up, to clobber you. But I got to him first.'

A large, empty Newcastle Brown Ale bottle was lying on the ground, near where I'd had my own skirmish.

'Jesus, thanks Andy,' I said.

After we had got the three prisoners in the back of our van, which was a tight squeeze, Andy carefully picked up the beer bottle as evidence. We took the three prisoners to the nick, put them in the cells and called out the doctor to check over Andy and the one I'd kicked.

The yob would live, declared the doctor. He'd be minus four teeth after tonight, but he'd live. It turned out that over thirty young men had come over from Newcastle for a weekend in town and someone in the pub had made the mistake of saying that Manchester United were a better football team than Newcastle. As it turned out, all three of our prisoners were from the Newcastle contingent.

I always thought it was a pity when Geordies caused problems because most of them were great folk.

We didn't see the two C.I.D. men again that night, which was just as well because Andy Wyatt was about fit to thump them for leaving us in the lurch. By the time the sergeant had done all of the paperwork necessary for the three prisoners it was almost 4am. I made us a brew.

'That's a hell of a deep voice you've got when you're angry, Steve,' said Sergeant Wyatt, as we sat with our cups of tea. 'You even made *me* bloody jump when you shouted about releasing dogs.'

I grinned. It was a compliment. One very quickly learns in the police which colleagues can be trusted to keep their nerve and pull their weight in a big fight.

'Have you got any reports that you can be getting on with until six o'clock?' he asked me. 'Obviously you'll have to stay in the nick, now, seeing as we've got customers in the cells.'

I told him about the reply from Australia regarding the late Mr Malinowski, then added: 'I think I should do a forwarding report asking that we notify the Polish Embassy in London rather than try to approach the Polish police, directly. That's bound to be a potential minefield in respect of interpreters. What do you think, Sarge?'

'Sounds good to me,' he said. He was staring at the name of Bydgoszcz on the reply from New South Wales. 'I bet there's no bugger in Cumbria that can even pronounce that word... "Bid-go-snoring," maybe.' Then he gingerly touched the cuts and swellings on his cheek and forehead. 'Damn, that's gonna be sore tomorrow. I'm glad you dropped him for me, mate. Thanks.'

I laughed. 'Oh sure, Sarge. He was going insert a bottle in my skull 'til *you* stopped him. It's me that's thanking you.'

'Oh well that's alright then; we'll call it quits,' said Sergeant Wyatt. 'Anyway, I'm meant to be back on at 9am so I'd best be off to my bed.'

On my last two night shifts, the Saturday and Sunday, it was Carol Clarke who was the sergeant on 5pm-1am. I knew that she'd been on 9am-5pm on the Friday, when most of the enquiries had been taking place about the robbery but when I went in, at 9.45pm on the Saturday, she told me that the C.I.D. were making no headway with it. There had seemingly been no witnesses to the incident and a check for fingerprints had come up blank.

'I'll tell you what, Steve,' she said, after we'd chewed over the topic of the robbery, 'those clowns from Newcastle are still in town so the pair of us will go out in the van together until I finish duty. There's no point in you being out alone on foot. If they see you on your own and any of them recognise you, you can guarantee that they will want revenge for last night.'

I can't say that the prospect of doing the foot beat on my own had bothered me; it was the job. But it was still a very nice change to have a warm seat and someone to chat to for half of a night shift. And there was one other thing – whenever I was close to Carol. It was her perfume. In fact, sometimes it was hard to tell whether it *was* a perfume or whether it might just be her. Either way, I wasn't complaining. It still used to amuse me, though. Given her predilection for the martial arts, that delicate, tempting scent sometimes seemed a bit out of place. Eau de punch-up might have been more appropriate!

On the Sunday night, we already knew that the Geordies from Newcastle had gone home but Carol decided to come out with me in the van again. About half past midnight, I was just about to drive her back to the nick for her one o'clock finish when BB sent us to a "two-vehicle, damage-only, R.T.A." on the road up to Leathermere. It was straightforward when we got there. The information had been accurate; nobody was hurt. It was just a case of recording the details and getting the two damaged cars safely away from the scene. It all took a couple of hours, though. Those jobs could be a bit tedious sometimes.

It was heading for 3am when I drove us back into the police station yard. Carol was rummaging in her handbag, looking for the keys to her own car so she could put some of her things straight into it. She was still sitting there, searching, when I got out of the van.

As I turned towards the back door of the nick, a figure lurched at me out of the shadows – someone had been lying in wait. I managed to dodge the first punch he swung but he was coming quickly and body-charged me into the side of the van. He stank of whisky – that much was immediately obvious. He punched me lower down but missed my stomach and hit my ribs so it did little harm. Then I pushed him back and clobbered him, right on the chin-end. It sent him staggering backwards and his drunken legs couldn't keep pace, so down he went.

By this stage, Carol had leapt out of the van.

'What the bloody hell is going on?' she shouted, and was round the van to help me in a flash. Maybe for a moment she'd thought that the Newcastle lads *had* come back for a bit of revenge, I don't know, but there would be no stopping her if it came to blows.

I reached down into the shadows where my attacker had fallen, grabbed him by the lapels of his leather jacket, and hauled him to his feet. And when I saw his face in the little bit of light from one of the nick windows, I got the shock of my life.

Carol was the first to speak. 'Well, well, well, Dick Price. It looks like you've got some explaining to do.'

'What the fuck are *you* doing here?' He spat the words at her. Then he started ranting. 'This bastard has cost me my *job*,' he cried, and tried to pull himself free from my grip.

'Don't be so pathetic, Dick,' said Carol. 'It was your own doing, you evil little shit. Everybody in this nick wishes that you could be sent to prison for it and it's just your good luck that you won't be.'

'What? For shagging his whore?' said Price.

I slammed him bodily against the wall of the police station for that one and I was moments from re-arranging his face when Carol shouted: 'Don't, Steve. Don't hit him.'

I kept him pinned there but did what she said.

'Right,' she said to me. 'Do we arrest him and have all this get into the newspapers, or do we send him on his way?'

'It's your choice, Sarge,' I said. 'I want to lock him up but we both know what that'll mean.'

'Will you trust me to deal with it my own way?' she said to me.

'Yes. If we have to,' I said.

'Okay, then let him go,' said Carol.

Price's pathetic grin was sickening. He'd obviously thought he'd made a major mistake by attacking me in front of a witness when I should, by rights, have been on my own. And now he was going to get away with it.

But his expression changed, a second or two later. He looked as though his balls had passed his tonsils, and that could be no surprise given the ferocity of the kick that Police Sergeant Carol Clarke had landed between his legs. Price slumped to the ground, gurgling. Carol dropped to one knee, pinned his neck to the ground with her fingers on a pressure point and grabbed at what was left of his battered testicles with her other hand. She made him scream like a wounded pig.

'This,' she announced to him, in a frighteningly chilly voice, 'is for women. And *this*' – his screams hit a new pitch – 'is for one woman in particular. And if *I* – she was shouting now – 'see your wanking, ugly fucking little face in this town ever again, I'll rip your balls right off and push them into your eye sockets, you twat. *Understood?*'

He was literally begging for mercy by that stage. If it hadn't been for what he had done to Susan Watson, I would have felt sorry for him. We left him groveling around on the ground and went inside.

'A question, Sarge.' I said.

'What is it?' said Carol.

'How come you didn't let me get my revenge but then you did him over?' I said.

'Because *you* would have marked him, and given him something visible to complain about, you dozy pillock. But anyway, I don't know what you mean; nothing even happened out there did it?' she said, with a completely straight face.

Chapter Twenty-Seven

The Rewards of a Brew

On the Monday and Tuesday – my two days off – the county was overwhelmed by blizzards. Several sections of the A66 main road, running west to east over the Pennine mountains to County Durham, were blocked by deep drifts and the majority of minor roads around central Cumbria had suffered the same fate. It was years since the fells and valleys of Lakeland had seen anything like it.

By the time I started work again, at two o'clock on the Wednesday afternoon, all the main roads around Hawthwaite had been ploughed clear and the council workmen were making good progress on the side roads in the valleys. Amongst all the other things in my tray, I'd been allocated three shotgun certificate renewals to do and it was the third of these that caught my eye, as I glanced through them: William Hodgson, High Outgang Farm, Snabside; Elizabeth's father!

It was a quarter to four and starting to get quite dark by the time I'd got some other little jobs done and had driven to High Outgang, along recently-ploughed roads. Mrs Hodgson opened the door when I knocked.

'Come *in*, lad. Whatever are you doing up t' valley at this time on a day like this?' she said.

'I've been sent to check Mr Hodgson's shotgun for his certificate renewal,' I said. It was a half lie – there was no rush about this job at all, nobody had "sent" me. It could easily have waited until the snow had gone, even if that had taken weeks, however, if I'd waited, somebody else might have done the job. None-the-less, I could barely say: "*I've come to gaze longingly at your daughter!*"

'Well, you've timed it well. Policemen and farmers are both alike; you can all smell a pot of tea brewing at five miles distance. Come in t' kitchen,' she said. 'We're just going to have a bite.'

I didn't expect to find what seemed like half the population of the valley in their kitchen. There were seven men in there – four sat on chairs, two leaning against the rail on the Aga stove and – just beyond them, Bill Hodgson, standing with his hands on his hips having a laugh at something that had just been said. And then there was Elizabeth.

'Elizabeth, set another place at t' table, lass,' said her mother. 'We've got a guest.'

Everyone looked up. The banter was immediate.

'Hey up, Bill; they've found out about you growing cannabis in your henhouses,' said one man.

'Nope,' said another. 'His cows have reported him to t' R.S.P.C.A. for not warming his hands afore he milks them.'

'Nay,' said a third. 'It's for that harem of exotic dancers that he keeps on the quiet, up in his top barn. They've not got work permits.'

'Well, do you wonder?' said the first. 'Bill doesn't know what work *is*. He makes Martha and Elizabeth here do it all. A work permit would be an unknown concept to him.'

'Hey,' said Bill, with mock indignation, 'at least when *I* have a lazy day I still get up at the crack of dawn and make an early start on it.'

When the laughter died down, I said: 'Nothing quite that exotic. I just have to check your shotgun for the certificate renewal.'

There was an even bigger roar of approval.

'Well don't ask him which end of it does the killing, because he doesn't know!' laughed one man.

'Take no notice, lad,' said Bill, chuckling. 'They're just jealous of my quick thinking, that's all.'

More laughter.

'Go on then, Bill, tell him what you did. Make a confession to the constable,' said the laughing man.

'I shot a fox in that bit of woodland, just a'back of t' house,' Bill said to me. 'The little bugger had dug it way into the hen run and killed some of my best layers. My first shot missed and the second only wounded it. And I had no more cartridges left so when it went limping off, I ran after it and hit over the head with the stock of the gun, to kill it.'

'And broke the bloody stock clean off his gun,' howled another of the men.

'Aye,' said Bill, ruefully. 'I had to pay for a new stock.'

'Well you were only meant to crack its skull,' said one of his taunters, 'not knock it through to bloody Australia.'

Elizabeth and her mother had finished putting the food on the huge table in the middle of the kitchen. 'Come on, you lot,' said Mrs Hodgson, 'afore any of this gets cold.'

'You'll have some tea with us, won't you?' Bill said to me.

'Thank you. That'd be first rate,' I replied.

Lakeland farm teas were legendary but the spread in front of us all, that afternoon, was like nothing I'd ever seen before. Sandwiches, ham and egg pie, scotch eggs, meat and potato pie, pork pie, sausage rolls, scones, buns, apple pie and cakes. It struck me as a wonder that the table didn't collapse. Bill pulled a chair out for me, to the left of his own, so I sat. I asked the only question that I could think of that might sound sensible in front of Elizabeth and her parents: 'Have you had to dig any of your sheep out from the snow drifts, then?'

'Aye,' said Bill, to my relief. 'That's what we've been doing today. All these fellas mucked in and gave me a hand. I'd brought all my sheep down off the fell a few weeks ago but there's been that much snow that about fifty of them got buried in drifts a'back of t' intake walls. So we've had the dogs sniffing for them, and us digging them out. It's a lot of years since we've had snow like this.'

'Do you think you've got them all?' I said.

'Aye. We did a head count and got the last one out about twenty minutes before you came.'

'He's got a special technique for counting sheep, has Bill,' said one of the men. 'He just counts all the legs and divides by four!'

That brought another roar of laughter.

'Anyway that's the police for you,' said the man on Bill's right. 'They always come right after all t' work's been done.'

After about an hour, one of the group said: 'Well that was a grand bit of scran, thank you, Martha, but I'd best get away home now.'

Three others took their cue from him and within two minutes the farmhouse kitchen was emptier and much quieter. Bill pointed at the two remaining men, diagonally opposite me at the far end of the table, and said: 'Do you know these two rogues, Steve?'

'Yes, indeed I do, by sight at least,' I said. 'Gawen Crosier, huntsman of the Forndale Foxhounds, and his whipper-in who, unless I'm much mistaken, is your son, Mr Hodgson.'

Both of them nodded a greeting to me and we chatted for a few minutes. But my attention was wanting to focus on someone nearer to me than them, on my left. Since the other four men had gone, there was now no-one actually between myself and Elizabeth.

'Days off?' I asked her.

She smiled as she spoke: 'Yes, today, tomorrow and Friday.'

'Did you manage to get there yesterday, in all that snow?' I said.

'Yes, I stole Dad's Land Rover for the day, so it was no problem. It was quite a lot of fun, driving it in all that snow, actually,' said Elizabeth. 'I heard that you'd been in, asking questions, the night of the robbery. Any luck with that yet?'

'No, nothing yet,' I said. 'It's a bit of a dead loss at the moment, to be honest. But how did you know it was me that was at the hospital asking questions?'

'You think that nurses don't discuss the new bit of "talent" at the police station?' she teased.

'Talent?' exclaimed Gawen Crosier, grinning. 'Whatever do you think policemen could possibly be talented at?'

'Even I'm struggling to answer that,' I offered.

After more laughter and plenty two-way teasing, the two hunt servants had to be off to see to their hounds. To my dismay, though, Gawen came around the table and kissed Elizabeth goodbye.

'I'll pick you up at eight on Friday night,' he said. Elizabeth simply smiled and nodded to him. Maybe they *were* more than "just friends," after all.

At least the two men's departure gave me the chance to actually get on with the task I had come for, even if it left me feeling demolished. Whilst Mrs Hodgson and Elizabeth were busy washing dishes, I stayed at the table with Bill and examined the side-by-side, twelve-bore shotgun that he brought from the next room.

'Do you shoot much vermin?' I asked.

Elizabeth has just come back to get dishes from the table and now it was her turn to laugh: 'No, he doesn't. He fires a lot of cartridges but it's very rare that he actually manages to *shoot* anything.'

'Cheeky bugger!' said her dad, grinning again.

'William!' interjected Mrs Hodgson, who had overheard him: 'You can swear all you like at our Daniel – he's a man. But I will *not* have you swearing at Elizabeth.'

'Well… They're *both* enough to make a bloody vicar swear, sometimes,' he said, mischievously.

'*William!*'

'Yes, Martha. Alright, alright,' he said, smiling.

As I drove slowly back down the valley, I mused over the fact that while I'd been on nights – with time to think – I had almost reached a decision on what to do about my love life in respect of Samantha and Cassandra but now I felt as though I was back to square one. Seeing Elizabeth again, had upset the apple cart once more.

On the Thursday afternoon, I was on foot patrol down the bottom end of the town when it dawned on me that it was about ten days since I'd been to see old Jack and have a brew with him. So I walked down to his bungalow, knocked at the back door, and let myself in.

'How-do, Jack,' I shouted from the kitchen. 'It's only me – Steve. I'll just put the kettle on.'

'Good lad,' he shouted back, as well as he could still shout.

I made him a cup of tea and myself a coffee then took them through and sat down with him for a chat.

'How've you been keeping?' I said.

'Ayy, nobbut middling. I've had a la'al bit of a cold but it's easing off now,' said Jack.

'Did you hear about that bit of excitement at the garage, round on Broom Levels, last week?' I said.

'The robbery, you mean? Aye, I did. How long did it take you to get the little buggers?' he asked.

'We haven't got them yet, I'm afraid,' I said.

'What? You mean you don't know who it *is*?' he said, clearly surprised.

'No. We've got nowhere with it,' I said.

I thought he'd gone silent but when I looked at him he was sat quietly laughing to himself.

'What's up with *you*?' I had to smile as I asked him because the old lad was obviously enjoying himself greatly for some reason.

'Well,' he said, between bouts of silent chuckles, 'you young fellas with all your fancy gadgets that you have nowadays, and you have to come to a half-crippled old bugger like me to find out who did your crimes! It was Gareth Fitzgerald's son and Jeremy Haston's son, off the Hill Foot estate – that's who it was.'

'You mean Jamie Fitzgerald and David Haston?' I said, astonished.

'Aye, that's them,' said Jack.

'Can I ask how you know?' I said.

'You can ask but I'll nutt tell thoo,' he laughed. 'Just take it from me that you'll find the money hidden underneath the Fitzgeralds' garden shed, unless it's been moved. Not *in* it, mind you... *under* it. Somebody saw them put it there – obviously not me, but I can't tell you who it was.'

'Jack, you're brilliant,' I said as I gulped down the last mouthful of my coffee. 'You'll not be too surprised if I tell you I have to be going.'

'Aye, I thought you might,' he said. 'Just don't tell a soul how you found out about it, alright?'

'Oh, I won't. You can bank on it,' I said.

The same two detective constables that didn't come to help Andy Wyatt and I in the big fight were in the front office when I got back to the nick, as was Inspector Sumner. As soon as the detectives' backs were turned I excitedly beckoned him to come out of the room. We went up into his office and closed the door.

'You look as though you've got St Vitus's dance with all that twitching and winking, Steve. What on earth is the matter with you?' he said.

'I know who the two robbers are and I don't want those two C.I.D. pillocks to steal our glory,' I told him.

'How did you find out?' he asked.

'From one of my coffee spots.'

'And is it good information, do you think?' asked the inspector.

'Well, I've been told where the money is hidden. It's in a garden. Underneath Gareth Fitzgerald's garden shed to be precise. It was his son, Jamie, and young David Haston that did the robbery, by all accounts,' I said.

'Really?' he said. 'Well Gareth's not a bad chap; it's just his son that's wayward. But Jamie has never pulled a stunt anything like this before. I hadn't really considered him and David Haston for this job, to be honest. I would have thought it was out of their league; they've just been small-time pains in the arse up until now. Do you want me to come with you if you are going to go and arrest them?'

'By all means, Sir. I'd prefer there to be two of us,' I said. 'And it *is* your police station!'

The Inspector made his excuses to the C.I.D. men and we slipped out to the van. I don't think either of us could believe our luck or our eyes when we saw Jamie Fitzgerald walking along the pavement as we drove along Broom Levels towards Hill Foot. I pulled up alongside him and got out. He took one look at the expression on my face and took off. He managed to run about a hundred yards along Broom Levels, then down somebody's private drive, through their garden, over a fence and halfway across a big field before I caught him. I grappled him to the ground but he turned over, wanting to fight.

'It's your choice,' I said, 'but we know it was you that did the garage. If you want a fight then I guarantee that I'll make a bloody mess of you, so what's it going to be?'

He stopped struggling so I rolled him face down and handcuffed him behind his back. He was only nineteen but he was built like a brick wall – not the "medium build" of the descriptions – so I was glad he gave up so easily.

'Now,' I said to him, 'we've got your mate, Haston, and he's told us that the money is hidden under your dad's shed. Is there anything you want to tell me before we go up there and dig it out?'

'It was David that hit the guy,' said young Fitzgerald. 'He hit him twice. I told him not to.'

'Okay, son,' I said. 'You are under arrest for robbery and for assault occasioning grievous bodily harm,' and I cautioned him.

'I've told you once,' he said. 'It was David that hit the guy in the garage, not me. I was getting the money. I *told* him not to.'

I got my radio from my tunic: '8-6-8 to Inspector Sumner, over.'

'Are you alright, Steve? Where are you?' said the inspector.

'I'm in the middle of the field at the back of the private bungalows. I have the prisoner, and he's given me a straight cough. He's owned up to it,' I said. 'I'll bring him back to the road the same way as we ran, sir, over.'

'Well done, Steve. I'll bring the van along towards you, out.'

Then I heard a rather puzzled voice on the radio: 'C.I.D. to Inspector Sumner, over.'

'Go ahead,' said Brian.

'Is your prisoner in connection with the garage robbery?' the detective constable asked.

'Affirmative,' said Brian.

'Can we assist?' asked the detective.

'Negative, thank you. This is Steve's "collar," over,' said Brian. Silence.

We took Jamie Fitzgerald to his house but left him locked in the back of the van whilst we went into the garden. I took my torch with me to the shed and was soon able to find some loose stones at the back corner. A little bit of rummaging around soon revealed two carrier bags, which I pulled out from underneath the woodwork.

The inspector looked in the top of the first and said: 'That's it. It's here.' Then he closed up the bag again.

The other bag was bigger and had two parka jackets bundled into it.

I went back to the van and put both bags in beside the front seat. The inspector had gone to knock on the Fitzgeralds' door to tell them that we had been in the garden and removed items from under the shed. He then came back and got in the front passenger seat.

'Right,' I said to our rear passenger, 'we'd better go and see if we can find your friend, Haston, now and lock *him* up, too.'

'You said that you *had* him!' said young Fitzgerald.

'Oh well… It just goes to show that you mustn't believe everything you're told,' I said.

'You shit. You liar… You *cheat*!' he yelled.

'You robber. You crippler. You bloody-well shut up, or *you* get your face re-arranged,' replied Inspector Sumner.

We nicked David Haston at his home about five minutes later. Only his mother was there with him at the time and she was devastated when it dawned on her what he had done.

The two C.I.D. men weren't best pleased, either, when we returned to the police station with our two prisoners and the case all sewn up. For "uniform" to beat the plain-clothes boys in a serious crime inquiry was as big a delight for us as it was a humiliation for them.

'You know what?' Brian said to the detectives. 'If you two hadn't let my two men down by failing to help them in the big fight the other night, we wouldn't have made the arrests without you there.'

Chapter Twenty-Eight

A Turn-up for the Books

I knew that somehow I had to tell Samantha that I had been out with Cassandra; my conscience wouldn't stop nagging me about it. But I'd been a coward; I was dreading upsetting her. She'd told me repeatedly that she wanted me to be her first; that it was something special that she wanted to share with me. And here I was going to have to tell her that I'd been out with somebody else. I wasn't proud of myself.

The first chance I got to speak to her was when our shifts overlapped, the following Monday – her on 9am-5pm, me still on my 2pm-10pm late shifts.

'Hey,' she said, when we met in the corridor at the nick, 'I heard that you got the arrests for the garage robbery. That's wonderful, I'm so proud of you.'

'Thanks, Sam,' I said. 'Listen, it's been ages since I've seen you. Can we go for a drink later this week?'

'Of course. I was just going to ask *you*,' she said. 'You're on two-to-ten tomorrow, then two rest days, then earlies, right?'

'Yes.'

'So how about Wednesday evening?' she said.

I picked her up at seven-thirty on the Wednesday. She looked lovely but she seemed a bit reserved with me; her kiss had nothing like the passion of our previous encounters. I had left this far too long. She'd been sat there waiting for me to phone or whatever, but I'd been so wrapped up in my shifts and deciding what to do that I'd virtually ignored her.

I drove us to the Lord Leathes again, and we got our cosy bench, near the fire. I brought our drinks from the bar and sat – trying to gather my wits and my courage for the imminent upset.

'Steve?' said Samantha.

'Yes,' I replied, still half distracted by my thoughts.

'Steve, when I was up home, at Carlisle, last weekend I met an old boyfriend that I haven't seen since we were at school together. I have to tell you about it,' she said.

'Oh, okay.'

'There's no easy way to say it Steve, but I have to be honest with you. We had sex.'

She obviously took my stunned silence for distress: 'I'm so, so sorry, Steve. I was madly in love with him for years at school but I never really expected to see him again. And it just sort of happened. And I feel awful after all I'd said to you.'

She was getting upset but for a dramatically different reason to the one I had anticipated. I felt as though I'd been let off the hook. Did I need to damage her teenage confidence by telling her that I, too, had had sex with someone else? I couldn't see a single good reason for it so I gently and briefly played the part of the wounded soldier.

'Blimey, Samantha, that's come as a bolt out of the blue,' I said.

'I'm so sorry, Steve,' she said. 'But if I told you I didn't love him, I'd be lying to you. I sort of always have.'

'Well, it happens to us all. I'll have to get over it.' I said.

Samantha would never ever know – or need to know – how utterly relieved I was that I hadn't taken advantage of her or hurt her feelings. She was a lovely girl.

On the Friday morning, Inspector Sumner came to work just before 9am, walked straight into the refs room where I was sitting having my sandwiches, and said: 'Ah, Steve; my office now, please.'

I was a bit taken aback. I followed him up the stairs wondering what I might have done wrong.

'Come in, lad. Shut the door and sit down,' he said.

Shut the door? This *must* be a serious bollocking if I had to shut the door.

'I've got three lots of results that I want to discuss with you. Don't look so worried. One of them has to be in private, that's all,' he said.

'Oh, thank God for that,' I said. 'Phew.'

'Right; first. The promotion results are in. You will get yours as normal in a sealed envelope within the next few days but sometimes one gets to find out things early when one is in charge of a police station. For example, the powers that be might just telephone to say that one of my men has not only passed the sergeant's exam with flying colours but has actually managed to finish in the top one percent in the country and is therefore eligible to apply for a place at "Brands Hatch",' said Brian.

Brands Hatch – a Formula 1 motor racing circuit – was the police nickname for the Bramshill Police College, down south; the place where the real high fliers from all the English and Welsh police forces went. I was stunned.

'You mean…?' I couldn't finish the sentence.

'Yes, lad. I *do* mean. I do bloody mean! You were in the top one percent nationally. Congratulations, Steve; it's absolutely marvellous.' He stood up, reached across and shook my hand. 'Don't panic about the Bramshill thing; there's no mad rush. It's up to you whether you are interested in that and I've been told that you'll have several weeks to think about it. But if you say yes and get through the interview it means rapid promotion. You will be a sergeant in one year and an inspector in two – astronomical stuff!'

I just nodded. I thought I'd done okay in the exams but I had no idea I'd done that well. All I could think of was the look, the joy that I knew would be on my mother's face when I told her. And Dad would just be quietly proud; nothing effusive.

'Now, the second thing,' continued Brian Sumner, 'is that the Polish Embassy have replied. They have tracked down Pietr Malinowski's parents at long last. It looks like the Embassy staff are handling all the arrangements for getting his body home to Poland. A hearse is apparently being sent up from London, today, to collect the coffin and take it to the airport to be flown back. I've told them to phone here for the keys to the mortuary but I think it'll be well after you've gone off duty by the time they get here. I just want to say I was pleased with the way you sorted it all out and worded all your reports.'

'Thank you, sir,' I said.

'Nooo, don't thank me yet; there's much better to come. Read this. It's the result of the investigation you instigated with the Divisional Chief Superintendent. I think you might like it even more than your exam results.'

He pushed a report across the table to me. Even though triggering the enquiry *had* been my doing, I was taken aback by what I read.

'Right, come on,' said the inspector. 'You and I have some business to attend to at Penrith.'

We arrived at the address in question about half an hour later. Brian Sumner had briefed me carefully on exactly what to do. I knocked. The door opened.

'Good morning,' I said. 'Can we come in?'

He was rubbing his eyes as we entered. 'What do *you* want.'

'You, actually Dick… Richard Price, I am arresting you on suspicion of the theft of a wallet and its contents, that had been reported as lost to the Hawthwaite Police Station, and on suspicion of the subsequent fraudulent use of an Access credit card from that same wallet.' And I cautioned him.

'Bollocks,' said Dick Price. 'You could never prove that.'

'Oh, but Dick,' I said, 'we already have. It was you that was sent to search the riverbank for Professor Rankin's wallet on the nineteenth of December. And you found it, didn't you? Not only did you pay for your brand new sports car in cash, but some of the money was in fifty-pound-notes. And some of *those* were still in the car dealer's cash float in his safe when enquiries were made there. Did you never consider that the professor might have been such a fastidious little chap that he actually kept a note of the sequential serial numbers of that bound wad of brand new fifties?'

'What?' said Price.

'Yes,' I said. 'And some of them have got your prints on them, too. Had you forgotten that the force has every officer's fingerprints on record? And the authorisation slip from the fraudulent use of the credit card is being analysed against samples of your handwriting from work.'

'I want my solicitor,' said Price.

'I'm sure you do. It will be arranged after we charge you, back at the nick. Come on,' I said.

Nothing bad about Susan Watson would get in the newspapers from *this* offence. Dick Price was now almost certainly going to get the prison sentence that he deserved, even if it was for different offences. Judges always hammered police officers who betrayed everyone's trust by committing crimes, and rightly so, too.

The undertakers with the hearse from London had phoned Hawthwaite Police Station for directions when they had reached Forton Services, on the M6 near Lancaster, at noon. They came for the mortuary keys at quarter past two and brought with them the necessary paperwork from the Polish Embassy for the release of the body.

Once Inspector Sumner and I were back at Hawthwaite, after depositing Price in the cell he so richly deserved, I hung on deliberately and went to the mortuary with the London undertakers to let them in. They had brought a coffin for Pietr, and the three of us lifted him in. It was a strange sensation for me. Nobody would ever understand why such a seemingly accomplished rock climber would do something so basic as going back to the lip of a completed climb and then slip off, but at least we were as content as we could be that this was what had actually happened. And now, at last, the unfortunate man was going home.

Cassandra phoned me at my parents' house, that afternoon: 'If I came up to Hawthwaite for the weekend, would you be doing anything?'

'Only my morning shifts,' I replied. 'So as long as you don't completely exhaust me before I go to work, I'm all yours.'

'Good,' she replied. 'Meet me at my place at seven, this evening. Bring your things – you'll be staying if you want to. We might go out… And there again, we might not.'

We didn't go out. And we didn't go out on the Saturday night, either, and I was knackered the next morning.

The Sunday morning was a bit frosty but not too bad. I did reports until nine, had my sandwiches, and then went out in the van at quarter to ten. The streets were quiet, apart from the cars of some churchgoers. But as I reached the west end of Main Street, a van went past me in the opposite direction – a Mini van – a blue Mini van – a blue Mini van with a *roof rack*. I turned the police van around as fast as I could. I'd lost sight of him for a few moments after he'd gone round a junction, but got him in view again as I turned into Fairfield Street and he was passing the police station. I caught up with him moments later in Anne Street, switched the blue lights on and pulled him in. I glanced down at the rear driver's-side corner as I walked past to speak to him but there was nothing; no sign of any damage at all. Bluff was my only possible hope.

'Good morning, sir,' I said. 'Two and a half months ago, on Christmas Eve, this van was involved in a fail-to-stop collision outside the Terriers Inn, at Snabside, at half past nine in the evening. Why did you not stop at the scene and why did you not report it?'

'Bloody hell,' he spluttered. 'I didn't think you'd still be looking for me now!'

The best of it was that if he had denied it, I wouldn't have had a hope in hell of ever proving it. But he didn't; he coughed it.

As I spoke, I thought of the dismayed newly-weds who'd had their car off the road ever since Christmas. And I took disproportionate delight in saying to the shocked driver: 'Sir, you are not obliged to say anything unless you wish to do so...'

END

ABOUT THE AUTHOR

The author behind the pen-name of Steve Shearwater was born and raised in one of the quiet and beautiful valleys of the Lake District National Park in what was then the county of Cumberland, now Cumbria, in the very north west corner of England. In that remarkable setting, he enjoyed what can truly be called an idyllic rural childhood.

At the age of 16, he was one of only four young people to be selected out of the year's 115 applicants for places as police cadets in what was then Hull City Police, now Humberside, on the east coast of England. Much of the next three years was spent attending the city's College of Commerce to gain police-related qualifications. However the cadetship also included industrial and community attachments, designed to let young cadets experience various aspects of 'real life'. Of course, the other part of real life that cadets start to encounter occur when accompanying officers on patrol duty and seeing crime scenes, arrests, road crashes, injured people and death, up close – things which inevitably accelerate the process of simply growing up.

At the time of transitioning from cadet to constable, 'Steve' chose to transfer back to his home county of Cumbria. By then, however, he had already realised that – at that time – there were about twenty times more road deaths than murders each year in Britain and because of that startling fact he decided to focus his career on traffic enforcement and safety rather than crime. (That ratio is now down from 20:1 to a mere 3:1, with road deaths down by about three-quarters in hard numbers – a huge success in which the British traffic police have played a major role.)

After several years on routine patrol duties in various small towns, in three of the four geographic divisions within Cumbria Constabulary, 'Steve' joined what was then called the Traffic Department – nowadays the Roads Policing Unit – and took his career forwards in that field.

In parallel to his working life, 'Steve' developed a deep and passionate interest in the history and culture of his home county, something which now adds tremendously to his writing about the area. His other interests include photography, wildlife, travel, and in earlier years mountaineering and mountain rescue.

He has travelled very widely within Africa, India, North America, and Europe.

24933678R00160

Printed in Great Britain
by Amazon